Bodie had memorized all the pertinent information about her that had been provided in the case file from his chief.

Yet nothing in Bodie's research had prepared him for his less than professional reaction to her in person. After all, he pursued justice and bad guys, not laughter and cowgirls turned potential suspects.

And Sarah Rickelle, the cowgirl before him, was just that. *A potential suspect.*

She stroked her index finger gently over the tiny duckling's head and eyed him from beneath the rim of her cowboy hat. "I believe I saw your motorcycle parked near my pasture earlier." Accusation was there in her words and suspicion in her shadowed gaze.

Bodie nodded, kept his stance casual and his story uncomplicated. "Took a wrong turn. I ended up finding your bison, not your farmhouse. They were less than thrilled to see me." Same could be said about her.

Her mouth pulled to the side. "Is that so?"

Dear Reader,

Welcome back to Three Springs, Texas. Three Springs has become one of my favorite places, and I always look forward to revisiting this lively, close-knit community. I hope you enjoy meeting a whole new cast of hardworking cowboys and strong-minded cowgirls and catching up with old friends along the way.

In *Kissing the Texas Ranger*, Bodie Hopson returns to Three Springs for an undercover assignment. Bodie is intent on closing his case quickly and hightailing it out of town. After all, Bodie hasn't considered Three Springs home for years. Yet when Bodie meets local farmer Sarah Rickelle, the reasons to stay start outnumbering the ones to leave. If this work-first, serious-minded ranger and breath of fresh air, dedicated farmer can open their hearts to each other, they might find a love worth building a future on.

The seasons are about to change in Three Springs, Texas, where help is always welcome at the harvest and late-night sweet treats are always best when shared. So, grab a spoon and a stool at the kitchen counter. We'll have the ice cream and the latest town gossip ready to share.

Happy reading!

Cari Lynn Webb

KISSING THE TEXAS RANGER

CARI LYNN WEBB

Harlequin
HEARTWARMING

If you purchased this book without a cover you should be aware that this book is stolen property. It was reported as "unsold and destroyed" to the publisher, and neither the author nor the publisher has received any payment for this "stripped book."

ISBN-13: 978-1-335-46010-3

Kissing the Texas Ranger

Copyright © 2025 by Cari Lynn Webb

All rights reserved. No part of this book may be used or reproduced in any manner whatsoever without written permission.

Without limiting the author's and publisher's exclusive rights, any unauthorized use of this publication to train generative artificial intelligence (AI) technologies is expressly prohibited.

This is a work of fiction. Names, characters, places and incidents are either the product of the author's imagination or are used fictitiously. Any resemblance to actual persons, living or dead, businesses, companies, events or locales is entirely coincidental.

For questions and comments about the quality of this book, please contact us at CustomerService@Harlequin.com.

TM and ® are trademarks of Harlequin Enterprises ULC.

Harlequin Enterprises ULC
22 Adelaide St. West, 41st Floor
Toronto, Ontario M5H 4E3, Canada
www.Harlequin.com

Printed in U.S.A.

Cari Lynn Webb lives in South Carolina with her husband, daughters and assorted four-legged family members. She's been blessed to see the power of true love in her grandparents' seventy-year marriage and her parents' marriage of over fifty years. She knows love isn't always sweet and perfect—it can be challenging, complicated and risky. But she believes happily-ever-afters are worth fighting for. She loves to connect with readers.

Books by Cari Lynn Webb

Harlequin Heartwarming

Three Springs, Texas

A Proposal for Her Cowboy
The Rancher's Secret Crush
Falling for the Cowboy Doc
Her Cowboy Wedding Date
Trusting the Rancher with Christmas
The Texas SEAL's Surprise
His Christmas Cowgirl

The Blackwells of Eagle Springs

Her Favorite Wyoming Sheriff

The Blackwell Belles

The Cowgirl's Christmas Reunion

Visit the Author Profile page
at Harlequin.com for more titles.

To my husband,
who claims he does not get enough credit.
This one is for you.

Special thanks to my writing crew—
I would be lost without you. To my daughters for
reading and plotting and keeping it real along the
way. To my family for ensuring I remember to laugh
and for their unwavering support. It takes a team
and I'm so glad you are part of mine.

CHAPTER ONE

MINUTES BEFORE SUNRISE, Sarah Rickelle was wide-awake. And she was not counting sheep to put herself back to sleep.

She was counting bison. *Her bison.* From her bedroom window. The same as she had been doing every morning for the past twelve days. Ever since her fourth bison had disappeared, Sarah had been up before dawn, waiting for the sun to grant her enough light to count her seemingly dwindling herd.

She counted now.

No. It couldn't be.

Recount.

One short. *Not again.*

Recount.

Still missing one.

Sarah pushed her panic aside and raced into her closet. Grabbing a pair of overalls, she quickly dressed and headed downstairs. She slowed only to tiptoe by her grandmother's closed bedroom door in her socks, avoiding the creakiest of the farmhouse's original wooden floorboards. Her grandmother's eyesight might be failing her, but her hearing was as fine-tuned as it had been when she had caught Sarah trying to sneak out of the house in high school so many years ago.

Setting her cowboy hat on her head, Sarah snatched her boots from the mudroom and eased the back door shut.

A bundled-up figure yelped from the porch chair. Her arms flailed, knocking her oversize hood off her head.

"Grandma Rose," Sarah sputtered. "You startled me."

"Feeling is mutual." Her grandmother replaced the hood of her dark brown sweatshirt and wilted into the chair cushions. "You put an extra zing in my pulse just now too."

Sarah dropped into the chair beside her grandma. "What are you doing?"

"Same as you." Grandma Rose tugged on the strings of her hood, tightening the fabric around her face.

Sarah doubted that. Then she took in her grandma's full attire. A pair of old forest green waders that sagged on her grandma's petite frame, and extra-large rubber boots. *On second thought.* Sarah kept her words mild, but her suspicion was more than obvious. "What are you wearing?"

"This is the best camouflage I've got." There was a boast in her words, quickly followed by uncertainty. Then her grandmother said, "But you should really change."

Sarah ran her hand over her favorite red-and-white pin-striped overalls. "Why?"

Her grandma leaned in and whispered as if they were sitting in a crowded conference room, not the only ones around for miles. "We want to blend in out in the pasture, so our bandit doesn't see us."

Sarah stilled. "Our bandit?"

"You know, the one helping himself to our bison." Her grandmother frowned and eyed Sarah over her eyeglasses. "Another one is missing, isn't it?"

So much for keeping things entirely to herself. Sarah should have known better. Her grandmother's rheumatoid arthritis was severe. Her once flame-colored hair was now muted like a smothered fire, and streaked with silver. Yet, despite her body's betrayal, Rosemary Rickelle's mind was sharp, and what she often called her gut's hunch was rarely—if ever—wrong.

Still Sarah hesitated, not wishing to overload her grandma with one more worry. She started, "How did you..."

"It's why you're sneaking out before sunrise," Grandma Rose cut in. "Although I've been telling you since you were a teenager that the *sneak* in your sneak is all wrong. It's simply too loud. You always give yourself away."

Sarah snapped her mouth closed. Sometimes no response was the best approach.

"My eyes might be failing me, but I've got the

hearing of a honey badger." Her grandma patted her hood-covered ears.

"Is that a thing?" Sarah asked. Because some conversations were too good not to participate in, especially with her grandmother. "I don't think I've heard that a honey badger has really good hearing."

"Of course they do." Grandma Rose smarted and asked, "How do you think they find the bees to eat their honey? They hear 'em buzzing."

Sarah chuckled and finally stuffed her feet into her work boots.

"Don't think you're going out there without me," her grandma warned.

"I wouldn't dare," Sarah said.

"You just did dare." Grandma Rose accepted Sarah's assistance out of the chair, then added, "But I was on to you. It's my honey badger–like ears."

"Come on, then." Sarah kept her grandma's arm linked around hers and walked toward the stairs. "Let's go check the herd."

Unfortunately, the count came up the same in the pasture. The female was not with the herd. She hadn't wandered to their favorite watering hole nor was she wallowing in the dirt. Most of the herd was up and grazing, their tails swishing calmly. The slow-to-rise others regarded Sarah with casual interest.

Two hours after sunrise and the start of their bison search, Sarah was back in the driver's seat of the UTV and shaking her head over yet another section of intact fencing. There were no signs of a predator attack. No obvious tampering with the locks on the gates. No evidence the bison had spooked and clamored through the fence.

Sarah was forced to admit she was definitely one bison short. She was anything but calm. That made five bison she had lost in a matter of months. At this rate, her herd would be cut in half by the year's end, and her last-ditch effort to earn a profit on the farm would be just that—in a ditch.

Grandma Rose's voice cut into the silence and Sarah's building unease. "Do you know what this clue hunt is missing?"

"Clues." Sarah started the UTV.

"Yes, our search has come up rather dry." Grandma Rose fiddled with her aviator-style sunglasses, which she'd pulled from the hoodie's front pocket when the sun first appeared. Her grandmother mused, "It is quite a clean crime scene, isn't it? On TV, this would be a possible inside job."

"Except we are the only two insiders on the farm," Sarah countered, and drove toward the last section of pasture fence.

Grandma Rose hummed, then lowered her tinted sunglasses to her nose and peered at Sarah. "Where were you at approximately three this morning?"

"In my room." Sarah shook her head yet played along. "And I don't have an alibi."

"At least one of us does," Grandma Rose replied.

"How do you have an alibi?" Sarah asked.

"I happened to be eating the last of the cinnamon-plum streusel cake at three this morning," her grandmother admitted unapologetically. "The empty cake pan is in the sink."

"Grandma." Sarah chuckled. "I thought we were curbing your late-night snacking as recommended by your doctor."

"Dr. Colborne suggested I cut back," Grandma Rose explained. "There was nothing mentioned about a full stop to my late-night munchies."

Sarah's shoulders shook silently.

"It's a good thing too because now I have evidentiary support for my alibi." Her grandmother nodded.

"Evidentiary what?" Sarah repeated.

"You really need to join me when I watch my afternoon crime shows." Grandma Rose nudged her elbow into Sarah's arm. "Obviously, I've been taking detailed notes."

"I'll have to leave the note-taking in your hands." Sarah parked the UTV near the corner of the pasture. "I need to arrange the harvests and move the herd." Perhaps the back wooded rangeland would prove more of a deterrent for their would-be bison bandit.

"Leave it to me. We will be expert sleuths in no time." Her grandmother straightened. "However, we are missing one important staple of every investigation."

Besides evidence of a theft, Sarah was not sure what else was needed. Still, she asked, "What is that?"

"Coffee." Her grandmother patted her stomach.

"It would certainly sharpen our senses. All the good detectives on TV drink coffee."

Sarah glanced at her grandma. Her grandmother liked to boast that age had not taken two things yet: her grit and her wit. Yet, that grit was looking slightly frayed around the edges of her slight grin to her pale cheeks. Sarah said, "Breakfast it is."

Sarah made a U-turn in the prairie grass and that was when she spotted a motorcycle parked underneath the trees lining the main highway. A dirt road cut through the trees and led straight to the last gate on the bison's current pasture. Sarah frowned. There was no rider in sight. No rustle of the branches. No movement at all. Still, she finally had something worth investigating further. After she dropped her grandma at the farmhouse.

The ride back was quiet, given Sarah set a fairly quick pace in the UTV. She slowed to drive around the stables and parked in the driveway. Anxious to get back to her motorcycle mystery, she jumped out and hurried around to her grandmother's side.

"Mav is up to mischief again." Her grandmother pointed to the duck pen Sarah had built a few weeks ago using an old storage shed near the orchards.

Sarah frowned at the open gate. "Not again."

"That dog is something of an escape artist," Grandma Rose said, amusement in her tone.

Sarah would be impressed with the golden retriever's abilities if the dog wasn't also releasing the duckling flock on the daily, along with the miniature donkeys too. Sarah had rescued Mav last year and the ducklings were recent rescues themselves. The unlikely group had bonded immediately. Now Mav protected the ducklings as if the flock was his. And the flock followed him everywhere.

Sarah rubbed her forehead. "No matter what I do, Mav finds a way to open every gate around here."

"Have to get more creative." Grandma Rose climbed out of the UTV. "I'm sure Mav is taking them to the pond for their morning swim."

Sarah calculated how quickly she could return the flock to the duck pen and get back to the pasture. With luck, the ducklings would be her only delay. She said, "You should probably start breakfast without me."

"I'll keep the coffee warm." Grandma Rose linked her arm around Sarah's and together they headed for the farmhouse.

Her grandmother was in seemingly good spirits, despite another missing bison and their predawn trek in the fields. Sarah helped her grandmother up the stairs and into the mudroom, then asked casually, "Grandma, where is your cane?"

"I don't quite recall." Her grandma hedged.

Sarah bet it was buried at the bottom of her grandmother's closet, where Grandma Rose stashed things she deemed no longer useful. Sarah said, "I'm going to look for it later. It's meant to assist you."

"You know…" Her grandma unclipped the buckles at her shoulders, shimmied out of the waders and dropped them on the wooden bench Sarah's late grandfather had handcrafted. Then she sat, tugged her fuzzy socks over her dark leggings and put on a pair of running shoes. Finally, she grinned at Sarah and said, "You do make a good point about that cane."

Sarah hummed in response, not quite buying Grandma Rose's hasty agreement. Her grandmother hadn't used the cane once since her physical therapist had presented the intricately carved piece to her months ago. Sarah asked, "What point is that?"

"The cane could come in handy if we encounter our bison bandit," Grandma Rose explained. Her expression brightened. Anticipation filled her words. She made a slicing motion with her arm. "I could take him out at the knees with a proper wielding of my cane."

"Maybe you should watch a different TV show this afternoon," Sarah suggested.

"I can't learn that maneuver from TV," Grandma Rose assured her.

Sarah relaxed.

"I'll have to ask Dustin at my physical therapy appointment this week," her grandmother said easily and stood. "Dustin will show me the proper maneuvers."

Sarah winced. Not exactly the kind of thing she wanted to encourage. But Sarah could tell from the set look on Grandma Rose's face that she would not be deterred. That left Sarah tasked with solving the thefts—and soon. Before her grandmother put her amateur sleuthing ideas into action.

"Now you best get after Mav and his flock." Grandma Rose grinned and made a shooing motion toward the back door. "Don't want anything to come across those little ducks. I've grown rather fond of them."

"Me too," Sarah confessed. She was also quite fond of her grandmother's smile. And ensuring her grandmother stayed on her farm would keep her grandmother smiling. That was all that mattered to Sarah.

Sarah switched her work boots for a pair of rubber rain boots, headed outside and sprinted toward the pond. With luck, she would outrun that bad vibe inside her.

Someone was stealing from them. And she did not know who or why.

She supposed she could call the sheriff, but she doubted they had any experience dealing with livestock theft. Besides, calling in law enforcement made it seem even more serious.

Stop kidding yourself.

It already was quite serious. The last of Sarah's savings had gone into the purchase of the bison. And the end-of-year deadline her parents had set loomed larger by the day. Sarah had to turn the farm around. Otherwise, her parents planned to sell the property and move her grandmother into a seniors' living community. Then Sarah would be left with nothing.

Talk about a make-or-break moment. She was living in one now.

Yet, Sarah had promised to help her grandmother stay in her home. So, she would handle things, and if she had to smile to keep her grandma from worrying, she would do that too. Whatever it took.

ONLY THE UNPREPARED relied on luck.

And special ranger Bodie Hopson was never unprepared and hardly ever lucky.

Although his first day back in Three Springs, Texas, after a decades-long hiatus just might prove to be the exception. After all, Bodie was entirely *unprepared* for the sight before him.

Easing his motorcycle to the side of the road, Bodie cut the engine, dropped his feet to the gravel and removed his helmet.

Then he counted. Twelve tiny, pale yellow ducklings to be exact. All of which fluttered like dandelion fluff around one wet cream-colored golden retriever smack in the middle of the road. The large dog sat perched on the gravel and eyed its flock, as if personally accounting for each duckling.

Just then, a shout came from inside a thicket of dense trees and overgrown brush beside the road. "Heads up, Mav," a woman called out and added, "Rover is speeding your way."

The dog barked once and then gave a full-body shake, spraying water droplets in every direction. The ducklings chirped and flapped their barely there wings. The bushes swayed. Then, out darted the smallest yet fastest duckling of the flock. The tiny fuzz ball on twin toothpicks zigzagged in the entirely wrong direction. Bodie hopped off his motorcycle and scooped up the wayward duckling as it tried to sprint past him. Rover peeped once at Bodie, then collapsed on Bodie's palms as if exhausted from its adventure.

The brush swayed again. Only this time, a cowgirl with brambles stuck in her deep brunette braids and a laugh like sunshine appeared. "Rover is certainly keeping me on my toes, Mav." She knocked several twigs off her straw cowboy hat and released more of her bright, off-key laughter. "Who would have thought I'd be outdone by a duckling of all things."

And who would have thought Bodie, a cynic by nature and one nurtured by his long law enforcement career, would be caught off guard by a cowgirl in red railroad-striped overalls and matching tall red rain boots. Bodie tucked Rover closer to his chest, as if the baby duck would cover the sudden uptick in his pulse.

The cowgirl caught sight of Bodie cradling the baker's dozen duckling. Her eyes widened briefly. Then she shook her head at the dog and said, "Thanks for announcing we had a visitor, Mav." Her disappointment was fleeting and replaced by amusement when she added, "We seriously need to work on your guard dog skills one of these days."

And Bodie seriously needed to remember his objective. His reason for being back in Three Springs.

He was here on a special assignment. He was working a case right now, even if it was a far cry from what he really wanted to be doing. Still, work was what he did best. It was all he ever wanted to do.

"Good morning." Setting her cowboy hat back in place, the cowgirl joined Bodie.

Although her smile and words lacked the same cheer from only a moment ago. As if she pressed a dim switch on all that sunshine. And wasn't that disappointing.

"Thank you for intercepting Rover and saving me from another chase through the weeds." She plucked the duckling neatly from Bodie's palms and added, "Rover prefers to go his own way."

And surprise, surprise, Bodie suddenly wanted to go whatever direction this cowgirl was headed, if only to hear her laugh again. That was unexpected and entirely unacceptable.

Bodie had memorized all the pertinent information about her that had been provided in the case file from his chief. Yet, nothing in Bodie's research had prepared him for his less-than-professional reaction to her in person. After all, he pursued justice and bad guys, not laughter and cowgirls turned potential suspects.

And Sarah Rickelle, the cowgirl before him, was just that. *A potential suspect.*

She stroked her index finger gently over the tiny duckling's head and eyed him from beneath the rim of her cowboy hat. "I believe I saw your motorcycle parked near my pasture earlier." Accusation was there in her words and suspicion in her shadowed gaze.

Bodie nodded, kept his stance casual and his story uncomplicated. "Took a wrong turn. I ended up finding your bison, not your farmhouse. They were less than thrilled to see me." Same could be said about her.

Her mouth pulled to the side. "Is that so?"

"I was told to turn at the double fence line with the fig trees." Bodie propped his sunglasses on his head and kept his expression neutral.

"Those are pines out at the pasture." She pointed over his shoulder. "Those are fig trees behind you. They're part of our orchard."

Bodie kept his gaze on her. "Well, I won't make that mistake again now that I know." He also would not mistake the gleam in her gaze for anything other than doubt. His farmer was not buying his explanation. Not even a little bit. There was value in skepticism. He would give her that.

"But I don't know why you are here." She leaned down, released the duckling to join with the others, then straightened. Her hands disappeared into the deep front pockets of her overalls. "Why are you here exactly?"

Bodie assumed her cell phone was in one of those pockets. He appreciated both her caution and her vigilance—those would serve her well. Although he did not appreciate getting caught scouting her pasture earlier. Rookie move that. Time to do what he did best and improvise.

He shifted his expression into apologetic. "Sorry. I should have led with that." He motioned in what his former partner called that useless flutter thing he did so naturally with his arms. The one that made him look more like a pushover than a go-getter. Then added, "Lacey Nash told me you were looking for a new ranch hand. But maybe she was wrong."

Sarah tucked her elbows into her sides and arched one eyebrow. "You know Lacey Nash."

Side note: his farmer was not a pushover either. Bodie scratched the back of his head and tried for an easy grin. "Deputy Nash and I go way back."

All the way back to their childhood days when Lacey's mom had married Bodie's dad. Back when Lacey was more interested in riding horses than taking an oath to serve and protect her fellow citizens. And Bodie was more interested in graduating from high school and making a reputation for himself that looked nothing like his father's.

"Then you won't mind if I text Lacey real quick," Sarah said. And lo and behold, she pulled her cell phone from the pocket of her overalls.

Bodie shook his head. "Don't mind at all." Even if it was entirely unnecessary. After all, he was one of the good guys.

Sarah tapped rapidly on her phone screen. Her phone pinged back. Her smile expanded and her soft chuckle filtered into the space between them like one of those catchy radio songs that got stuck in his head all day.

Now Bodie minded very much. He minded not being the recipient of her smile. And he very much minded being cheated of that sunshine all over again. He wanted to wave his fingers over her phone screen or do something—anything—to pull her focus back to him. He crossed his arms over his chest and locked his stance. He had never fidgeted in his life, especially not for attention.

Sarah finally stashed her phone in her pocket and glanced at Bodie. Once again, she pressed that dimmer switch and dialed herself into reserved. "Deputy Nash says you never could tell the difference between poison ivy and a regular vine, so it figures you'd mix up your foliage too."

A minor but easy-to-remember truth inserted into a cover story to give it depth. His little stepsister was proving her own law enforcement expertise. The big brother in him couldn't be prouder. Although, he felt the slightest pinch of guilt for having to pull Lacey into his subterfuge for his case, given his stepsister and his farmer were friends. Bodie nodded. "Lacey is not wrong about that."

"Well, your lack of green thumb aside, Lacey claims you can handle yourself on the farm." Sarah's shoulders relaxed. "If you're interested, I've got an opening for a ranch hand."

Bodie was more than interested. After all, he meant to close his investigation quickly. He extended his arm toward her. "Bodie Taylor."

Not quite his full name, but that was all he could give her. His father was the long-standing sheriff of

Three Springs County. Growing up, Bodie had only ever visited his dad and stepmom over the summers. He wasn't that awkward, lanky teenager any longer, however the Hopson last name would no doubt connect him to his father and ruin his cover.

Her handshake was brisk and efficient. She gave him her full name and welcomed him to Rose Rickelle Family Farm then added, "It's named after my great-grandmother, but around town we're referred to as the Crossroads R&R, given our location literally straddles county lines. We harvest our crops in one county and our newest venture is bison in the other."

Bodie already knew that and more about her and the Rickelle family farm. Thanks to the detailed case file he'd memorized. Now, thanks to her open attitude, his investigation just got that much easier.

He had already boasted to his chief he would have this case officially wrapped up and the report written before the first cheers at this coming Friday's happy hour. Despite his sister's claims about her farmer friend, Bodie was certain this was nothing more than a small-time farmer in a small town running a small insurance-fraud scheme. Once Bodie proved as much, he could get back to the southern part of the state where his undercover work made a real difference. It was where he belonged. Because he never intended to call Three Springs, Texas, home for long.

"I believe in a hands-on interview approach," Sarah explained. "Basically, we get to work and take it from there. If you don't like the job, there's no sense wasting time on the paperwork."

"Jumping right in," Bodie said.

"That a problem for you?" She tipped her head and considered him.

"As it happens, I'm partial to jumping right in." He dropped his sunglasses back in place before he edged closer to determine if those were gold flecks in her hazel eyes or simply the sun playing tricks on him.

"Great." She whistled for the dog and gathered the flock. "When can you start?"

Bodie did a quick duckling head count and asked, "Does now work?"

"Better than you can imagine." Her grin spread from one cheek to the other.

All that wattage in her smile aimed at him was like the jolt of touching two live wires together. The sensation was not entirely pleasant yet not entirely unwelcome either. And mostly exhilarating.

Some might definitely claim it was Bodie's lucky day. If Bodie subscribed to such things, he would have agreed. As it was, he knew two things for certain.

One: luck was fickle and always changing.

Two: even the simplest cases had a way of becoming complicated very quickly.

And there was something about this cowgirl farmer with her imperfect-yet-endearing laugh and her flock of adorable ducklings that nudged at his long-forgotten heart.

If that wasn't the worst sort of complication, Bodie didn't know what was. Fortunately, he was somewhat of an expert at avoiding heart-related complications like that.

Besides, he dealt in facts, not emotions.

The fact was he had a job to do. A case to solve. Justice to serve.

Because the truth was, Bodie had not gotten to where he was by leading with his heart. And he most certainly did not intend to start now.

CHAPTER TWO

THE MYSTERY WAS SOLVED.

Her new hire owned the motorcycle Sarah had spotted in the bison pasture earlier.

His wrong turn story sounded plausible.

Her friend Lacey Nash had vouched for him.

Even more, he wanted to work, and Sarah needed the help. As it was, she was barely outrunning exhaustion on the daily.

Bodie Taylor was an answer. A timely solution, she supposed.

Her friends would no doubt call Bodie refreshing eye relief from the acres and acres of crops currently growing on Sarah's farm. And declare the tall, blond, and entirely too handsome cowboy a welcome addition.

Why then was Sarah feeling slightly unsettled?

She slanted her gaze toward Bodie. He was pushing his motorcycle up the driveway, having claimed he didn't want the growl of the engine to startle the ducklings.

Thoughtful. One more check mark in his favor.

Sarah touched her cheek, wondering if her cheeks looked as flushed as she felt.

As it was, Mav was trotting ahead of them, straight up the driveway, his tail wagging and his head held high. The flock was busy waddling after the dog, all fluff and peeps. Even Rover kept pace, taking up the rear. All was as it should be.

Only Sarah was not feeling much like herself. She wanted to blame the stress of the bison thefts.

Bodie parked his motorcycle beside her truck, turned, and headed right for her. As if he was in a hurry to return to her.

Thump. There it was. That sudden race in her pulse. That flush in her face. All over again.

Same as she'd felt when Bodie had lifted his sunglasses earlier, revealing his impossibly blue—yet oddly haunting—eyes. Paired with his brooding manner, he had fairly poked an audible sigh right out of her. Worse, when he had cradled Rover protectively against his chest, an adorably perplexed look on his face, Sarah had wanted to hold onto him. She still did.

Bad luck there. The one cowboy to pique her interest in far too long was her employee.

But blurring the boss-employee boundaries would only burden her already teetering too-full plate. Besides, she did not have the bandwidth to navigate a relationship right now. And her goal list certainly did not include another bruised heart.

So, there would be absolutely no embracing her cowboy. Now. Or later.

Time to get down to business. Her words matter-of-fact, Sarah explained, "We've got corn and sorghum crops soon to be harvested. In the spring, it's soybeans."

Bodie caught Rover before he darted in the opposite direction and shooed the duckling in line with the others.

Sarah stopped her smile before it caught hold. Attentiveness was obviously a necessary attribute for any good employee. She recited more farm facts. "The orchards are plum and fig. Both fruits were harvested last month, and the remaining figs are in their drying season." She moved ahead of Mav, opened the gate to the duck pen, and waited for the ducklings to waddle inside. "The orchards were my grandfather's passion project." And were as much as part of the farm as the original farmhouse.

Bodie walked in behind Rover, shut the gate, then propped his sunglasses on his head and eyed her. "But not your passion."

Perceptive too, she noted. Yet, she didn't need to know any more of his attributes. She needed an obvious red flag. One that would curb her interest in the blue-eyed cowboy. She said, "I adore the orchards." Removing the lid on a steel can, she scooped out fresh pine shavings and scattered them on the floor of the duckling's brooder and rambled on. "I'm partial to the original orchard my grandfather started. The first trees were planted because my grandpa liked the fruits. It wasn't about profit or earning potential, but rather pure pleasure."

Bodie said, "And now it's about…"

"It's about income lines now." Not butterflies in the stomach and date nights. She checked the heat lamp on one side of the shed, then ushered the ducklings under it to fully dry from their swim in the pond. "Every part of the farm must earn. That means every plum eaten by a deer or squirrel is lost revenue. Every single dropped and dried fig not collected means less weight and less money."

"Nothing is insignificant," he said quietly, his gaze locked on her.

"Exactly." She nodded, noting there was nothing trivial about the way he considered her. As if he understood her. And there was nothing minor about the uptick in her pulse. Now, she was flustered. Surely that was a red flag. Sarah swiftly composed herself back into business mode. "Our newest addition is our bison herd." Thanks to her neighbor's recommendation. Artie and Pearl were convinced bison would turn the farm around.

"I think the only thing you haven't mentioned is a vegetable garden." His face and words softened.

She gave up collecting those red flags. Instead, she accepted that he was attractive and seemed like a good cowboy. There, she had acknowledged the problem, now she just had to manage it. She waved toward the farmhouse. "The garden and greenhouse are behind the main house. I'll give you a tour later."

"Another income stream then." He scratched his cheek.

She checked the ducklings' water and food supply, then walked out of the pen. "Our vegetables mainly go from our land to our table. But several local chefs get first choice of whatever they want for their seasonal menus."

"That's impressive." He sounded sincere.

She shrugged but could not stall her grin. "I won't deny a bit of pride that my produce is restaurant quality. Even if it doesn't change the bottom line."

Although some of the town locals kept encouraging her to expand, certain if she did she would find those ever-elusive profits. Yet that meant Sarah needed to locate the ever-elusive button that would grant her more time in a day.

"Do you do anything without considering the bottom line?" he asked, a slight tease in his words.

She couldn't afford not to these days. Still, she rose to the bait and countered, "Are you suggesting I'm all work and no play?"

He lifted his hands and shook his head. "I'm definitely not the one to comment on that."

She asked lightly, "So, are you telling me you don't have fun either?"

"It's been suggested on more than one occasion that I need to work less," he said flatly, a hint of dismay in his words. "Apparently, there is some mythical work-life balance which I apparently lack."

That she understood. But a connection with him

was not what she was after. She had only just admitted her cowboy problem. She said, "Well, if you like what you are doing, then work is fun, right?"

He fixed those ice-blue eyes on her and held her stare for a beat. Then another. His eyebrows flexed together slightly, as if she confused him.

That makes two of us, cowboy. But Sarah was working on a solution.

Finally, he asked, "Do you like what you are doing?"

She would when those bottom lines improved, and her bison stopped going missing. And when she knew for certain her grandma would spend her remaining days on the farm, as was her only wish. Sarah chewed on her lip and said, "Most days. What about you?"

His jaw tensed as if he caught his response, then he dropped his glasses into place and repeated, "Most days."

Suddenly, she wanted to know about those other days.

A hearty hello rang out. Mav barked happily and sprinted off.

Sarah spun around and cut off her curiosity. All she should want to know about Bodie was whether or not he could lift more than one hay bale into the stable loft without tiring, properly clean a grain bin, and get a temperamental old tractor to run.

She watched her grandma make her way across the extra-wide front porch toward the staircase. Finally, Grandma Rose braced her hand on the wooden railing, both looked slightly worn and a bit too rickety.

Bodie was in motion before Sarah could stop him. He was at her grandmother's side, assisting her grandma before Sarah could get to her. Before Sarah could explain her grandma was dogged about maintaining her independence and particular about accepting outside help.

Only Grandma Rose all but leaned into Bodie's side and practically beamed at him. As for Bodie, he was considerate and careful with her grandma, slowly assisting her down each stair as if he had all day to help her. Sarah cut off her sigh.

Her family was her responsibility. It was a duty Sarah willingly accepted and nothing she ever trusted to anyone else. Yet something about Bodie's protective nature and confidence tempted her to pretend she wasn't alone in watching over her grandmother and the farm.

Talk about a pickle of a revelation alright.

Because her cowboy employee would most likely be good for business. Yet Sarah worried he just might be trouble for her and her pocketed heart. But only if she let him. Sarah rolled her shoulders back and moved to join the pair.

Introductions complete, her grandma kept a firm grip on Bodie's arm and considered him beneath the brim of her emerald green flower-print bucket hat. "You've got a familiar look about you."

If by *familiar*, her grandmother meant *handsome*

in a clean-cut-chiseled-jaw-broody-silent-but-strong sort of way, then yes, Bodie had that look down pat.

"I hope it's a good look," Bodie said lightly.

"That remains to be seen." Her grandmother's mouth pursed. She pressed her palm over her heart. "Although, it hardly matters what you look like if your insides are put together all wrong."

There was nothing forced about Sarah's sudden grin. Leave it to her grandmother to dig right to the core of things.

Bodie never missed a beat. "I like to think my mind knows where my heart is going."

Sarah's eyebrows arched at the certainty in his bold words. Sarah's heart and mind were aligned too. Now, she focused on things that brought her happiness and paid little mind to her heart. These days, without her heart on her sleeve, there were a lot fewer bruises. And that she didn't mind at all.

Her grandmother's gaze sparkled in the late-morning sun. The approval in her tone tempered her warning. "All the same, I'll be keeping my eye on you."

Same as Sarah would be keeping a close eye on the pair.

The rumble of an engine and double honk of a horn filled the air. Sarah watched a dust cloud float over the driveway. A familiar silver truck pulled in and parked.

Sarah's best friend, Sawyer McGowan, jumped out and hollered, "Sarah-Belle, tell me you love me."

Sarah opened and closed her mouth, then slanted her gaze toward Bodie.

He watched her, his gaze cool and collected, and intensely curious.

Her cheeks heated.

"Come on, Sarah-Belle," Sawyer urged. "I'm waiting for those three words."

Sarah tugged her gaze away from her new ranch hand. Sawyer and Sarah had been friends since the eighth grade. He had always been charismatic, and outlandish commentary was sort of his trademark. Still, she frowned at her long-time friend. "Sawyer, what are you talking about?"

"I bring you your favorite doughnuts from Double Dutch and still I can't get any love from you." Sawyer revealed a to-go box from behind his back. "What is it going to take?"

Sawyer had hinted over the years that he saw Sarah as more than just a friend. But Sarah wanted to keep things between them friction free. She feared dating Sawyer would be a fast lane to ruining their friendship.

"Please be serious, Sawyer." Sarah chuckled, as she often did to soften her rejection, then shook her head. "Come and meet Bodie. He's getting a feel for working here to see if he wants to sign on with us full-time."

Funny, when she considered Bodie, it wasn't friction she felt. Her cowboy had definitely caught her interest. Yet, mixing business with personal was another fast lane to trouble. So, she would stick to the slow lane and keep her feelings to herself.

Introductions and handshakes complete, Sawyer opened the doughnut box.

Sarah was about to reach for her favorite—the triple chocolate peanut butter—then she paused. Her grin faltered. "Hold up. Sawyer, you only bring me doughnuts when you need to apologize."

"Well, I brought you something else." Sawyer skipped his gaze away before he lifted the box closer to her and said, "Maybe eat a doughnut first. Chocolate is your happy place."

Sarah knew that look. Equal parts guilty, apologetic, and hopeful. Sarah ignored the sugar rush and started toward Sawyer's truck. "What did you do, Sawyer?"

"Now, Sarah-Belle." Sawyer thrust the to-go box at her as if to stall her, then added, "I know we talked about you not wanting to take in any more rescues."

It was not a matter of want. She really could not afford to. The farm was barely breaking even. The renovation list was growing. Every animal Sarah added strained those resources she needed to ensure her grandmother had a reliable home to spend the remainder of her years in. She sighed. "Please tell me you didn't bring any more rescues here."

"Look, I had no choice," Sawyer stated, his shoulders slumped.

Her stomach twisted. Sawyer was always hard to refuse when he gave her that particularly defeated look. Still, she attempted to stand her ground. "You always have a choice."

"Not this time. I met the family outside Old Town Pet Market this morning. They were in a real panic." He leaned into his truck and took out a basket, as if he sensed he gained the advantage. "You know the story, Sarah-Belle. The family got two piglets from a bad breeder. I had to help them out. I knew you wouldn't say no to harmless piglets. It's a win all around."

Sawyer always had the best of intentions. Yet, those good intentions often seemed to become Sarah's responsibility somehow. She refused to look in the basket and shook her head. "I can't keep them. I know nothing about pigs."

"That never stopped you before," Sawyer countered, then traded Sarah the basket for the doughnut box and added, "You knew nothing about miniature donkeys. Now, Tansy and Pepper act more like house pets than wild animals. They're thriving and obviously meant to be here with you."

Snort. It was the cutest barely there snuffle she'd ever heard. Sarah couldn't resist peeking into the basket. Inside, two of the tiniest, sweetest piglets were nestled together in a fleece blanket. One was cottonball white and the other was black and white. *Snort.* Even their petite snuffles were precious. Sarah's resolve melted as Sawyer and she both knew it would.

The basket cradled against her chest, Sarah glanced at her grandmother and Bodie, who watched her across the driveway. She asked, "What are we supposed to do now?"

"I will call the Baker sisters," Grandma Rose suggested and pulled her cell phone from her sweatshirt pocket. "Breezy and Gail will know what to do. They have pigs themselves. Been raising them for years."

"See. Assistance is a phone call away." Sawyer beamed and helped himself to a doughnut. "It's all going to work out. Like I always tell you it will." He aimed the chocolate doughnut at her. "You really need to stop doubting me."

Her always-optimistic best friend really needed to listen to her. Sarah pushed her words and expression into stern and said, "This is it, Sawyer. I'm pressing Pause on any more rescues. I'm running out of space."

"Not likely." Sawyer took a bite of his doughnut and frowned around the mouthful. "You have more than seven hundred acres out here."

"Not all farmable," Sarah argued. She had land in abundance, but not profitable acreage.

"You can't refuse." Sawyer polished off the doughnut, brushed his hands on his jeans, and brushed off her argument. "It's not in your nature, Sarah-Belle. That's a compliment, by the way."

She had lost count of how many times she had been told what was and what was not in her nature by well-meaning friends and family alike. Sarah ground her teeth together.

"You're a rescuer, Sarah-Belle," Sawyer added,

seemingly pleased with his advice. "Just accept what we already know to be true about you. Like I always tell you, it's not a bad thing."

Translation: *Don't try to be someone else. We won't stand for it.* Sarah adjusted her grip on the basket and widened her stance. Still, the past rolled through her, bringing its own insistent reminder.

What happened to you, Sarah? You're the happy-go-lucky one. Always easy-breezy. Always full of light. That's the woman I fell in love with, not... Sarah cut off her ex-boyfriend's parting words and turned away from Sawyer.

Across the driveway, her grandmother greeted Breezy and Gail Baker and introduced Bodie over a video call. When Breezy announced Bodie had a familiar look about him, Sarah wedged herself beside Bodie until her face appeared on the screen and asked everyone to please focus on the piglets.

Minutes later, Breezy and Gail insisted the baby pigs be taken directly to the local veterinary clinic in downtown Three Springs. There, Dr. Paige Bishop and her staff could teach Sarah how to care for the little ones properly. The Baker sisters promised to stop in as soon as they returned from visiting their nieces in Santa Fe. With that, the video call ended.

"You must get the piglets sorted today." Grandma Rose stuffed her phone into her pocket. "Then I can look after them tomorrow while you're seeing to the sheep."

"Sheep," Sarah repeated and looked at Bodie as if he knew what was going on.

Bodie shrugged.

"Yes, I took the call when you were out chasing the ducklings," Grandma Rose explained and tugged on the chinstrap of her bucket hat. "I believe he told me he was Sawyer's contact. Said he plans to bring the sheep here tomorrow. I told him that would be fine."

Sarah's fingers dug into the basket.

Sawyer bit into his second donut as if he needed the sugar rush and grinned around the bite. "You remember I told you about Eric Haydon being interested in leasing your southern pastures for his flock?"

Being interested and dropping off sheep were too different things. Sarah blew a strand of hair out of her eyes. "But the troughs in the southern pasture need to be reactivated."

"You can't turn him away," Sawyer said.

Or rather, she could not afford to turn away another potential revenue stream. Sawyer was not wrong there.

"You need to meet Eric at the pasture first thing in the morning to negotiate the lease pricing," Grandma Rose stated.

She needed to find her missing bison. Catch her bison bandit. Check the crops and arrange the harvest. Now head to the vet. And ready an entire pasture. *Welcome to farm management. Now gather your grit and step up or...*

"What will it take to get the troughs working in the southern pasture?" Bodie asked.

Sarah held his clear and exceedingly calm stare, felt herself steady and her focus return. Perhaps she'd made a good hire after all. She explained, "We need to run all-new pipes from the natural spring to the holding well, then out to the troughs in the pasture."

"I've got the afternoon free. Can't think of any place I'd rather be than here with you, Sarah-Belle." Sawyer polished off his doughnut and smiled as if he was now in his happy place. "Of course, I have the equipment we're going to need." Sawyer's smile grew. "So, are we doing this?"

Bodie nodded at Sarah. The motion small and clipped.

A barely there acknowledgment, yet Sarah felt as if that overfull plate she carried suddenly weighed just a little bit less. She glanced at Sawyer. "How quickly can you have your tractor to the southern pasture?"

"I can be there by the time you return from your vet visit." Sawyer headed for his truck. "But I need to leave now to get the supplies."

"Bodie and I will meet you out there." Sarah watched Sawyer drive away, then turned and pressed the piglet basket into Bodie's arms and said, "Let me get my keys and we can leave too."

Bodie's words were measured. "You want me to go with you to the vet."

Sarah grinned at the sudden wariness on his face and nodded. "Yes, I do."

Both eyebrows climbed up higher on his forehead.

"Never hurts to have an extra set of hands and extra set of ears." Grandma Rose patted Bodie's arm and continued, "Looks like that's you this time around, Bodie. Now, you two have fun learning about piglet care."

Fun was not part of this. This was work. A typical day on the farm Sarah needed to keep running for her grandmother.

And if Sarah looked at Bodie and considered a different sort of fun, well, even a workaholic cowgirl was entitled to dream, wasn't she?

CHAPTER THREE

How had he gotten here?

Stuck inside a sterile veterinarian exam room with two undeniably cute piglets and the most enchanting cowgirl Bodie had ever come across.

He should hightail it away from there and leg it straight out of town.

He was precariously close to being in over his head. Something he had never been during his long career in law enforcement. Bodie would have laughed at this nonsense, but he was too busy getting his focus straight and his head back in the game.

"It's not working," Sarah whispered.

The anguish in her quiet words and alarm on her face had Bodie shoving away from the wall where he'd taken up his post and squeezing in beside her on the exam room floor.

"I'm following the instructions. He won't eat." A hitch snagged her words, releasing another wave of worry. She stammered, "If he doesn't eat, he'll…"

"That's not happening," Bodie cut in. Not on his watch and not to his sweet-natured farmer, who he kept conveniently forgetting was also his potential suspect. Bodie carefully scooped up the piglet and arranged the black-and-white tuxedo pig on his lap. "Let's take it from the top."

"I did everything." She grabbed the instructions from the tiled floor. Her hand shook. The paper quivered. "Several times. He doesn't understand what to do without his mama. We need Dr. Bishop."

Unfortunately, the veterinarian and her vet tech were on an emergency call treating cattle bloat at a farm near the edge of the county line. And Verna, Dr. Bishop's receptionist provided printed, not hands-on, care instructions, claiming she'd been hired for front office work only. That left the baby pigs' care in the hands of Bodie and his farmer.

He took Sarah's hand in his and squeezed her fingers until she looked at him. The panic in her hazel eyes might have unsettled him if he was allowing his cowgirl to get to him. His words gentle but firm, he said, "We can do this."

She held onto his stare. Same as she had at the farm earlier when she'd learned about the sheep. As if Bodie was her anchor. As if he wanted to be that for her. Wishful thinking got him nowhere fast.

Her fingers tightened around his. One exhale, then an inhale, and the panic receded from her wide eyes. And didn't that make him feel rather selfishly pleased with himself.

Sarah ran the back of her hand across her cheek, swiping at a stray strand of brunette hair and finally whispered, "Together."

She might have shouted the one word, given the way it echoed inside Bodie. He wanted to cheer as if he'd won something precious. He batted more of that reckless wishful thinking aside and concentrated on the piglet. "Okay. Walk me through the instructions."

Sarah released him and reached for a clean rag, then read the steps out loud. Bodie wrapped the cloth around his finger as instructed and dipped it in the tray of goat milk Sarah slid closer. Squeezing out the excess, he tapped the rag gently on the piglet's mouth. No response.

Another dip. Another tap. Nothing.

Once again. Same result.

Sarah was pressed against his side. So close Bodie felt her tense. He knew without looking her panic was building again. Seeking a distraction, he asked, "Could you check the temperature of the goat milk? I think it has gone cold."

"Right." Sarah was suddenly in motion. "Of course, no baby likes cold milk." Certainty strengthened her words. Seconds later, she was clutching the jar of goat milk and hurrying out the door.

Even better his cowgirl was no longer panicked. Bodie grinned and ran his other finger over the piglet's head. "Okay, little dude. It's you and me now. You have to learn to eat on your own." Bodie dipped the rag back in the flat tray, soaking up more milk. "Otherwise, you're going to break my farmer's heart, and I can't let that happen."

The piglet blinked at him from eyes surrounded by two patches of dark bristly hair.

Bodie pointed his rag-encased finger at the baby pig. "No judgment. I fully recognize I might be the one doing the breaking. But I'm just doing my job." *Keep telling yourself that, Hopson.*

The piglet snorted and resisted Bodie's encouragement to suckle.

Sarah returned and filled a new tray. Bodie switched to his pinkie finger. On the third swipe, he felt the slightest suckle on his fingertip. Wonder filled his words. "He's doing it."

Sarah gasped and leaned over Bodie's shoulder. "You did it."

"Now what?" Bodie asked, knowing he sounded a bit thunderstruck.

"Now touch his snout to the milk in the dish." Sarah pointed to the flat tray of goat milk on the floor. "He's got the taste for the milk. He'll know what to do next."

Bodie set the baby pig on his feet near the tray, then gently pressed the piglet's black-splashed snout into the milk. Seconds later, the baby pig stuck his front legs in the dish and lapped at the milk. "Look." Awe coated Bodie's words. "He's eating on his own."

"One down." Sarah smiled and transferred the cottonball–colored piglet to Bodie. "I'll watch this one while you teach her the lapping ways."

Bodie arranged the tiny baby pig in his lap and

chuckled quietly. "Never imagined I would be teaching a piglet how to eat."

"Stick with me." Sarah hovered over the tuxedo piglet. "Lately, every day on the farm seems to be one surprise after another."

The day was something of a surprise for him. But in his line of work, Bodie never much cared for surprises of any kind. Although, today might prove to be the exception. And wouldn't that be the biggest surprise yet. He cradled the girl piglet in one arm and dipped his other rag-covered pinkie finger in the goat milk. "Do surprises bother you?"

Because he was not all together comfortable himself and it had nothing to do with the hard floor he was sitting on. And everything to do with the intriguing cowgirl beside him.

"Certainly, keeps things interesting." Sarah lifted one shoulder and added, "I did data entry and administration at a manufacturing company before moving in with my grandma. There were few if any surprises at work, which was good for the company."

"But bad for you," he guessed.

She sat back and slanted her gaze toward him, her expression bewildered. "How do you do that?"

"What?" *Read you.* He wanted to tell her it was his job. All part of his extensive training. Yet, he kept forgetting he was working a case. That she *was* his case and not just simply an intriguing cowgirl he wanted to get to know better.

"Never mind." She shook her head.

Bodie nodded, relieved she hadn't pressed, yet oddly disappointed too.

"Looks like mine is done eating." Chuckling, Sarah caught her baby pig before he sat in the milk dish.

"Now, this one is hungry." Bodie grinned at the tug on his fingertip, set his baby pig down, and pressed her cotton ball–colored snout into the dish. Fortunately, she took to eating right away.

Sarah bundled her little guy in a fleece blanket and stood. "I'll get Verna and see what Dr. Paige wants us to do next."

Bodie had his baby pig nestled inside the basket when Sarah returned with the receptionist. The conversation flowed from vaccinations to supplements to incorporating creep-feeding, with more color printouts courtesy of Verna. They were given a children's playpen for a temporary pigpen, several plush toys, and a heat lamp. Then Verna sent them on their way with an assurance Dr. Bishop would stop in at the farm to do a complete exam within the next day or so.

They were across the street when a wheezy voice called out, "Howdy, Sarah!" Seconds later, a burly cowboy lifted Sarah straight off her feet.

Sarah embraced the cowboy, who looked to be only a few years older than Bodie, aside from the gray sprinkled in his dark hair. Boots back on the sidewalk, Sarah smiled. "Hey, Jonah. How are you?"

Jonah. Bodie ran through the file he had memorized on Sarah. Jonah Kersch was her insurance agent. The one who recorded her multiple missing bison claims. The last of which triggered the attention of the internal auditors at Jonah's national insurance agency. Somehow, that had triggered the attention of Bodie's chief and ultimately Bodie's new assignment.

"My ears are full." Jonah tugged on his earlobe, his demeanor good-natured. "More rumors being spilled than lemonade over at the diner."

"Anything I should know about?" Sarah asked. Her words were upbeat, almost off-hand.

Yet, there was tension in the arch of her eyebrows and a strain around the edges of her smile. Bodie straightened.

Jonah sank his fingers into his thick beard, peppered with even more silver hair and considered Sarah. "Just tell me you got nothing new to report. Tell me all is well at the Crossroads R&R."

The corner of Sarah's bottom lip disappeared for the briefest second.

So quick to be unremarkable. Yet long enough for Bodie to notice. As if that small press of her teeth into her lip was a reminder to herself to clip her first response.

Bodie was instantly alert.

Sarah exhaled on a low chuckle and released the brightness in her smile. Then she motioned to the basket Bodie held and said cheerfully, "It seems I'm welcoming pigs onto the farm now."

"Sweet little additions, but they won't stay small for long." Jonah laughed.

"I've got space for them to grow in," Sarah stated. "I just need to build it out."

That would be another farm expense. Bodie doubted Sarah had foreseen a pigpen build when she'd filed her last bison claim several weeks ago. Sawyer's piglet delivery had seemed to set her aback.

Jonah hooked his thumbs in his belt loops. "At this rate, if you keep collecting animals, you'll be able to open your own petting zoo soon."

Sarah adjusted her hold on the portable playpen. Her expression was thoughtful. "I hadn't considered a petting zoo."

"I'd be more than happy to run the numbers from the insurance side of things." Jonah grinned, as if relieved he had offered her viable business advice.

When all the seemingly helpful insurance agent had offered Sarah was nothing but more work. And in return, a commission for himself. Bodie's jaw clenched.

Sarah's smile remained in place. "What could it hurt, right?"

It could hurt if his farmer was stretched too thin. Working herself to the bones so to speak. Bodie tried to refocus. She was his potential suspect, not his to worry over.

"It's good to be open to new business possibilities," Jonah added.

Sarah nodded. "Definitely."

But why would she need to add another revenue stream if she was collecting the insurance claim money? That was the scam. Fleece the insurance company to make quick cash. Yet, the past few hours with Sarah, she had been nothing but thoughtful and compassionate. Was her good nature all an act to cover up her fraudulent behavior?

The cynic in him wanted to believe no one was this genuinely kind. His gut told him he just might have met the outlier. Bodie frowned and considered the possibility someone was stealing her bison.

That did not sit well. Not at all.

Jonah turned to Bodie, but his words were for Sarah. "You have yet to introduce me to your new cowboy."

"What? Oh no, he's not my..." Sarah paused. Her cheeks deepened to an interesting red color.

Bodie would have liked to count how many shades of red her cheeks could turn. Or he would have, if he was really her cowboy. Instead, he forced himself to look away from his farmer's pretty flushed face and adjusted the basket in his arms to shake the insurance agent's hand.

Sarah recovered and added, "This is Bodie Taylor, my new farmhand."

Jonah held onto Bodie's hand a beat longer. "You sure got a familiar look about you."

First, Sarah's grandmother. Then, the spirited Baker sisters. Now, the insurance agent. Bodie suspected his *familiar look* had something to do with his father, Wells Hopson, the long-time sheriff of

Three Springs County. For years, Bodie had never considered how much or how little he looked like his dad. It was not like father and son were close. They'd been more like strangers for the past decade or so.

Now, hours into his return, Bodie was beginning to worry he might have underestimated their resemblance. He said casually, "I've been told I look like one of those famous action stars. I can't ever remember his name."

Sarah slanted her gaze at him and tipped her head. Her eyes widened. "Do you mean Hudson Rhodes from those spy movies?"

Any name was better than Sheriff Wells Hopson, his father. Bodie nodded.

"Now that you mention it, I can see the resemblance." Jonah released Bodie's hand. "Well, I'm glad Sarah got herself some help." The insurance agent eyed Sarah and added, "Folks will be settled knowing you and Rose aren't out there alone."

"Is there something going on that has folks concerned?" Bodie asked mildly, once again circling that other possibility.

"Usual concerns," Jonah said smoothly, but a deep crease appeared between his eyebrows. He studied Bodie again, as if reevaluating Bodie's claim about looking like some famous action star. Jonah shrugged. "You know, upcoming harvests. Managing crop disease. Monitoring the weather. It's a lot for anyone to manage on their own."

Now the insurance agent was withholding information too. Most likely because he wasn't certain if Bodie could be trusted. In small towns like this one, Bodie knew the locals protected each other.

"Well, no one needs to worry about me," Sarah announced. Her smile barely creased her cheeks, giving away her false bravado. Still, she charged on, "I've got everything handled."

Surely, she wasn't implying she was handling the bison thefts herself.

Sarah continued, "We really need to get these guys home and settled in."

Jonah touched his forehead. "I'll be in touch with a petting zoo insurance quote."

Sarah and Bodie headed for the truck she had parked across the street. He asked, "Does the diner have sweet potato fries and milkshakes?"

"Yes, but their homemade pies are even better." Sarah chuckled. "You hungry?"

Yes, but for information. Gossip in the busy diner was a good place to start. The locals would have theories about the livestock thefts. Proving those false would serve to strengthen his insurance-fraud theory. "I'm always in the mood for any kind of sweet treat."

She laughed and shook her head. "I will have to remember that."

And he would have to remember how the gold in her eyes practically sparkled when she truly laughed. If only to make them shimmer again.

At the truck, Sarah inventoried their piglet supplies and frowned. "I left the heat lamp in the exam room. Be right back." A quick jog across the street and she disappeared inside the clinic.

Bodie reached for the passenger door, but a uniformed officer grabbed the handle and swung it open first. Then the officer faced him and grinned. "I thought the case was bison, big brother."

Bodie smiled at the tall woman dressed in the perfectly pressed tan slacks and coordinating shirt of the Three Springs County Sheriff's Department. A buckskin deputy's hat was propped on her head, but her trademark red hair was still visible. He hadn't seen his stepsister in almost ten years. And that had been for her mother's funeral and their visit had been too brief and all too painful. Lacey and he had traded phone calls and texts here and there over the years when Lacey was stationed overseas, and Bodie was working long hours.

He was more than glad to see her now. Lacey radiated joy. And that made him happy. Despite the tension between him and his father, Bodie had always adored his little stepsister and her mom from the very first time he had met them.

He wanted to hug her but feared blowing his cover if a customer in a window seat at the diner took notice. Instead, he said, "Afternoon, Deputy. Thanks for the cover story assist earlier."

"Nice work on getting inside quickly." Lacey pointed into the basket, amusement in her words. "I'm assuming Sarah hired you then, since you're already transporting livestock."

"First vet visit." Bodie nodded and kept an eye on the door to the clinic across the street.

Lacey tipped her head and considered him. "Wow."

"What," he said, although he already had a sinking suspicion of where she was going.

"I just never realized how much you look like Swells," Lacey continued, amazement in her words.

Swells being Lacey's childhood nickname for her super-stepdad, Wells. And there was the confirmation Bodie needed. He frowned. "I never wanted to look like my dad."

"You never wanted to be like him either," Lacey pointed out. "But you got Wells's DNA from the same eye and hair color to the shared passion for law enforcement. Even you can't deny that."

Yet, that was where the similarities ended. After all, Bodie hadn't walked out on his wife and three young children like his father had, choosing his career over family. And worse, leaving his ten-year-old son to pick up the pieces. Yet, Bodie had long since moved on from the upheaval in his childhood. If only he could leave the past where it belonged—behind him.

Bodie lifted his eyebrows at Lacey. "How about we concentrate on my case and not the Hopson family gene pool?"

"It's not a bad thing to be like your dad," Lacey countered.

Bodie kept silent. There was not time enough for this debate. Not to mention, Lacey and he had agreed to *disagree* when it came to Bodie's father a long time ago. He asked, "Have you heard about any other livestock thefts in the area?"

Lacey shook her head, then said sharply, "Although that doesn't prove your theory about this being a cut-and-dried insurance-fraud scheme."

"It certainly bolsters it," Bodie argued. "Don't let your friendship with Sarah skew your objectivity, Deputy. You know I'm just looking at the information I have in front of me."

Lacey frowned, not bothering to hide her displeasure.

Even though he was perhaps a notch less than certain about Sarah's guilt too, he was not about to admit it to Lacey. Instead, he said, "I will concede our farmer is nice."

"And really pretty," Lacey added.

Pretty didn't begin to describe Sarah. Bodie barely dipped his chin in acknowledgment.

Lacey's smile grew anyway.

"But," he said, grinning when his stepsister's smile drooped. "Nice people are not exempt from making poor and often desperate decisions."

Lacey notched her fingers around her utility belt. "Well, cynics aren't exempt from admitting some people just might be honestly good through and through."

"Well, I think you, my favorite stepsibling—" he started.

"Your only stepsister," Lacey corrected, amusement in her gaze.

"Let's concentrate on what matters," he said. "I think you, little sister, are genuinely good." Bodie smiled at her. "Satisfied now?"

"Not quite," Lacey said.

"It's all the time we have. Sarah is on her way back," Bodie lowered his voice. "Don't blow my cover."

"As if, but you might want to get over to the general store, buy a baseball cap and cover up those baby blues before you blow your own cover," Lacey warned, then touched his arm and added, "Promise me you will keep an open mind. You know as well as anyone things are not always as they seem."

He also knew some things were exactly as they seemed. Like facts were indisputable and not all relationships should be fixed. And it would serve him well to remember that.

"By the way, my daughter very much wants to meet her uncle Bodie in person," Lacey continued. "Don't disappoint Aspen or you'll have to deal with me."

"Understood." Bodie tracked Sarah's progress across the street.

"You can't keep avoiding us," Lacey cautioned. "I've missed seeing you long enough."

He had missed her too. More than he realized. More than he was ready to admit.

Lacey greeted Sarah with a warm hug. The same kind of hug Bodie had wanted to share with his stepsister earlier. The kind that spoke of long-standing affection and friendship.

And one Sarah returned warmly.

Bodie couldn't quite recall the last time he had been embraced with such enthusiasm. He wrapped his arm tighter around the piglet basket. He knew one thing. If he ever held so much sunshine, there was a chance he might not let go. Good thing he made it a rule not to embrace potential suspects.

"Just met your new arrivals to the farm." Lacey tipped her head toward the truck and continued, "I was telling Bodie about the rodeo this weekend. There's a two-night celebration at the Owl, starting Friday night. There will be line dancing and a live band out on the patio. Everyone will be there."

A night out with his farmer. The idea was intriguing. Pulling his farmer close for a slow dance under the stars was even more appealing and very tempting.

"It's date night for Caleb and me," Lacey added, then said, "You and Bodie should join us."

Yes. No. Bad idea. Friday was the day Bodie intended to hand in his case report to his chief. The one where he marked Sarah as guilty for insurance fraud. Once Bodie did that, he doubted his farmer would talk to him let alone dance with him. Bodie swallowed hard around the sudden knot in his chest.

"Thanks." Sarah avoided looking at Bodie and said, "A live band sounds fun, but…"

"Stop right there," Lacey interrupted and held up her hand. "Let's leave it at *fun* so I can hope you will show up."

"Fine. We will leave it at that." Sarah laughed, climbed onto the bench seat in the truck, and gestured for him and the piglets to join her.

Lacey wished them both a good afternoon and headed down the sidewalk.

Bodie made his way to the passenger's side, determined to leave his fascination with Sarah right there on the sidewalk and get back to his job.

After all, undone by a farmer—no matter how enchanting—was not ever going to be part of his official report.

CHAPTER FOUR

IF SARAH WAS still leading with her heart, she might be tempted to call Bodie Taylor her own personal boon.

But her heart was unpinned from her sleeve and buttoned up in her pocket.

So now, Sarah was left wondering if her new ranch hand was too good to be true.

Because her cowboy was proving to be quite perfect in almost every way, from his reliability and calming presence to his seeming ease at understanding her. He was someone she could get used to having around, but she wasn't interested in forming a cowboy habit.

That left her no choice. She had to find his flaw—the flip side of her cowboy so to speak. Because even Sarah, with what others referred to as her inexhaustible optimism, knew too good to be true only happened in the movies.

Sarah took her foot off the gas and the truck coasted along at a modest speed. "You never mentioned how you and Lacey know each other."

"I've known Lacey since before Lacey's deputy

days and even before her overseas tours with the military." Bodie adjusted the blanket around the piglets and said,

"Lacey was racing horses across the prairies in those days." He lowered the volume on the radio and asked, "What were you doing back then?"

"When I wasn't helping my grandparents on the farm, I was joining everything I could at school and volunteering at the local animal shelter." Trying to find where she fit in.

"Idle time hasn't ever been part of your vocabulary, has it?" He grinned at her.

"My family is always on the go, literally and figuratively," she said. "It's what I know. Besides, you can't be productive without being active."

"Is that the Rickelle family motto?" he asked.

She nodded and explained, "Growing up, my parents worked a lot and loved to travel as often as possible. Whenever a location spoke to their inner wanderlust, they would pack me and my siblings up and off we would go."

He scratched his chin and glanced at her. "You don't have the same wanderlust."

"I never had it." She was meant for settling, not jet-setting like her family. One more thing about her that perplexed her parents. "I was just starting high school when my parents divorced. My mom took a job in New York while my dad remarried and moved overseas. They both said I could join them. But I asked if I could live with my grandparents here in Texas instead."

"Your parents were good leaving you behind?" he asked.

"They wanted me to be happy," Sarah said, then admitted, "I suspect both my parents were somewhat relieved." She didn't just suspect it. She knew it. She'd seen it firsthand when her dad and his new wife had dropped her at the farm and never looked back.

"Why would you say that?" Bodie's words were bewildered.

"I was the surprise child." Sarah signaled and turned onto the highway. "My sister is seven years older than me and my brother nine years. I caught my family completely off-guard." And she mostly still did. She added, "They love me though."

"But," he pressed.

"But I don't think they quite get me," she confessed. Not like her cowboy seemed to. Yet, he saw the upbeat cowgirl too. The one everyone wanted to be around. *This isn't the woman I fell in love with. I don't understand you anymore.* Sarah cleared her throat and silenced the past. "My brother is an accomplished architect in Manhattan, who travels more than my parents ever did. My sister has a PhD in biochemistry and lives in London. Then there's me—the farmer."

"You are also the one looking after your grandmother and preserving the family legacy," he countered. "You should be proud of that. They should too."

She had to save the farm, if she intended to preserve the legacy and all before her parents' year-end deadline. She straightened on the bench seat and said, "Enough about me. I'm supposed to be interviewing you."

"What do you want to know?" he asked.

Everything. Simple things like black coffee or flavored. Night owl or early bird. Worst Halloween candy. Favorite Thanksgiving side dish. Then the not so simple like the story behind the thin scar on his right temple that curved into his hairline. And who caused such a haunting glint in his deep blue eyes.

Hello, way too personal. After all, this was not a date. It was entirely too comfortable and not the least bit awkward and nothing like one of her typical first dates. Now, Sarah was stuck on the idea of a date with her cowboy.

She drummed her fingers on the wheel. Then completely ignored her newfound professional distance and blurted, "Did you and Lacey ever go out?" Sarah wrinkled her nose.

"Friends only." He shook his head abruptly, then looked at her. "What about you and Sawyer?"

"Same. Friends only." She made a left onto the dirt road that led to the farmhouse. "Although, we went to prom together, but it wasn't a *date* date."

"What about now?" he asked.

Sawyer was interested in going out with her. But Sarah's interest...her gaze slid across the truck cab, landed square on Bodie, and stuck as if it really was a first date. She rushed on. "I'm too busy to even think about dating anyone." Yet, clearly that didn't stop her from considering it, although not with Sawyer. The truck hit a pothole and bumped him closer to her on the bench seat. She asked, "What about you?"

"What about me?" he countered, and flashed her a one-sided grin.

"Do you date?" She secured her hold on the wheel and prepared for another bump.

"That depends," he teased. "Are we talking a *date* date? Or…"

Chuckling, she leaned over and shoved his shoulder lightly. "Stop stalling and answer the question."

"Yes, I have dated," he answered, then quickly said, "Right now, I'm currently single."

And wasn't that welcome news. Sarah barely stopped herself from grinning cheek to cheek. As his boss, of course, the information pleased her. She wouldn't need to be concerned about upsetting his girlfriend if they had to work late into the evenings, which happened more often than not on the farm. The road smoothed out and Sarah relaxed.

"I've decided it's easier to keep my relationship status right where it is," Bodie explained, his words casual and cool. "So, I'm not looking to *date* date or anything like that."

His guarded expression hinted at a relationship gone bad. Sarah knew all about those. She watched the high roofline of the farmhouse come into view and said, "Being single certainly makes life a lot less complicated."

"Well, now I know how you feel about love and relationships," he mused.

"Tell me I'm wrong," she challenged.

"I can't," he admitted, although frustration was there in his words.

"Let me guess." Her gaze drifted over the cornfields. The harvest was coming soon, as was the end of their conversation. "You got burned in your last relationship and came to Three Springs for a fresh start." She knew something about that too.

"You sound rather pleased with your assessment," he said.

"I'm right, aren't I?" It certainly explained the haunted look in his eyes.

"Something like that." He shifted the piglet basket in his arms as she stopped the truck in the driveway and cut the engine. "But that's all the questions we have time for now." He opened his door and looked over his shoulder at her. "We've still got the hands-on part of the interview to get to in the south pasture."

Bodie got out, called a warm greeting to her grandmother sitting in a rocking chair on the front porch. At the hood of the truck, she took the basket from him and he leaned down to give Mav a full body rub, earning the dog's complete adoration and total loyalty.

As for her employee, well, Bodie had already earned the job. If it hadn't been the way he watched over the ducklings, then it would have been his understated cowboy chivalry with her grandmother.

If not that, then his composure at the veterinary clinic. He'd looked after everyone Sarah cared about. He won Sarah over alright.

Good thing he was intent on securing a job and not something like Sarah's heart. Otherwise, Sarah worried she just might need more than her pocket to protect her heart from a cowboy like him.

Now, FOUR HOURS later with hundreds of yards of pipe laid in the southern pasture and the troughs full of fresh spring water, Sawyer drove Sarah's truck back to the farmhouse. Sawyer's plan was to shower and change and celebrate their job well done with drinks and dinner. For Sarah, there was still work to be done.

Sarah, the shortest of the trio, sat in the middle to make the seating arrangements more comfortable for everyone. She struggled not to slide around on her truck's vinyl bench seat. She was afraid to drift into Sawyer's side and give him the wrong impression. Yet, she also worried if she collided with Bodie, she just might want to stay there.

It seemed every bump Sawyer hit and every curve he took jostled Sarah ever closer toward her cowboy. Finally, she propped her boot against Bodie's as a sort of brace to hold herself still and tried to concentrate on her evening task list.

However, bedding down the horses or checking corn silks or watering the garden was not top of mind. But rather what was, was cuddling on the back porch swing and counting fireflies all while enjoying more of that get-to-know-you kind of conversation with her cowboy.

Two potholes and a tight, quick turn later, she found herself sealed right up next to Bodie knee to hip. Only to discover what she already suspected. It was not the most uncomfortable place to find herself. Definitely not the kind of information she needed about her new hire.

Sarah readied herself for the next bend in the dirt road. After all, this was not a porch swing and cuddling was frowned upon.

Only the curveball came from her best friend.

Sawyer lowered the volume of the country song playing on the radio and asked, "So, Bodie, how long have you been in town?"

"Just got here in fact." Bodie lifted his arm and propped it on the back of the bench seat behind Sarah, as if inviting her closer.

She absorbed another bump and still found herself tucked neatly against Bodie's side.

Don't sigh. Sarah held her breath.

Don't rest your head on his shoulder. Sarah stiffened.

Don't get confused. Employees weren't meant to snuggle.

Before she could scramble away, Sawyer took the next turn and filled the silence. "Do you need a place to stay, Bodie?"

Sarah pressed her lips together while she stayed sealed against Bodie's side.

Bodie never reacted as if he was more than content with her in his personal space. Instead, he asked casually, "Do you know someplace reasonable in town to rent?"

"I can do better than a place in town." Sawyer grinned over at them. "My parents have an apartment over their garage. I've been renovating it when I can. It's nothing fancy, but it has the essentials. I'm sure they'd be happy to let you use it."

Sarah frowned. What was Sawyer doing? Sure, she was hiring Bodie. But that didn't mean she wanted him only a hop, skip, and a jump away, did she?

"My parents' place is right down the road from Sarah," Sawyer explained. "Our families have been neighbors for decades."

"That would be convenient," Bodie said mildly.

Sarah wiggled and scooted herself away from Bodie.

"It would certainly make for a short commute to work." Sawyer chuckled.

Sarah crossed her arms over her chest and pressed back into the vinyl seat, trying to lock herself in place. Then she told herself the idea of Bodie being so close did not appeal to her, not even a little bit. *Tell me lies.*

"You okay, Sarah-Belle?" Sawyer glanced over at her. His eyebrows pulled together. "You seem a little tense."

That could be from my disappearing bison herd or my dwindling savings account or my growing interest in my cowboy employee. Take your pick.

Sarah shook her head, keeping her words untroubled and easy. "I'm rearranging my to-do list and trying to prepare for the sheeps' early arrival tomorrow."

"The sheep are going to be really great," Sawyer assured her. "Trust me. You'll be leasing out even more land before the year is over. Everything will work out."

Not if her entire bison herd went missing. Jonah had all but confirmed rumors were already starting up about Sarah in town. She could not afford to become known as the farmer who lost valuable livestock too. If her parents found out, they would most likely expedite the sale timeline.

"You believe me, don't you?" Sawyer reached over and touched her arm. His words were encouraging. "It's all going to be fine. It always is."

"I know." Sarah pulled out her trademark smile. The one she had perfected as a kid. The one guaranteed to put everyone around her at ease.

"There's the cowgirl I know." Sawyer grinned as if satisfied she was back to herself again.

Sarah ran her palm over her jeans. Her hand collided with Bodie's. A flutter of her fingers and she could tangle them with his, capture that composure of his and hold on. She didn't so much as flinch. Just kept her hand right where it was as if welcoming even the smallest connection to her cowboy.

Sawyer turned onto the private road leading to her farm and his parents' place then said, "Bodie, grab your motorcycle and follow us. You can meet my folks and check out the apartment. If it doesn't work for you, we can ask around town about rentals when we go to eat."

"Sounds good." Bodie nudged Sarah's arm and whispered, "Does that work for you?"

There was a lot about her cowboy that was working for her. Yet, her lack of a dating life was not a problem in need of solving. Besides, Sarah had left love and its expectations behind a few years ago. These days, she preferred to *do* what made her happy, rather than *be* someone who was unhappy.

She met her cowboy's stare. *Could I be happy with you? Never mind. Don't answer that.* Sarah held onto her smile and nodded. "Whatever works for you is fine with me."

Bodie's gaze sharpened. He opened his mouth.

But Sawyer's phone rang. The shrill sound filled the cab and interrupted whatever he might have said.

Sawyer tossed his phone to Sarah and said, "Tell me who's calling."

Sarah read the name on the phone screen. "It's the mayor."

"Sorry. I have to take it." Sawyer took the phone back and answered. Two curves and no potholes later, Sawyer hung up and explained, "I need a rain check on those drinks. Mayor Molina needs me at the rodeo grounds. They've got dozens of hay bales to move tonight to get ready for the rodeo this weekend."

Sarah was barely paying Sawyer any attention. They had rounded the last curve on the private road. The Crossroads R&R main gate came into view along with the trio gathered there. Her grandmother and Sawyer's mom, Pearl, rummaged through a tall cardboard box. Sawyer's dad, Arthur, stood on a ladder propped against one of the main gateposts.

Confusion filled Sarah's words. "What are they doing?"

Beside her, Bodie straightened and leaned toward the dashboard.

"What is my dad doing on a ladder?" Sawyer slowed the truck. His words came out even slower. "He's not supposed to be on a ladder with his bad hip and knee."

Bodie reached for the door handle.

"I have no idea." Sarah swatted Sawyer's arm. "Drop us off here." Grandma Rose held up what appeared to be a red bubble light, like the kind that used to be on the roof of a police car. Sarah continued. "Take the truck up to your parents' and get your equipment. I'll pick my truck up later."

Bodie was out, his boots planted on the gravel road before Sawyer had come to a complete stop.

"You need some backup?" Sawyer asked, a hint of disbelief in his words. "Because they are up to something."

"We got this." Sarah scrambled across the bench seat and jumped out. "You don't want to leave the mayor waiting any longer."

"Text me an update," Sawyer called out before

Sarah shut the passenger door and joined Bodie near the main gate.

Bodie grabbed the ladder and fixed his gaze on Sawyer's father balanced on the top rung. Sarah quickly introduced Bodie to Artie and Pearl McGowan, then set her hands on her hips and asked, "What is going on?"

"You should know." Artie waved the cordless drill he gripped over his head and added, "It's the thing now to install cameras all around your property. Everybody is doing it."

Bodie shifted his grip, as if preparing to prop his hand on Artie's lower back and stop the older man's swaying. Bodie's gaze never strayed from Artie.

Sarah switched her focus to her grandmother and Sawyer's mother hovering near the cardboard box full of what looked like scrap metal and old parts.

"We need to keep a closer eye on things around here." Grandma Rose cradled the bubble light, an authority to her words and expression.

Pearl yanked a spool of electrical wire out of the box and nodded with that same conviction on her softly weathered face. "A proper security system is very important as you know."

Security system. Sarah smashed her lips together. *Let them get it out. All of it.*

Grandma Rose fiddled with a button on the bubble light and set the red light to flashing, then she declared, "Well, it's past time we got our own security."

"Us too." Pearl winced from the red light blinding her. She shaded her eyes with one hand to peer at Sarah. "We've decided the entire neighborhood could use a better security system."

The entire neighborhood was their two properties. As of right now, they did not have any kind of security system other than heavy-duty gate locks.

"We gotta protect what is ours." Artie pressed the button on the cordless drill as if to punctuate his words. "That's exactly what we're doing."

Sarah flinched at the red flashing light before snatching it from her grandmother and searching for the off switch.

Undeterred, Grandma Rose plunged her arms into the cardboard box and yanked out a matching bubble light. Grinning, she said slyly, "We can't have our bandit helping himself to any more of our bison." Grandma Rose paused and looked for the power switch on the second light, then considered Sarah. "What's wrong? Surely, you know we would've gotten more than one bubble light at the junkyard. Can't have a proper security system without these."

Sarah wasn't sure what she knew at the moment.

"We've got a security map drawn up and everything." Artie drilled into the wooden post. "We just need to get our first red light installed."

Wood shavings sprayed into the air, floating down into Bodie's hair. He never flinched, just kept his composure and his focus on Artie. Even his words sounded dry and indifferent. "Artie, do you think you could show me that map? I'm wondering if the light should go on top of the Crossroads sign."

Artie paused and peered at the metal sign. "Sure would be more visible from the farmhouse up there." Artie worked his way off the ladder. "You got the height to get it up there. We can trade places."

Sarah relaxed once Artie was standing on the ground.

Artie dropped the drill into his tool bag, then tugged a piece of yellow notebook paper from his shirt pocket and handed it to Bodie. "Got any other ideas? We should make those changes now and then get busy."

Bodie unfolded the paper, his movements measured as if slow was the busiest he moved. He studied the map intently as if he truly was coming up with suggestions.

Sarah silently willed her cowboy not to encourage them.

"We got plenty of lights." Grandma Rose tested the second bubble light and grinned when it flashed. "The bison bandit has finally met his match now."

Sarah cleared her throat and said, "I haven't filled Bodie in yet on all that."

Bodie's all too perceptive gaze met Sarah's over the top of the map.

"Well, why not?" Grandma Rose flipped off her light and frowned at Sarah. "Bodie won't be talking out of turn around town, if that's what has you worried."

Talk was already going around town. But that news would only make her grandmother fret. As for Bodie, he was proving to be levelheaded and dependable. Yet, that hardly meant she intended to confide in him. After all, real cowgirls handled their own business their own way and were better for it. Sarah tugged her gaze away from Bodie.

Grandma Rose whispered above conversation level, "If you haven't noticed, Bodie is a cowboy of few words."

"Nothing wrong with that." Artie crossed his arms over his chest and lifted his chin. "Some of us cowboys like to consider our words for a spell and get things right before we share 'em." He nudged his elbow into Bodie's side. "Isn't that right?"

Bodie nodded and wiped his hand over his mouth, seemingly sticking to his cowboy-of-few-words nature.

"Smooth talk only gets a cowboy so far anyway." Grandma Rose waggled her eyebrows at Sarah. Her gaze gleamed. "Don't you agree, Sarah?"

She thought there was much more to the cowboy watching her now. Amusement tempered the icy blue color of his eyes, yet his gaze fixed on her with an unapologetic intensity. Warmth spread across Sarah's face. She touched her cheeks as if that would stall her sudden blush and blurted, "Can we please focus?" Flustered, she paused and waved her hands around. "How exactly does this security system work anyway?"

"It doesn't really work." Artie shrugged at Bodie

and confessed, "We didn't have time to order those fancy cameras."

Bodie seemed to still.

Grandma Rose switched her light on. "It's more of a deterrent."

Deterrent. Sarah swallowed her groan and glanced at Bodie. The bright red light swirled across his face. He never flinched. It seemed her cowboy was entirely unflappable. And suddenly, she wanted to find out—if anything—ruffled him.

Bodie folded the map and stuck it in his back pocket. "How does this security system work?"

Grandma Rose rummaged inside the box again, pulled out a gearshift and handed it to Bodie. "These are our cameras. See it looks like one of those cameras on the sticks that the younger folks walk around town with."

Artie touched the metal stick Bodie held, then continued, "Rather inspired really."

But those were car parts.

Bodie lifted the gearshift to his eye and looked inside, as if he seriously believed it could pass for a security camera. Then he said, his words thoughtful, "So, the bison bandit is going to see these and think his every move is being recorded."

That was supposed to sound ridiculous, only the way her cowboy talked it sounded reasonable. Sarah clutched the bubble light.

"Exactly." Approval smoothed across her grandmother's face. "When our bandit sees the cameras, he'll think twice about helping himself to our herd."

"How many do you have?" Bodie asked.

That was borderline encouragement. Sarah rolled her lips together.

"More than enough," Artie assured him. "Scoured the entire junkyard to find what we needed this afternoon."

Bodie returned the gearshift to the box.

Sarah appreciated Bodie's restraint and patience. The trio always meant well. She never wanted to injure their feelings, and it seemed neither did Bodie. Another point in her cowboy's favor.

"Don't forget the lights." Pearl pointed at the bubble light Sarah still held. "Those will flash when the bandit trips the trigger at a pasture gate. When those flash, we will know exactly where he is on the property."

"But you won't be chasing down the bandit," Sarah warned.

"Of course not," her grandmother huffed. "We'll call the appropriate people."

Relieved, Sarah finally grinned.

Then her grandma added, "Unless the appropriate people are occupied with other more important duties, then we'll have to take matters into our own hands."

Sarah frowned and shook her head.

"I've got both of our UTVs gassed up and ready to drive," Artie said.

Time to stop this. Sarah swallowed to keep her voice from climbing an octave higher, then asked,

"Did you already install the lights and cameras out at the pastures then?"

"No, we just got started here at the main gate," Artie announced. "We had to collect our equipment and tools first."

Pearl checked her watch and said, "Now we need to get the shepherd's pie in the oven."

"Artie, Bodie, and you should have time enough to install the rest of the system before dinner is served." Grandma Rose smiled as if everything was settled.

"Come on, Rose. I want to take a turn through the greenhouse. The pie might need a touch more rosemary." Pearl linked her arm through Grandma Rose's and the two women started up the driveway toward the farmhouse.

Sarah touched her forehead and stopped short of squeezing her temples.

"Everything we need is in there." Artie pointed at the cardboard box, then patted his pockets. "Now if I can find my keys for the UTV, we can be on our way too."

Bodie picked up the tool bag and handed it to Sarah. "Ready?"

Sarah gripped the leather handle and eyed him. "Are we really doing this?"

"We are until we come up with a better idea." He reached for the cardboard box and grinned at her. "Who knows? It could be fun."

CHAPTER FIVE

WHAT DO YOU HAVE, HOPSON?

Bodie set a screw into the base of the last red bubble light, adjusted it on top of the pasture fence post, and ran through what he had.

A pretty farmer with an almost endearing lack of agribusiness focus and an obviously deep loyalty to those she cared about.

Whir. First screw set, he moved to the next.

A likable best friend who seemed genuinely sincere in wanting to be seen as more than a friend by said pretty farmer.

Whir. Second screw set.

A frail but very witty grandmother with more farming experience under her boots than Bodie's family combined.

Whir. Third screw set.

Finally, a well-meaning, more-than-kind couple who were adamant about protecting their neighbor. Even going so far as assembling and installing a fake security system, convinced it would stop anyone up to no good.

Bodie would have laughed. But Artie was passionately adamant the security system was a surefire deterrent. While Bodie was less inclined to believe the system was value-added, he was aligned with Artie's steadfast desire to help Sarah and her farm anyway he could.

Bodie placed the last screw, drilled it into the wood and declared the light secure.

So, what did he have?

Nothing. Nothing that was substantial to his investigation.

However, he did have something else—an urge to look after his farmer. One that was becoming more undeniable the longer Bodie was around her. Nothing for it now but to get himself some distance and much-needed perspective.

Bodie checked the trip wire then swung the pasture gate open. The bulb light swirled red instantly. Out in the field, the headlights on the UTV flashed on and off, signaling to Bodie that Sarah and Artie could see the bulb light. Bodie locked the gate, double-checked the trip wire and light, then packed up Artie's tool bag.

Artie slowed the UTV and waved to Bodie. "That's a wrap. We can call it a job well done."

It was a job complete. As for a job well done, Bodie still needed to do that. He dropped the tool bag into the bed of the UTV and folded himself into the back seat.

Artie pumped the gas and sent the UTV lurching over the dirt trail that cut across the prairie. Artie's lead foot across the open land kicked up the wind inside the cab, preventing conversation. Finally, the trail narrowed through the trees and Artie was forced to slow down.

Sarah lifted her cowboy hat off her head, smoothed her hair back and said, "Artie, I wanted to bring Bodie by to see your apartment."

"It's spacious. Good view of our land and Sarah's from the bedroom too." Artie twisted to glance at Bodie. "It's possible those alarms might be visible from there. That could come in handy."

Bodie ran his fingers over his head and nodded. Although, it wasn't the alarms that caught his attention, but rather the unobstructed view of Sarah's land.

Fortunately, Sarah pulled the conversation back on track. "Bodie would like to rent the place."

"Of course." Artie grinned, then added, "Can't stay there tonight though."

"I can clean if that's an issue," Bodie offered.

"The place is spotless, but the power is out again on our property. Unfortunately, the generator needs fixing too." Artie parked the UTV in the driveway and cut the engine. "We're all hunkering down with Rose and Sarah tonight. Lucky for us, we can take shifts watching for our red-light alarms to go off."

Sarah looked at Bodie, her eyes wide.

"Even better, we can caravan together if any of the alarms go off." Artie hopped out and hollered to Rose and Pearl, who were sitting in the rockers on the front porch. "Set another place at the table. We got one more staying the night."

"That's not necessary." Bodie joined Artie in the driveway and said, "I can get a room in Belleridge."

Relief smoothed over Sarah's face.

"Why would you do that?" Rose stood and stepped over to the porch railing. "We've got a perfectly good bed not being used and more than enough room."

But that put Bodie closer to his farmer, not farther away. He really needed to find his perspective, not scramble it up even more. Bodie searched for an excuse.

Sarah tucked her hands into the pockets of her overalls and said, "We can't make Bodie stay if he'd rather head to an inn."

He should be thankful Sarah was letting him off the hook. No awkward excuses needed on his part. Instead, he was disappointed. And if that wasn't baffling, he wasn't sure what was. Time to wish them a good evening and be on his way.

"Bodie must stay," Rose scoffed. "If the bison count comes up short in the morning like it did today, you can take Bodie on your sunrise bandit hunt and not me."

Sarah blanched.

Just like that, Bodie was back on the hook. He eyed his farmer. "You went looking for your thief?" He didn't want to consider what they intended to do if they had encountered the person.

"I went looking for my missing bison," Sarah clarified and started up the front porch steps.

"And the bandit," Rose insisted. "After all, the

bison wouldn't be missing if there wasn't any bandit."

"As it happens, I never did care much for a hotel room." Bodie followed Sarah onto the porch. "Hotel rooms are usually too cold and the beds too hard." He gave his farmer a quick grin.

Sarah pursed her lips, looking none too pleased about her additional overnight guest.

Bodie wanted to laugh and decided he'd made the right choice. His farmer unsettled him, and he was more than thrilled to return the favor.

"Well, we've got a better breakfast than anything you'll get at the inn." Rose beamed her approval and waggled her eyebrows at Bodie. "We also offer midnight snacks if you're of a mind for late-night munching."

Bodie's grin reappeared. At least one of the Rickelle family members wanted him around.

"Grandma," Sarah warned.

"What? I'm not saying I'll be having any late-night treats," Rose argued, yet the gleam in her crafty gaze gave her away. "It's just important for our guests to know we have them on hand."

Sarah rolled her eyes and said dryly, "Most people prefer to sleep through the night and eat during the day."

"Good thing too," Rose declared. "All those sleepyheads leave more for us midnight-treat seekers." Rose held her arm out for Bodie and said, "Come on. I'll show you where you can wash up for dinner, then we'll get you settled in proper."

Bodie linked Rose's arm through his and walked inside the farmhouse. He knew his farmer kept a close eye on him. No matter that. His secrets weren't up for the telling. But hers, well, those he intended to uncover—and quickly. Because the closer he got to his farmer, the closer he wanted her.

But his farmer was a cowgirl who deserved to be loved for a lifetime. And Bodie was only meant to be there for now.

Bodie snagged a seat at the dinner table near Rose, trying to maintain some distance from his farmer. Sarah sat at the other end, closest to the kitchen. Sarah was up and down most of the meal, making sure everyone had whatever they needed. The conversation was relaxed and entertaining and centered around the two families' long history. The older trio was eager to share stories of Sarah's farm rescues as a teenager. As it happened, Bodie was even more content to learn about his kindhearted cowgirl. Dessert was almost finished when the conversation shifted in Bodie's direction.

Pearl swallowed the last bite of her shortcake, declared herself too full to move, then said, "Bodie, I hear you come with an impressive reference from our very own Deputy Nash."

Bodie swallowed and set his fork gently on his plate. "Lacey and I go way back."

Rose shared a look with Pearl, though neither woman commented. As for Artie, he was concentrating on polishing off his second serving of strawberry shortcake in short order.

"Bodie and I ran into Lacey downtown this afternoon." Sarah scooped out more whipped cream from the bowl. "Bodie introduced her to Gladys and Gilbert."

"Who?" Bodie asked.

"The piglets." Sarah dipped a strawberry into her whipped cream and took a bite.

"You named them already," Bodie said and scratched his cheek. "Isn't there an unwritten rule about naming your livestock?"

"They're family now," Sarah replied, as if that settled it.

As if that was all it took to become her family. But what would it take to become *hers*? That couldn't be top of mind. Or even up for discussion. Bodie pushed his chair back and gathered the empty dessert plates.

"Guests don't clean up around here," Rose stated.

Bodie smiled. "But grateful farmhands do."

Rose grinned and tipped her water glass at him as a toast, then shifted her gaze to Sarah. "Did Lacey mention when the sheriff and Lilian are getting hitched?"

The sheriff, as in Bodie's dad, and Lilian Sloan—Bodie's soon-to-be new stepmother. As if Bodie was anxious to welcome another stepparent into his circle. By his mother's third divorce, Bodie had stopped using *stepdad*, and simply referred to his mother's husbands by their respective number. Seeing as his mom sought solace in the French Riviera after her fifth divorce earlier in the year, Bodie assumed it would not be long before she returned with number six on her arm. Unlike Bodie, his mother was never content on her own for long.

"I think the entire town is checking their mailboxes daily for the save-the-date card for the sheriff's wedding." Pearl chuckled, handed Bodie her plate, then thanked him.

Rose hummed her agreement. "The sheriff has looked after us for many years. Now we are all excited to see him happy again."

Bodie wasn't exactly excited to see his father again after so many years apart. Anxious, perhaps, and not for the wedding. It was no secret as a kid, Bodie had blamed his dad for his parents' divorce. His mom never discouraged her son's feelings while his dad always put in his best effort whenever Bodie had visited.

Yet when Bodie recently consoled his mother as she cycled through another partner, Bodie started to wonder if having his guard up against his father all these years benefitted him or Bodie's mom more. Bodie stacked the plates and worked on keeping his expression indifferent.

"I'm sure as soon as the wedding day is officially set the entire town will know." Sarah finished her strawberries. "And their calendars will be marked."

Bodie glanced up. "Won't it be a rather large wedding if the entire town attends?"

"Do you dislike the spectacle of a wedding?" Sarah watched him. There was a faint trace of amusement in her gaze. "Or is it the public celebration of love?"

Both. Bodie supposed that answer would not be well received.

Sarah arched an eyebrow, as if daring him to be honest.

Rose mused, "Spectacle or not, it only matters that two hearts aren't alone anymore."

Perhaps. But Bodie was good on his own and that mattered too.

"Well, there's nothing for it." Artie laughed and took Pearl's hand in his. "We're a close community and the sheriff is one of ours. Same as Lilian Sloan."

"And we can't wait to celebrate what they found together," Pearl added.

But what had Lilian and his father really found? A temporary solution to not being alone. What happened when that wasn't enough? Bodie already knew. He had a ring his ex-fiancée had returned to him. If that wasn't proof enough, he had only to go through his mother's growing collection of signed divorce papers. He would leave the celebrating to the town and his calendar open. Bodie carried the dishes over to the kitchen sink while the older trio debated what card game to play.

Sarah was right behind Bodie and nudged him out of the way. She turned on the faucet and said, "You really don't need to do these."

"What can I do then?" he asked and propped his hip against the counter.

Sarah watched him, bit her bottom lip, then blurted, "Did you have a bad marriage? Is that why you don't like weddings?"

"That's my mother's area of expertise." Bodie watched her eyes widen and added, "I had a fiancée." Back when he believed he could get love right.

Her eyebrows pulled together. "Then you believe in love," she said, a faint thread of surprise in her words.

He believed his family excelled at getting love fantastically wrong. As for himself, he wasn't interested in a second strikeout. Once was enough. But when he looked into Sarah's intriguing hazel eyes, he considered stepping back into the game. That was only love trying to play him for a fool again. Good thing he was one step ahead.

A movement over Sarah's shoulder caught his attention. He frowned at the sliding glass door. "I don't mean to alarm you, but Mav is outside on the porch with two horses. I think they might want to come inside."

"That's Tansy and Pepper." Sarah's shoulders shook with her soft chuckle. "They're miniature donkeys, but they think they're house pets. Mav taught them the art of begging for treats."

Bodie rubbed his chin. "Should I let them in then?"

"You should start drying." Sarah tossed a dish towel at him. "Then we can head out and bed down the farm for the night."

Apple treats for the donkeys and the Jersey cow,

Olive, and the evening chores complete, the household headed to their own rooms. Bodie stood at the wide window in the guest bedroom and stared at his reflection in the windowpane. Some would say it was all falling into place rather neatly and seamlessly for him.

Between the job on his suspect's farm and now an apartment that supposedly offered a view of his same suspect's pastures, Bodie would have full access to what he needed to prove his insurance-fraud theory and close his case.

If his farmer was moving bison from one pasture to another to hide them, Bodie would be able to see it in real time. *Gotcha.*

Or if his farmer was miscounting and altering her own records. *Gotcha.*

Honestly, those theories made his skin prickle. Much like wearing a fitted wool turtleneck sweater on the hottest summer day. Ironically, he was starting to feel like that *gotcha* just might be aimed at him.

Especially since Sarah had been nothing but attentive and thoughtful all evening. She'd even stopped in the greenhouse to grab fresh mint for Pearl's migraine and an aloe vera leaf cutting for Artie's sunburned cheeks after they'd finished the evening chores. Not to mention, she'd added Pearl's groceries to her own shopping list to pick up the following day.

Perhaps his farmer was spending her insurance claim money on her neighbors and the community.

Talk about grasping at straws. Bodie ran his fingers underneath the collar of his denim button-down and rubbed the back of his neck.

A small red flash caught his attention. Bodie scrubbed his hand over both eyes. He'd tested and installed more than a half dozen of those bubble lights today. He wouldn't be surprised if the red flare was simply a lingering aftereffect in his vision. He pressed his forehead against the windowpane. Sure enough, the red blinked again. Nothing for it now but to check things out, even though he suspected it was most likely an electrical short in the wiring.

Bodie crossed the bedroom, then was downstairs and outside in seconds. He stuck to the shelter of the trees lining the road until the main gate came into view. As he suspected, it was closed. Still, he kept to the shadows, listened to the night and watched the bulb light flicker every ninety seconds. Definite electrical short.

He heard his farmer well before he saw her. Or, more preciously, he heard her talking, assuring herself it was nothing. *That everything was fine.* Finally, she came into view. Her dark hair was undone and floated around her shoulders in delightfully messy waves. The pocket on her bulky hooded sweatshirt bulged and only one leg of her plaid pajama pants was crammed into her red rain boot. She clutched the handle of what looked like an extra-large stainless-steel tumbler.

His farmer was disheveled, utterly distracting, and Bodie was entirely too captivated.

Sarah swiped at her cheek, knocking her hair away from her face, and muttered, "See. Fine. All good."

Before Bodie could alert her to his presence, the dry leaves behind him crackled. The branches above his head swayed. A low growl filled the silence.

Sarah yelped and spun toward him.

A bright light wobbled across his vision, blinding him. Now he knew what was in Sarah's pocket—a flashlight. Bodie raised his arm and blocked his eyes from the erratically bobbing light and called out, "Sarah! It's me. Bodie."

The beam stilled, then swung back in his direction. Confusion was there in her whispered "Bodie."

"Yeah." He stepped out from the protection of the trees. "And maybe a racoon or two."

"Racoons," Sarah whispered, her confusion even thicker now. She aimed the flashlight over his head. "Are you sure?"

"I think I caught a ringed tail in the branches earlier." And the unpleasant scent also gave his nocturnal buddies away. Bodie scanned the trees. "They tend to avoid the spotlight. I'm sure they are already on their way out of here."

"We should whistle too." Sarah never turned off her flashlight. "I heard that scares them off as well."

"Or we could head back to the farmhouse." Bodie walked over to the bulb light and flipped the switch to Off. "And we can leave them to their nighttime foraging."

Sarah joined him at the gate and handed him the stainless-steel water bottle. Then she tugged hard on the lock. Once. Twice. Finally, she nodded as if satisfied. "Everything is as it should be out here."

"Faulty wire." Bodie watched her fiddle with the lock again and kept his words casual. "Those lights became vintage several decades ago."

"True." Sarah's grin was quick and small. Still, the worry in the crease between her eyebrows lingered.

Bodie gripped the tumbler handle and wished he could take her hand in his. But he knew he wouldn't stop there. He'd tuck her right into his side. If he left it at that, then maybe all would be fine. Except the cowboy of few words wanted to make her promises. Impractical and impossible ones.

But she wasn't his. And he wasn't staying. He belonged elsewhere, chasing bad guys, not on a farm caring for a farmer.

After all, he'd taken an oath to serve and protect. He'd dedicated his life to his duty. There simply wasn't room for anything more, even if his farmer tempted him to... Bodie sidestepped that thought and got his focus straight.

"This is empty." He lifted the water bottle between them and eyed her. "What did you intend to do with it?"

"It was the first thing I grabbed on my way out the door." Sarah snatched the tumbler back and started up the driveway. "There's a good weight to it. It's hefty and solid. It would certainly cause damage if wielded appropriately, don't you think?"

His farmer, a possible thief and a tumbler. There was an image he did not want to entertain. Never mind the first thing she grabbed was a water bottle and not him. Bodie clamped his jaw tight, certain those promises would spill out into the night air and stick between them like a swarm of gnats.

She slanted her gaze at him and frowned. "You're thinking I can't handle myself."

He was thinking he wanted to be the first person she turned to for whatever.

"Well, I can," she argued, as if his silence counted as agreement. "I knew nothing was happening at the main gate." She rounded on him and halted all their forward progress. "Do you know why?"

Bodie shook his head and tried not to marvel at the way those brunette waves in her hair fairly vibrated and her eyes sparked. His cowgirl was riled and Bodie was hooked all over again.

"Because he wants my bison." She speared her arms to the sides as if shaking off her frustration. The tumbler swung in her tense grip. "And do you know what is not here at my main gate?"

Bodie arched one eyebrow and said mildly, "Bison."

"Right." Just like that, she deflated. Her shoulders sagged as her exhale came out in a long sigh. She peered at him. "I can handle myself."

She had backbone. He would give her that. Heck, he admired that about her. Still, he knew firsthand how courage wasn't always enough to win against someone bent on doing wrong. He followed her toward the farmhouse. "Even so, maybe you should keep the tumbler for nightcaps and let law enforcement do what they are trained for."

"I will call the sheriff's department if there is a real problem," she assured him and then considered him a beat longer. "I could say the same thing to you. You came out here alone and without even a water bottle."

Well, he was law enforcement. Bodie opened the back door, motioned her inside and told himself it was not *concern for him* he heard in her words. He said, "I'll make a call too if I think there's trouble."

She faced him. Her gaze searched his. Her words were hesitant. "For what it's worth, I'm glad you were out there with me tonight."

And didn't that make him want to sweep her into his arms and promise something like always. He tapped his finger against the tumbler. "I wouldn't turn down a nightcap."

"That I can handle." Her smile was slow and stretched into her cheeks. "Follow me."

Anywhere. Bodie winced. He lingered in the mudroom, wiped his boots on the mat again, and put much-needed space between him and his farmer. Then, he headed into the kitchen and pulled up short.

Rose sat on a barstool, her cotton robe buttoned under her chin and her feet covered in fluffy slippers. She gripped a spoon in one hand and a pint of chocolate cherry vanilla ice cream in the other.

Sarah set her hands on her hips and frowned. "Grandma, we talked about this."

"Bodie and I talked about a late-night sweet treat." Rose aimed her spoon at Bodie. "Utensils are in the drawer beside the refrigerator. You'll find pints of butter pecan and salted caramel ice cream in the freezer. I'm sure you could use a bite after your midnight stroll."

Sarah opened and closed her mouth. "Our what?"

"Your grandpa and I used to take starlit strolls." Rose waved her spoon between Sarah and Bodie, then grinned slyly as if in on the secret. "We'd hold hands and let the moon guide us. I know the best spot to count the stars and sneak a good night smooch, if you're of a mind for that."

A good night kiss under the stars with his farmer. Yeah, Bodie could be of a mind for that sort of midnight stroll.

"Grandma," Sarah mumbled and wiped her hand over her face.

But not before Bodie caught her blush.

"Oh, I get it." Rose stuck her spoon in her ice cream and smiled knowingly. "You want to discover your own special smooching spots."

Sarah groaned and her cheeks darkened.

his farmer's long-time friend might have something to do with his feelings for his farmer and nothing to do with his case. Nothing about that realization was good.

Clack. Clack. Clack.

Bodie flinched.

Rose caught him and arched an eyebrow. "What's the matter? You never heard a barn owl before?"

"Owls hoot," Bodie argued, leaning into his lessons from his elementary-school days.

"Not the barn owl," Rose countered, and moved to scratch Olive's ear. "And not Gizmo. He's not sure about you." Rose eyed him as if she wasn't so certain about Bodie, either. "He's just letting you know it."

Bodie rubbed the back of his neck. "Where is Gizmo?"

"Sarah's grandpa built an owl roost at Sarah's request when she was a little girl." Rose pointed to the pitched roof of the stable barn. "The hole is hidden up under the eaves. Gizmo can see you quite well."

Bodie shaded his eyes and squinted. Seeing nothing but shadows, he returned his attention to Rose and asked, "When will Gizmo decide I'm okay to be here?"

Rose shrugged and studied him. "When will you admit you are not a farmhand?"

About the same time he confessed this case had him more than a little twisted around. So, not ever.

"Don't try convincing me otherwise," Rose continued and tapped a finger against her temple. "I may be decades away from my spring chicken years, but that doesn't mean the tack isn't still sharp up here."

Bodie couldn't help but grin. "I don't think you look a day past fabulous."

"I always did appreciate a charmer." Rose smiled. Her words were wistful. "My husband, Teddy, was one. Never could hold onto my anger when he was around." She paused and pointed at Bodie. "But charm can't change the facts. You got no experience."

"That would be true for farming," he admitted. "As for the horses and stables, those I already took care of this morning, and I challenge you to find fault in there."

"You got that familiar look about you again." Rose's mouth quirked up at the corners. "You sure remind me of someone. The name keeps slipping past me. It'll come back. You can count on that."

Bodie didn't doubt her. Nothing for it but to stop acting like his father. Not that he knew exactly how his dad acted these days. Still, a baseball cap would be his first purchase. He couldn't remember the last time his father wore anything other than a cowboy hat. Surely that much hadn't changed.

"Now, there's more work to be done before nightfall, and while you may not have the know-how, you've got the strength and willingness." Rose gave one last rub under Olive's chin, slipped another apple from her pocket and started walking toward the pasture. The cow followed docilely behind her.

"Let me guess," Bodie said and fell in step beside Rose. "You're going to be my know-how."

"Of course." Rose led Olive into the pasture, gave her the apple, then stepped out. A big smile stretched across her face. "I haven't had this much fun in an age. If my granddaughter replaces you for experience, what will I do then?"

He was more than certain the wily older cowgirl would come up with something, and no doubt it would be entertaining.

"I'll tell you." Rose arched an eyebrow at him. "I will be back in my rocking chair on the front porch. A person can only rock so long before they've rocked themselves into a permanent boredom."

Bodie shut the gate and locked it. "Well, I would like to stick around." After all, when he got his feelings and his perspective untwisted, he would remember he had a case to solve and a job he intended to return to. He added, "And I would hate for you to be bored."

"Well, let's get to it." Rose tightened the strap of her bucket hat under her chin. "We need to scour the storage barn to see what we can use for an outdoor pig paddock. We sure can't keep Gladys and Gilbert in a playpen for much longer."

With those orders, Bodie set off to learn the farmhand ropes from an expert. The storage barn picked through, Rose and Bodie spent the lunch hour watching how-to videos on assembling the best pig paddock. However, they disagreed on which pigpen to build. Fortunately, Sarah returned in time to cast the deciding vote and convince her grandmother to get ready for her afternoon doctor's appointments.

"Bodie should come with us," Rose called over her shoulder. "He can pick up the supplies we need at Country Time Farm & Ranch Supply while we're at the doctor's and physical therapy."

Sarah turned to him. "Are you okay with that? Because I can take care of it another time."

He was not letting her off the hook that easily. He wanted to help her. Besides, any excuse to spend more time with his farmer was a good one in his mind. He picked up a piece of paper from the table. "We already made a supply list. I know exactly what to get."

"Looks like we are all headed into town," she said.

Rose returned, her bucket hat back on her head. "Don't forget we're stopping in at The Silver Penny after physical therapy."

"Tess Sloan owns the general store, and she is the chocolatier extraordinaire," Sarah explained on their way outside.

Bodie connected even more dots—except these were related to him. Tess Sloan was married to Carter Sloan, who happened to be the oldest son of Lilian Sloan. Bodie supposed that would make Tess and him family of sorts after his father wed Lilian.

"Tess's chocolate confections are the best you've

ever tasted," Rose stated. "It's my incentive for getting through all those exercises my physical therapist makes me do."

"I can't wait to try some." Bodie helped Rose into the truck, hopped in beside her, and then they were off.

It took more than an hour and several trips around the large ranch supply store for Bodie to find the pigpen supplies and schedule delivery. Still, he was early when he entered The Silver Penny General Store and used the time to find a baseball hat before Sarah and Rose arrived.

Bodie stepped up to the counter and handed a distressed denim baseball cap to a woman with chin-length brown hair, striking green eyes, and the name *Tess* embroidered on her shirt. She shook his hand and introduced herself, then said, "I know who you are."

Bodie nodded and reached for his wallet.

"This one is on the house." Tess dropped the hat in a paper shopping bag and handed it to him.

"Consider it a welcome to the family." A refined older woman stepped beside Tess and smiled.

Bodie knew instantly he was about to meet his father's fiancée, Lilian Sloan. Her handshake was firm, her introduction quick. He said, "I wasn't aware you worked here too."

"My daughter-in-law took pity on me." Lilian wrapped her arm around Tess's waist and added, "I was a bit lost when I retired from the medical field."

Bodie had read Lilian's rather impressive online

bio and knew all about her accomplishments as a renowned heart surgeon.

"Don't let her fool you." Tess grinned. "Lilian is a guest professor at the medical college not far from here and the chair of her other daughter-in-law Maggie's rodeo committee. She also keeps her son Grant's medical staff in line and babysits whenever anyone asks her."

"I will not ever turn down time with my grandbabies." Lilian lit up right before his eyes. She went from the composed, unruffled former doctor to the approachable and devoted grandmother in seconds.

Tess chuckled. "And despite all that, Lilian still finds time to work here when I'm short-staffed."

"What can I say? I'm a sucker for the free chocolate samples." Lilian handed Bodie a waxed paper–wrapped caramel and said, "Enough about me." Then she tucked her hair behind her ear and shook her head. "I'm sorry. Lacey told us to be expecting you, but she didn't tell us how much you look like your father."

Tess tipped her head and regarded him. "It is really uncanny how much you look like Wells."

Bodie opened the bag and pulled out the baseball cap. He tugged the sales tag off and adjusted the brim low on his forehead. "How about now?"

"I'm not exactly sure what answer you would prefer to hear, so I'm not going to say anything," Lilian said.

"Thanks for this." Bodie touched the brim of the hat, then said, "So, Lacey has been talking about me."

"We're family," Tess replied. "We talk around the dinner table and everywhere in between about pretty much everything and anything."

"Even Wells talks about you and your siblings quite often," Lilian offered.

Bodie wasn't quite sure how he felt about that. All he knew was he thought about his dad more often these days. Ever since he'd lost his friend and mentor in the line of duty last year. His friend had left behind a legacy and no regrets. Yet when Bodie looked at his own life, all he saw were loose ends he needed to tie up. "I hope it's all good things my dad has told you."

"You'll have to join us at the dinner table if you want to know what gets said among family." Tess gave him a small grin.

Bodie tended to approach family dinners with caution, not enthusiasm. It had been at the dinner table when his mother had announced his parents' divorce. Later, the same table would play host to the introductions to their mom's current boyfriend— and sometimes future stepdads—as if somehow their favorite meal made the rotation of father figures easier to digest. Then there was his fateful dinner for two when Bodie's own relationship crumbled before the appetizers were served. His fiancée had handled her engagement ring with less care than the bread basket that evening.

The Sloans valued their family-dinner time. While he respected and envied them a bit, he would pass on joining in.

Tess glanced at Lilian, saw the older woman nod, then turned her attention back to Bodie and said, "I'm not one to talk out of turn, but there's something that needs saying."

Bodie stilled.

Tess met his stare boldly. Her words were soft and serious. "Whatever is going on at Crossroads R&R, Sarah and Rose aren't involved. I would bet my store on it."

Bodie kept his words low. "I'm sure Sarah would not want you to do that."

"It's what she would do for me." Tess blinked at him. "Around here, we look after our own."

"I'm starting to see that," Bodie said.

"You'll get used to it." Tess released her full smile. "And if you stick around long enough to call this place home, we just might look after you too."

Home. Bodie was not certain of the last place he had called home. He had an apartment where he slept and stored his tactical gear. His fiancée had claimed the one-bedroom unit had less warmth than a hospital room. Bodie had never given his place much thought, preferring instead to keep his mind on work. Now, his cowgirl's farmhouse had true warmth, a comfortable kitchen table made for gathering around, and a sense of... Bodie fiddled with the handle on the shopping bag and said, "For the record, we're on the same side."

"I'm glad you recognize that." Tess turned and asked a customer in the home goods aisle if she needed any assistance with picking out bedsheets.

Bodie nodded, unable to deny there was something appealing about such a close-knit community.

Lilian reached out and set her hand on his arm. "Your father and I are not expecting you to jump into the family with both boots and a Bundt cake."

"That's good to know." Bodie grinned. "I'm not exactly known for my baking skills."

"My sons will appreciate your sense of humor." Lilian chuckled, her expression softened, and she said, "Just know this. Whenever you are ready to join us, there will be a seat for you at our table. Whether that is now or next year."

Touched, Bodie managed a rather raspy sounding "Thank you."

"Family wounds heal when they are good and ready. It's not something to be rushed," Lilian continued in her succinct, straightforward manner. "That much I know from personal experience. You won't be getting an end date on healing from me."

Bodie said, "I appreciate that too."

"It's also why we are not setting an official wedding date," she explained. "That will happen when the entire Hopson family is healed."

Now Bodie both liked her and respected her.

The bell over the entrance chimed. The double doors swung open. Bodie caught a glimpse of a familiar green bucket hat before the tall endcap display blocked his view. But he recognized the cheery greeting all too well. Rose and Sarah were finished with Rose's medical appointments. The duo headed down a side aisle toward the confectionary at the back of the general store.

"I'll let you get back to work." Lilian smiled, then disappeared through a door marked Private.

Bodie turned and headed in the direction of his farmer and her grandmother.

"Tess, tell me you haven't sold out of your Black Forest dark cherry truffles." Rose stood in front of a large, refrigerated display case. The brim of her bucket hat was crinkled against the glass. "I'm going to need all you got today."

Sarah waited behind Rose and shook her head empathically at the general-store owner.

"Does this mean you've graduated from physical therapy then, Rose?" Tess asked and took a pair of gloves from a box on the counter.

"Dustin is keeping me on through the end of the year. He already booked all my appointments through to January," Rose harrumphed. "That's not the worst of it either."

Bodie grinned at the put-out note in Rose's words.

"I'm sure Dustin only wants what is best for you and your health," Tess said soothingly.

"Chocolate is good for my health." Rose accepted a sample dark chocolate from Tess and frowned. "It would be better for me if Dustin taught me something useful to do with my cane."

Confusion widened the shopkeeper's eyes.

Sarah groaned. "Grandma, Dustin holds a doctorate in physical therapy. He is not a self-defense instructor."

Self-defense. Bodie's good humor dipped.

"Well, he should be," Rose muttered. "I could get a two-for-one deal then." Rose turned and reached for a napkin. She spotted Bodie and brightened. "Bodie is here. He will agree with me that a cane is good for more than walking."

"I'm sorry I missed the conversation." He touched his baseball hat. "I was shopping for a new hat."

Sarah looked aghast.

"I would've suggested a cowboy hat." Rose stuck the rest of her chocolate into her mouth and shrugged at Sarah. "Well, it's what true cowboys wear around here."

"I've got a collection in storage." Bodie flicked the brim of the baseball cap. "Thought I'd change it up."

Rose hummed. "I tried to change things up today too. Not sure I would recommend it."

Bodie was changing things up again too. He wasn't going to entertain anymore reckless thoughts about his farmer. It really shouldn't be that hard. Bodie concentrated on the display case and asked, "How did the doctor's appointment go today?"

The strained silence pulled his attention back to his farmer.

A reserve settled into Sarah's hazel eyes, and she offered only, "It was fine."

The lack of assurance in her words told him it was far from fine. But his farmer wasn't sharing. They were both withholding information. He supposed that put them on even ground. Although, he didn't much care for it. He wanted his farmer to confide in him. Call him selfish. It wouldn't be the first time.

"It was fine, at least until we got to physical therapy," Rose muttered and tapped her finger on the glass. "Tess, give Sarah a piece of the dark chocolate toffee." Rose nudged her elbow into Bodie's side and whispered, "That's Sarah's favorite. It's something of a pique popper. And she's rather piqued with me."

Although Rose didn't sound bothered by that fact.

"Grandma." Sarah shook her head again.

"Better make it two pieces, Tess," Rose decided and held up two fingers. "You should always know when to double down. That's advice you all best remember."

Bodie was double downing on tying up and knotting off his awareness of his farmer.

Amusement flashed softly across Sarah's face. Her words were resigned. "Tess, we will take a dozen Black Forest truffles." At Rose's enthusiastic gasp, Sarah added, "To go, please."

"Told you," Rose said to Bodie. "Tess's divine chocolate works every time."

But his farmer hadn't taken even a small bite of toffee. Bodie suspected it had nothing to do with the candy and everything to do with Rose. The older cowgirl meant well, and it was difficult to be frustrated with her for wanting to protect her farm. He only wished the older cowgirl didn't feel like she had to.

Outside in the truck, Sarah turned up the air-conditioning and said, "Grandma, about today."

Rose shifted on the bench seat between Bodie and Sarah, then sighed. "I promise not to ask Dustin to teach me self-defense at my physical therapy appointments."

"And you will use your cane for walking," Sarah added.

Rose crossed her arms over her chest. "We haven't found my cane, so I don't see as how it matters much."

"I'll look for it when we get home," Sarah said.

"That'll have to wait," Rose mused. "We need to get building the pigpen and you got crops to see to. Harvest is right around the corner. You need a backup in case Sawyer's combine isn't up and running soon."

"Sawyer assured me his combine would be working," Sarah said. "The pigpen will have to wait. Bodie and I are moving the bison this afternoon to the western pasture."

Bodie congratulated himself for not flinching. Not even a little bit at that news.

"Good idea," Rose said cheerfully. "Take Mav too. He can practice his herding skills."

And perhaps teach Bodie a thing or two as well. How exactly was he going to fake his way through a cattle run?

"I know Mav is a retriever, not a herding dog."

Sarah chuckled and glanced at Bodie. "Still, I can't leave Mav behind. His heart is in the right place."

Rose patted Bodie's leg and said, "Sometimes that's all you need."

But Bodie had set his heart aside a long time ago. Left it behind and moved on. He hadn't needed it. In fact, he hadn't even bothered looking for it.

Now, he had to be careful. Otherwise, his heart just might find him and show him what he'd been missing.

CHAPTER SEVEN

THE NEXT DAY, Sarah still had her overnight houseguests, thanks to the electrician waiting on a special-order breaker panel for Pearl and Artie's ranch house. Pearl and Artie were up at their orchards, collecting apples and persimmons. Sarah had joined the couple to pick her own baskets of fruit while Bodie took care of the stables. Sarah congratulated herself for concentrating on the farm all morning rather than her cowboy.

Now, the lunch hour was closing in and Sarah hadn't seen Bodie since breakfast... When he had filled her coffee cup before she'd even settled fully into the chair beside him. When she had been stumped at how natural it was to have Bodie there. How ordinary it had felt when he helped clean up the dishes and they divided the outdoor morning chores.

Sarah grabbed the large fruit baskets from the passenger seat of the UTV and headed inside the farmhouse. She would have patted herself on the back, but her hands were full. Still, she smiled, acknowledging her restraint at not even scanning the property for a quick peek at her cowboy. She would see Bodie when she saw him.

As for that quickening of her pulse, well, she blamed it on the bushel of fruit she hefted onto the kitchen island.

Grandma Rose snapped the footrest on her recliner into place and yawned. "The piglets and I were taking a brief intermission after our lunch."

"Don't get up on my account." Sarah waved at her grandmother in the family room. "I'm just dropping these off. We can deal with them later."

"I'll sort through them." Grandma Rose settled into her chair. "I've got plans for bread, jams, tarts and pies." The footrest popped back out. "I'm going to take a minute to figure out what I want to make first."

Her grandmother needed to take a longer intermission. "I'll help you make whatever you decide." Sarah checked on the piglets huddled together in the pigpen. "Can I get you anything before I head out?"

"Got everything I need." Rose picked up the remote from the side table and turned on the TV, then added mildly, "Oh, by the way, I packed you and Bodie lunch."

"Bodie hasn't been in for lunch?" Sarah asked casually.

"He works as hard as you. I couldn't get him to come inside with me." Her grandmother flipped through the TV stations. Her words were cheerful. "Now you can grab Bodie and get to enjoying what the day is offering."

"What is that exactly?" Besides fence repairs, trough leak checks, and a grain cart tune-up.

"Whatever you want it to be." Delight spread across her grandmother's face, pushing aside any hint of fatigue. Grandma Rose continued, "You've got good food, good weather and a good cowboy. That's the recipe for a perfect day. It's time to shake things up and try something new."

Or, it was time to stay the course. Sarah could use the good weather and extra help to her advantage. She could finally tackle those tasks she'd been too busy to attend to. A completed to-do list would certainly be something new. Sarah walked into the kitchen.

Grandma Rose mused, "Nice day for a ride and picnic out at the grotto."

When was the last time she had ridden for pleasure? Sarah eyed the cloth lunch sack on the counter. Never mind that. She couldn't recall the last time she had been tempted.

"Everything will fit rather nicely into a saddlebag." Grandma Rose lifted her voice over the jingle on the TV commercial. "Ask your cowboy how he feels about an old-fashioned picnic."

Sarah snatched up the lunch sack. Because both she and Bodie needed to eat before they got to work on her to-do list. She smiled at her grandmother. "Thanks for lunch. Text me if you need something."

"I only need you to go enjoy yourself." Grandma

Rose lifted her phone to show Sarah it was within reach, then added, "You work too much."

"You always tell me hard work is good," Sarah argued, amusement in her words. "That it keeps the mind wrinkle-free and the body well-oiled."

"It's true." Grandma Rose shook her finger at Sarah. "But you must stop and enjoy yourself. Otherwise, all you're going to be left with is a pile of starch and a rash. No one wants that."

What Sarah wanted was to make sure her grandma was happy and could spend her last years in her home just as she wished. That would bring Sarah joy. If that meant Sarah had to set certain things aside for now, so be it. The fun would surely be around when she was ready to seek it out.

Sarah walked out the back door and paused on the porch. Mav barked. The sound drew her attention to the side of the house and straight to her cowboy.

Bodie and Mav were at the duck pen. The gate was propped open behind Bodie. Mav sat inside the pen, his fluffy tail wagging and stirring up the dirt. Bodie knelt, reached into his shirt pocket, then held out his palm. The first duckling pecked gently at his hand. Bodie grinned. The other ducklings chirped and fluttered their feathers as they crowded around Bodie. Mav barked excitedly again. Her cowboy laughed and talked to the dog.

Just a dozen or so long strides would put her right in the middle of the lively group. A quick jog and she could join the merriment within seconds.

Sarah stepped off the last stair, then turned to the left, away from the pen.

Sarah skirted around the other side of the farmhouse, stopped at the UTV to get Artie's gift for Bodie, then headed to the duck pen. Bodie inspected the latch on the pen gate. Mav watched him intently.

Sarah grinned and said, "You're thinking there is no way a dog should be able to open that latch."

Bodie scratched his head and nodded. "How does he do it?"

"I wish I knew." Sarah greeted the mischievous dog. "I'm thinking I might need a working camera so I can put it on this gate and watch what Mav does."

"That's not a bad idea." Bodie latched the gate and turned to face her.

But it was a bad idea to be standing within tripping distance of her cowboy. *If I fell, would you catch me?* The thought set her pulse to racing. She thrust a cowboy hat at Bodie and pushed her words through that breathless catch. "Artie wanted me to give this to you. He also told me to tell you being a cowboy means looking like one."

"Well, Artie would know." Bodie chuckled and swapped his baseball cap for the cowboy hat. His eyebrows lifted. "It fits pretty well."

It suited him very well. The black felt accentuated his sharp jawline. The brim shadowed his startlingly blue eyes, but not his undeniably pensive gaze. And his confidence all but amplified right before her eyes.

Now she knew what eye-catching looked like. She was definitely caught.

Bodie reached for the hat. "Does your frown mean I should stick to baseball caps?"

It would certainly give her eyes a reprieve. Who was she kidding? Her cowboy was handsome, hat or not. He drew her gaze whenever she was near him. Worse, something about him spiked her interest and made her much too aware of her pocketed heart. Sarah shook her head. "Keep it on. It suits you."

Bodie lowered his arm.

As for Sarah, she slipped on her sunglasses and vowed to keep her focus fixed on anything but her cowboy. Time to get back to work. Alone. Like she preferred. Yet she said, "I thought we could take a different ride around the property today." She paused, quickly devised an out and added, "If you're up for that kind of thing. If not, that's fine too." *Because I'm not confused about what this is.*

This was not a picnic date kind of thing where her feelings might get bruised.

Bodie tapped the brim of his hat higher and eyed her. "What's a different ride look like?"

Not a date. That was for sure. Sarah pointed to the stables and said, "Saddles and open trails."

Bodie grinned. "I'm all in for that."

Sarah was all in for some breathing space between her and her cowboy and if she had to saddle up to get it, so be it. She started toward the stables and set the expectation. "We will check on the herds and give the horses some much-needed exercise."

"What's in the bag?" Bodie walked beside her, and Mav followed behind them.

"Lunch." She lifted the cloth bag and shrugged, keeping her expression indifferent. "Grandma insisted we eat."

Sarah refused to call it a picnic or ask her cowboy how he felt about going on one. Because that teetered too close to things like feelings and diving deep beneath those layers of her cowboy. And that would tip her right into other things like dates and relationships. Both Bodie and she had agreed relationships were a complication they didn't need.

Bodie opened the door to the stables and smiled. "Can't think of a better way to spend an afternoon."

There was the problem. Sarah couldn't think of a better person to spend the afternoon with other than her cowboy. She stepped inside and pointed to a stall. "The dapple-gray one looking at us so earnestly is Calvin. He's been restless to stretch his legs in more than the pasture."

"Calvin." Bodie arched an eyebrow. "You named such a stunning gelding Calvin."

"Sure did." Sarah chuckled and walked over to Twilight's stall. The red-roan mare greeted her with an excited whinny. "Calvin is intelligent, reliable, and hard to spook. Everything a Calvin should be."

Bodie looked doubtful and greeted the dapple-gray. He whispered loudly, "Not to worry, Calvin. We'll find you a suitable nickname this afternoon."

Sarah laughed and handed the lunch sack to Bodie. "Grandma Rose assured me this will fit in your saddlebag. I'll find extra water."

"What do you have in your saddlebags?" he asked and took the cloth bag. "Our camping gear?"

"Tease me if you want." Sarah took a halter bridle off the hook outside Twilight's stall. "But I like to be prepared out there."

"I wasn't teasing," he corrected. "My father always told me if I was prepared, there would be no need to panic in any situation."

"He sounds like a very smart man." Sarah smiled.

Bodie turned away, but not before she caught his frown. Sarah explained, "I don't have camping gear, but I do have a first aid kit and a lot of other provisions just in case."

That earned only a nod from her pensive-looking cowboy. But Sarah was determined not to pry. After all, this was not a date, and he was not her cowboy to soothe. She got busy preparing her mare instead.

The horses saddled and warmed up outside the stables, Sarah guided her mare toward the road that bordered the cornfields. Bodie followed along with Mav beside them. Minutes later, they turned onto a narrow trail that cut through the forest and led out to the open prairies. The entire bison herd accounted for, Sarah relaxed and started to rediscover a bit of the joy in riding for pleasure.

Mav chased a butterfly through a patch of sunflowers.

Bodie guided Calvin beside her and tipped his head toward the excited dog. "Are the sunflowers another crop for Crossroads R&R?"

Sarah chuckled and shook her head. "I tossed the seeds out to see what would happen when I moved back here two summers ago." When she was following her joy and not profit margins.

"It's something." Bodie smiled at her. "It's like your own private field of sunshine."

Sarah took in the delightful yellow sunflower heads and slowed her horse. She heard the wonder in her words. "It makes me want to linger and chase butterflies with Mav."

"Me too." Amusement flashed across Bodie's face. "Now I sound as surprised as you."

"When was the last time you did something for pure pleasure?" Sarah slanted her gaze toward him. "The kind of thing that makes you lose all track of time and get completely caught up in the moment."

"I can't remember." He loosened his grip on the reins. His shoulders shook silently. "Now I'm frantically flipping through memories trying to find something. What about you?"

She watched Mav leap over a bush, his tail wagging, his ears flapping, all joy in motion and said, "I came back here to have more of those moments." Like the ones she remembered from her teenage years living with her grandparents.

"Let me guess," he said quietly. "It's been more work than butterfly chasing."

"That's part of the whole adulting deal, isn't it?" she asked.

"Seems to be," he mused. "But it also seems that you and I are seriously lacking on butterfly moments."

"It also seems we have this prairie to ourselves." Sarah's grin slowly spread across her face. She leaned forward and patted Twilight's sleek neck. "Interested in a bit of a race?"

Bodie's eyebrows lifted. "Thought you wanted to linger?"

Sarah chuckled. "Why do that when we can outrun the wind and touch the clouds?"

"Why indeed." One corner of his mouth lifted. "I'm in."

I could be too. If you called me yours. Sarah blinked and blurted, "Winner gets the last of the salted caramel ice cream that I hid in the back of the freezer."

With the reward settled, the race was on. Cowboy hats flew off and were left behind in the field of flowers. Laughter and good-natured ribbing spilled across the breeze. Unfortunately, it was a dead-even finish, and Mav failed to declare the winner. With the decision made to share the ice cream later and the horses drinking in the stream, Sarah wasn't in a rush to leave.

She divvied up the lunch Rose had packed and told herself it was far from a picnic. After all, they weren't at the grotto, and they were standing so Sarah wouldn't be tempted to stay too long. As it was, she ate slowly. But when she was tempted to share more than grapes with Bodie, she decided their late lunch break was over.

Still, she retrieved her cowboy hat in the sunflower field, then tipped her face toward the afternoon sunshine. Finally, she felt the last of her daily tension ease from her fingers and toes. She closed her eyes and sighed. "I need to do this more."

A shadow fell over her. She opened her eyes to find Bodie watching her. A small smile on his face. His expression was unguarded and his gaze warm. Awareness spiked inside her. Her breath hitched.

He took her hat and brushed off the brim. More of that warm appreciation filled his gaze. He said softly, "It definitely suits you."

I could say the same about you, cowboy. And what suited her then was chasing a different kind of butterfly. The ones that made her feel fluttery and excited and all too hopeful inside.

He set her hat on her head and trailed his fingers across her cheek. His touch light as a flower petal drew her to him.

Sunshine. Sunflowers. And a kiss from her cowboy. Surely those were the makings of a perfect day.

Sarah tipped her face up. He leaned in.

Mav barked excitedly.

Her cowboy seemed to catch himself.

And Sarah remembered chasing a cowboy wouldn't save the farm and ensure her grandmother could spend the rest of her years at home. She took a step backward before she stole a kiss and a glimpse into what her perfect day could have been, then said, "We're close to the sheep. We should probably head on over there."

Bodie smashed his cowboy hat low on his head and nodded. "After you."

The joy inside Sarah hung around. She was smiling into the sun when they crossed the bridge leading toward the sheep in the southern pasture and eventually the grotto. Perhaps her grandmother had been onto something after all. A picnic at the grotto sounded more than a little appealing. Now she was considering future plans with her cowboy. She sighed at her giddiness.

Bodie reined in beside her. Confusion shaded his words. "Are we moving the flock to this pasture then?"

"What?" Sarah blinked the sunbeams from her eyes and scanned the pasture. The very empty pasture. "No. They're supposed to be here." She tightened her hold on her reins and her sudden panic. "I'm sure they are here."

Bodie adjusted his seat in the saddle and gazed at the pasture.

Sarah dismounted and checked the gate. "It's latched and secured." She looked at Bodie over her shoulder and smiled around the unease in her words. "That has to be a good sign, right?"

Bodie frowned, looking less than convinced.

Sarah swung the gate open and motioned him inside. She mounted Twilight and joined him. "Let's split up and check the far ends of the pasture in case the flock is huddled there. And it won't hurt to inspect the fence along the way too."

"Text me if you find anything," he said.

"Same." Sarah turned Twilight in the opposite direction, finally dropped her forced smile and headed for the first section of fencing.

By the time she rounded the far side and noted no sheep and no holes in the fence, worry filtered through her. She pulled out her phone. No texts from Bodie.

Two days was all it had taken for Sarah to lose someone else's livestock. First missing bison. Now missing sheep. Was it a coincidence? Was it... Sarah refused to follow through on that thought.

Instead, she tracked the fence line down a dry, grassy knoll. In the gulch, she discovered the break in the wire mesh near one of the wooden posts and she dropped to her knees in relief. The sheep simply took advantage of a weak section in the fence and escaped.

This was nothing she couldn't handle. Nothing she couldn't fix.

After all, every farmer dealt with the very same issues with livestock and proper fences. She was no different.

Minutes later, she heard the thud of Calvin's hooves and called out, "Down here."

Bodie made his way to her and studied the steel-wire panel.

"This is where they got out." More relief worked through her rushed words. "Someone isn't trying to sabotage the farm after all."

Bodie eyed her. "What?"

"Never mind. This is good news." Sarah pointed over the top of the fence. "This pasture borders Pearl and Artie's land. With luck, the flock made its way there and Pearl is already looking after them." She tugged her phone out. "I'll call her."

Bodie nodded, walked over to Twilight and asked, "Have any wire cutters with you?"

Sarah told Bodie where to look for the tools, then greeted Pearl. Bodie was mending the hole when Sarah ended her phone call. She refused to give in to her unease and chose to be optimistic. "Pearl hasn't seen the sheep yet. She promised to call when they show up."

"They won't be seeing any sheep," Bodie said flatly. He rapped the hammer against the wooden fence post.

"Not if the sheep don't get there soon," Sarah replied, sticking to her resolve. "Artie and Pearl are headed to Amarillo for the night and leaving within the hour. Sawyer gifted them theater tickets since their power is still out." Sarah worked another smile into place. "Wasn't that kind of him? Pearl loves musicals."

"That was nice of Sawyer," Bodie muttered and banged the post again. "You can tell Pearl to worry about what dress to pack and not the sheep."

Sarah propped her hands on her hips and frowned. "But the flock is headed their way."

Bodie shook his head and pressed his palm against the wire panel, testing it. "They didn't leave this way."

Sarah crossed her arms over her chest and tamped down her frustration. "You're wrong."

"There are no hoofprints around me." Bodie's words were patient and straightforward. "Look closely at the gulch. See for yourself."

Look at me. Can't you see I need you to be wrong? This needed to be only a farm oversight. Easily corrected and simple to recover from. Sarah argued, "The gulch is covered in grass and weeds. You wouldn't see any."

"Nothing is trampled or grazed on either side of this fence," Bodie countered. "And you would've had fifty head of sheep going this way."

"Forty-eight sheep," she said and surveyed the admittedly undisturbed gulch on the other side of the fence. "And two guardian dogs."

Bodie ran the back of his hand over his mouth, but not in time to cover his frown.

Sarah stepped beside him and trailed her fingers over the mended wire fence. "Then what is this if not their escape route?"

"A lucky catch." Bodie collected the tools he'd dropped on the grass. "That is now repaired and won't be an escape hatch when the sheep return."

"But we need to find them first." Sarah winced at the strain she heard in her own words. Never mind that. She was cowgirl strong, same as her grandmother, and this was no time to lose her grit.

"I've got an idea which direction they are moving." Bodie headed up the knoll toward the horses. "Come on. I'll show you."

Sarah caught up to him and asked, "Are you some kind of wilderness tracker too?"

"Something like that." Bodie mounted his horse. "We need to get moving before we lose too much daylight."

Sarah wasted no time finding her seat in her saddle and urging Twilight close enough to Bodie that their knees collided. She asked, "What if you're wrong? What if the sheep really are on their way to Pearl and Artie's?"

What if this was some sort of wild-goose chase? She looked at Bodie's profile and reluctantly admitted the reserved cowboy seemed much too sensible for wild chases of any sort. Their earlier race across the prairie notwithstanding. Besides, what did he gain from all this? Still, doubt swirled. And Sarah marveled at her inner skeptic, unsure if she liked it or not.

"I'm not wrong." Bodie shifted to look at her. His gaze was thoughtful and solemn. "You need to trust me."

"I can't do that." Never mind that she didn't trust her own heart these days, her inner skeptic seemed to have taken full charge. The flinch around his eyes hinted that her refusal got to him. Well, he got to her too. She rushed on, "You don't understand. Between the stolen bison and now the missing sheep…" Her words trailed off.

So much was at stake. The farm. Her livelihood. Her grandmother's future.

She couldn't just trust that to a cowboy she'd only just met, could she?

"Let me show you what I found." Bodie reached over, placed his hand on hers and continued, "Then you can decide which direction we go to look for the flock. It's entirely your call."

Sarah searched his face, found only sincerity and a cool calmness that steadied her. Finally, she nodded and said, "Lead the way."

And she would follow, but not with her heart.

CHAPTER EIGHT

THE RIDE TO the opposite end of the pasture was silent—even Mav was subdued. Bodie dismounted in the corner where the forest bordered the field. He propped his boot on the thick bottom rail, grabbed the top of the closest post, and vaulted over the fence in seconds. Then he turned and waited for Sarah to do the same.

Her smile was completely gone. The shimmer in her hazel eyes was duller. He blamed himself for that travesty. He disliked even more how she flat-out refused to trust him. She hadn't hesitated or waffled. Heck, she hadn't even suggested she wanted to try.

It shouldn't matter. He shouldn't care. Bodie crossed his arms over his chest.

Sarah mimicked him and placed her boot on the bottom fence rung and hoisted herself up. The leg of her jeans got caught on a nail, snagging her in place. She gripped the top rung with both hands, shook her leg, and muttered, "So much for tucking my jeans into my boots."

Bodie moved quickly to free her. He set his

hands on her waist, lifted her up and over, then swung her down in front of him.

Her boots landed softly on the dirt. Her breath swooshed out. Her hands slid from his shoulders down to his forearms and stalled as she regained her balance. Bodie stared at the top of her straw cowboy hat and waited for her to look at him. Then he would know if the awareness he felt in the sunflower meadow still swirled between them. Or whether it was all one-sided and he was the only one mesmerized.

All he knew was he really wanted to kiss his farmer. Same as before.

Did he dare?

Because one perfect kiss—and he knew it would be—would have him wanting another and then one more.

Before he knew it, he would be kissing and confessing things like…what exactly?

That he got love wrong more than he ever got it right. That love was no longer on his achievement list. That now he was committed only to things he could do well, like his job.

But with her, he wanted to… Bodie released his farmer and retreated.

Sarah plucked a stray piece of grass from her jeans and said, "Thanks for the assist."

"Anytime." *I could be here for you any time.* If he was a different kind of cowboy. The kind who trusted his heart, knew how to love her the way she deserved. Bodie pointed to the ground and got back on track. "These hoofprints are fresh and lead into the forest."

"This trail leads to the back of our property." Sarah walked beside Bodie into the wooded area. "It's unfarmable acreage and the wilderness gets thicker the farther we go."

That was not the most welcome news. It meant predators and wildlife and more difficult terrain. Not to mention sunset was closer than he would have liked. Bodie said, "We need to move quickly to find the flock and return them." He held up his hands and considered her. "But this is your call."

Sarah bent and trailed her fingers over the trampled underbrush. "Let's get the horses and head in." She stood up and dusted her hands off. "You can take the lead."

It took more than an hour and a trek through a stream that was deeper than anticipated, but they finally located the flock grazing in a small glade. Their guardian dogs sat nearby, alert and attentive.

The head count complete, they worked their way through the herd from opposite sides and examined each sheep thoroughly. Mav trailed alongside Sarah and sniffed the sheep, as if greeting each one personally.

"No injuries so far." Sarah scratched a friendly cream-colored ewe under her chin and glanced over at Bodie. "Surprisingly, none of them seem too stressed."

"Same for mine." Bodie studied the skyline above the trees. Sunset was upon them. Frowning, he said, "But we won't be able to outrun the last of the daylight."

"Are you suggesting we camp here tonight? That's not an option." Sarah ran her palms around the sides of a ewe and inspected each of her hooves. Her words turned insistent. "We need to examine these last few and leave. Immediately."

"There's too much risk." Bodie patted a sheep between the ears and scooted around him to get to the next one.

"Then I'll go alone." Sarah met his stare from across the glade. Resolve pushed her chin up. "I'll be faster if I'm on my own anyway."

Bodie considered her. "It might be faster, but not safer by yourself."

"There's still some light left." She yanked her hat off her head and fixed her braids. "It'll be fine."

"The light is fading fast," he countered then repeated, "It's not safe."

She stepped awkwardly around a sheep, her every movement agitated. "I will be fine. Just fine."

But his cowgirl was clearly not fine. Worry made her face pale in the fading daylight. Panic was there too in her furrowed eyebrows and her sudden haphazard pacing among the flock. Even Mav sat and tracked Sarah, as if the dog understood she was the real flight risk. Bodie said, "I will keep watch tonight. Nothing will happen to the sheep." *Or you.*

"It's not..." She dropped her hat on her head and set her hand on an alert-yet-calm ewe, as if bracing herself. "I have to get back tonight." Her pacing picked back up. "You don't understand."

"Then tell me what's wrong," he urged. His mind jumped to the bison and started to run different scenarios. None of them were good. He shut down all the possibilities and focused on her. "Let me help you."

"You can't," she countered.

There it was. More proof she did not trust him. Still, he wanted to kiss her, soothe her, look after her as if she was his and this was the start of their relationship story. Where he proved he could show up for her. But this wasn't the beginning of *them*. It was simply a moment on a job like all his others. He couldn't make this one be anything different. Still, he said softly, "I can if you let me in."

"You can't help keep my grandmother safe." More of that steady resolve. She set about zigzagging around the sheep. Panic pushed through her words all over again. "You're here with me. Now she's all alone."

Bodie diligently and hastily worked his way around a dozen stationary sheep and closed the distance between Sarah and him.

"It doesn't matter." She wove farther out of reach and added, "My family is my responsibility. I gave my word." Dismay crowded her words. "But I don't know who to call." She squeezed between a pair of sheep then stalled out. "There's no one…"

There was someone. *Him*.

Bodie quickened his steps and reached for her

hand before she set off again on her erratic route. Her fingers were cold and stiff. He squeezed gently, guided her carefully around a ewe, and tugged her toward him. When she was close enough to easily embrace, he said quietly but insistently, "I'm here. You are not alone."

Her hazel eyes flared, settled on him as if she'd only just noticed he was right there beside her.

"Sarah," he said, his tone low. "Please tell me what's going on."

Her gaze slipped from his face to their joined hands and stuck.

Bodie stayed where he was, still and steady and ready to give his farmer whatever she needed.

Slowly, her fingers linked with his. Her breath evened out, next, her words tumbled free. "I need someone to stay with Grandma Rose. I promised Dr. Colborne and my parents that Grandma Rose wouldn't be left home alone, especially at night." She inhaled and exhaled, then continued. "Her eyesight has worsened a lot more than anyone anticipated. There's concern about her falling and injuring herself."

Worry was written all over her face. Yet, Bodie felt relief too. It wasn't about bison thefts and scams. This they could find a solution to together.

"I have to leave," she insisted, and tightened her grip on his hand. "If something happens to her and I'm not there."

That thought didn't need to be finished. Bodie would feel the very same if it was Sarah. He cut in, "If something happens to you on your way back tonight, you won't be able to help Rose."

"I know you're right." Frustration crowded her long exhale. She yanked her phone from her pocket with her free hand and clutched it. Her grip was as tense as her words. "I just don't know who to call. Pearl and Artie are in Amarillo for the night. Sawyer is on a job near the border in Llyne."

"There must be someone else," Bodie said. Rose and her family had been in Three Springs for generations. Surely there were any number of locals willing to lend a hand.

"Here's the thing. I don't want anyone to learn about the missing sheep. And I really don't want Eric Haydon to find out." She blew out another aggravated breath and studied him. "There, I said it." Her face scrunched up. "It's a good lease and Eric plans to rent more of my land for his livestock. We need that rent income more than ever. I can't lose his trust."

Bodie knew a little something about keeping things on the down-low. He also knew people experienced in doing the same. Bodie widened his stance. He knew where this was heading, and he needed to brace himself.

"You're extra quiet. That's not good." Sarah stashed her phone in her pocket and peered at him. "You're thinking I'm putting business above my grandmother's well-being." She dropped her head in her free hand and groaned. "I am. But I don't have a choice."

Looked like Bodie didn't have a choice either. He supposed there never really was a choice from the first time he'd met his farmer. He wanted to help her then and now. And not simply because he was doing his job. More than anything, he wanted her to smile again and know he was responsible for that. There he was, back to being selfish again.

"I'm going to text Lacey." He squeezed her fingers, then took out his own phone and started pressing the screen. "She isn't one who will talk around town."

Sarah chewed on her bottom lip and peered at his phone. "What did she say?"

Nothing he wanted to hear. He said, "Lacey is on the night shift tonight. Caleb is filling in at the bar."

Her shoulders sagged in defeat.

Down, but not out. Bodie supposed this moment was inevitable. After all, he knew one person who could be relied on—who his farmer would trust implicitly. The irony she didn't trust Bodie wasn't lost on him. "Lacey suggested someone else."

Sarah's head snapped up. Her gaze, wide and hope filled, locked on his. "Who?"

He cleared his throat, exhaled, yet his shoulders tightened. Finally, he said, "Lacey told me to call my father."

Sarah stiffened and dropped his hand. "You have family in town." It sounded like an accusation.

"It's complicated." Bodie pulled up his contact list on his phone. "I promise to explain everything, but first let me call my dad and make arrangements so Rose won't be alone tonight."

"How can you be sure your father will do this?" she asked.

"Because I know my father," he said, then added, "And so do you."

Sarah's gasp was soft yet sharp.

And it spurred Bodie into motion. There was no backpedaling now. He pressed the call button, raised the phone to his ear, and stepped away from Sarah.

At his father's greeting, he wove around the sheep to the edge of the glade and wasted no time filling his dad in on the current situation. His father listened, then simply reassured Bodie that both Lilian and he would stay with Rose until Bodie and Sarah returned, however long that was. Bodie ended the call and raised his face to the darkening sky.

There was a longer conversation required between father and son, and a past Bodie wasn't sure he wanted to revisit. But his father had opened the door just now, and Bodie would decide later if he was going to walk all the way through it or not.

Right now, what mattered was Rose's well-being and easing his farmer's worry.

Bodie walked over to Sarah, wiped his palms on his jeans. "Let me formally introduce myself." He held his hand out to her. "I'm Bodie Taylor Hopson."

She faced him and crossed her arms over her chest. Her eyebrows drew in. "As in Sheriff Hopson?"

"Sheriff Wells Hopson is my father." Bodie lowered his arm and stuck both hands into the back pockets of his jeans. "He and Lilian are headed over to the farmhouse to stay with Rose until we get back in the morning."

"Your dad is the sheriff of Three Springs." Her words were perplexed and came out in a slightly higher octave. At his nod, she gave a forced laugh and asked, "So, what are you? Like a deputy or something?"

"The deputy is my stepsister, Lacey." Bodie barely stopped himself from wincing.

"Lacey mentioned her stepsiblings. I should've paid closer attention to your names." Sarah rubbed her forehead. "Who are you then?"

"I'm a special ranger," he explained, and worked to keep his tone even. "Recently, I've been on undercover assignments on down south."

Her gaze snapped to his and sharpened. "And now?"

"Now, I'm on an assignment here in Three Springs," he admitted and went for full disclosure. She deserved to know the whole of it. He added, "I was sent to investigate the bison thefts."

She tensed and seemed to pull herself inward. "And me."

He nodded and said, "I'm sorry." And he meant it. There was one less false pretense between them now. But his growing affection for her, well, that would only muddy things up more. Best to pretend his feelings weren't real and not worth confessing.

"Don't apologize," she said, although uncertainty and hurt shadowed her gaze. "You're just doing your job and all that."

Her plain acceptance set him back. Bodie said, "I'd understand if you're angry or upset with me." He was upset with himself and his subterfuge.

"What will yelling at you solve? Will it prove my innocence?" Heat infused her words, conviction tightened her expression. "Which I am, by the way. Innocent, that is. In case you hadn't put that together yet." More intensity fused her words together. "I am not stealing my own bison. And I have no idea who is."

She wasn't entirely unaffected. She'd given him a deeper glimpse of her anger and hurt. That in turn gave him hope. She hadn't completely shut down and closed him out yet. Bodie exhaled and let his resolve show. "I'm here to figure out who is stealing from you and to stop them."

"Then I don't need to ask my grandmother to post my bail?" Sarah set her hands on her hips.

Bodie frowned. "You're not being arrested."

"Not right now," Sarah argued. "But every bison that goes missing without a suspect makes me look more and more suspicious. You can't deny it."

But he wanted to. Very much. He opened and closed his mouth.

"Before you ask, I don't have an alibi." She sighed, then added, "I have been alone and asleep in my bed each time a bison has been taken."

But she wasn't alone now. And she didn't need to be alone going forward.

Could he stay? His pulse stepped up a beat.

Would she want him to? His pulse notched up again.

Bodie collected himself and got back to matters at hand. He asked Sarah to walk him through each of the bison disappearances from the first to the most recent. They continued examining all the sheep for possible injuries while Sarah filled him in on her dwindling bison herd from her perspective.

Bodie's pulse returned to normal and his clarity with it.

After all, this was not some beginning for Sarah and him. It was not even a start, despite the spikes in his pulse earlier. That was only his heart trying to play tricks with him.

Good thing Bodie trained too hard and too long to let blips like that throw him off his game.

CHAPTER NINE

NIGHT WAS FULLY upon them when the horses were watered and bedded down, and the flock gathered in the center of the glade. Sarah unpacked her emergency supplies and gave Bodie a thick blanket before she took water and snacks out of her other saddlebag. Bodie walked over to the edge of the glade, sat and settled his back against a large tree trunk.

"I think we've exhausted the bison inquiries for the evening." Sarah dropped to the grass near Bodie, handed him a bottle of water, and added, "I know you are trying to help me. I really appreciate it."

Dare he hope she was starting to trust him too. The tension receded from Bodie's shoulders for the first time since he had told Sarah who his father was. Switching to a lighter note, he asked, "So, have I officially convinced you that you won't need to ask Rose to post your bail any time soon?"

"I've shelved the bail discussion." She chuckled and bumped her shoulder against his when she scooted beside him. "However, I think it's your turn now."

Her hand rested on his leg, and she leaned toward him, not away. All good signs there. "My turn for what exactly?"

"Twenty questions or however many you asked me." Sarah opened a bag of trail mix.

Bodie held out his arm, palm up, and said, "That's part of my job."

"Well, now I'm doing my part." She poured trail mix into his hand, then grinned. "Consider it a continuation of our job interview."

"I thought you preferred a working-while-interviewing approach." He separated the nuts from the dried fruit and chocolate candy.

"You passed that part." She shook the trail mix bag and picked out several pieces of dried pineapple, then met his gaze. Her words were straightforward and sincere. "The truth is, I want to know the cowboy who I'm spending the night under the stars with."

And didn't that just suit him all too well. "Fair enough." Bodie stretched out his legs and stacked one ankle over the other. "But in return, I want to know the cowgirl beneath the farmer."

"Fine." She tossed the dried fruit into her mouth, swiped her palm across her jeans, then shifted to face him. She extended her hand and asked, "Do we have a deal?"

Bodie tossed the last of his trail mix into his mouth, cleaned his palms on his jeans, and set his hand in hers. One small tug and he could pull her onto his lap. His fingers flexed.

One eyebrow arched as if she'd guessed his intention. "But I get a few bonus questions to make us even."

"Deal." He laughed and released her. After all, she wasn't his to hold under the stars, no matter how much the idea appealed to him. He leaned back against the tree and asked, "What do you want to know?"

She picked up the trail mix and eyed him over the bag. "Do you sing in the shower?"

"Always," he replied. At her surprised expression, he continued, "Wait. Doesn't everyone sing in the shower?"

Sarah shook out a handful of trail mix and studied him. "Is it loud enough others can hear you?"

"Absolutely." He swiped the bag from her and grinned. "Why sing if no one can hear you?"

Her laughter spilled out like a shooting star. She ate the chocolate candy, then the nuts, as if savoring the snack while settling on her next question. "What is your biggest irrational fear?"

That you might break my heart, even though I misplaced it a long time ago. He went with... "Barn owls." Then he arched an eyebrow at her and added, "That is a recent discovery." Same as realizing his heart might not be as lost as he thought.

"Barn owls," she repeated. Suddenly, her eyes widened. Her smile grew. "Did you meet Gizmo by chance?"

"Gizmo introduced himself," Bodie corrected her. "Let's just say your owl let it be known he is keeping a close eye on me."

"Gizmo is quite protective of those he considers his." Sarah chuckled. "He'll get used to you."

"And if he doesn't?" Bodie asked.

"You might have to stay away from the barn." There was a playfulness in her smile and tone.

"So, it's Gizmo over me," Bodie teased back.

"He was here first." Sarah shrugged one shoulder and failed to look apologetic. "Besides, Gizmo keeps the barn extremely rodent free."

"You don't like rodents?" Bodie handed her the trail mix.

"I like all animals," Sarah replied, and picked out more of the dried pineapple before she sealed the bag. "However, Calvin prefers not to share his house with the mice."

"I thought you told me Calvin is hard to spook." Bodie's gaze drifted over to the horses tethered to the high line Sarah had shown Bodie how to set up with a rope tied to two trees like a clothesline. Both Twilight and Calvin were grazing and content.

"Everyone has something that unsettles them," Sarah stated.

He returned his attention to his farmer and asked, "What unsettles you?" Something about being with her unsettled him—and Bodie was undecided if that was good or bad. All he knew was he wasn't in a rush for this night with her to end.

Her mouth twisted. Her gaze skipped away from

his. Perhaps he unsettled her too. Or, more likely, she was checking on the flock, ensuring they were not anxious now that it was getting darker.

"Let me guess," Bodie continued. "It can't be frogs and you take the ducks to the pond. But maybe snakes?" At her headshake, he said, "Spiders?"

Again, she shook her head, then slanted an amused look his way and said, "I'm fairly hard to spook, same as Calvin."

He appreciated her bravado and drawled, "Well, now I have to accept your challenge."

"I should warn you." She pointed at him, although her grin ruined her attempt at looking stern when she added, "Sawyer has been trying to spook me for years. He has failed every time."

"But I'm not Sawyer," he said.

Her eyes flared. Her gaze warmed. And color filled her cheeks.

That he noted with satisfaction and a whole lot of appreciation.

She sounded bemused. "Why am I looking forward to this all of a sudden?"

For the same reason he was. Bodie finally gave in. Wanting to hold even a small part of her, he took her hand in his and linked their fingers together.

Sarah scooted into him until her shoulder touched his. "Back to you. What is something your family would be surprised to learn about you?"

"That I miss them." Truthfully, he was more than

a little surprised himself. Even more that he admitted it to his farmer.

She was silent for a beat, then another, as if surprised too. Finally, she said, "You should tell them."

There were a lot of things he should tell his family. More things he wanted to tell them, especially his father. And now there was his farmer. Oh, the things he could say. He stretched his fingers and adjusted his position. "I'm still working out what to say."

She set her free hand over their joined ones. Her touch was like one of those weighted blankets, warm and calming and an instant fidget stopper. "How long have you been working on that?"

Years. "I know what you're thinking." Bodie sighed. "It's my family. The words shouldn't be so hard."

"I think sometimes because it is family the words are harder," she offered. Her next words were wry. "Unless, of course, it's Grandma Rose. She seems to have a knack for always knowing what to say in any situation."

"Well, I have not known what to say to my father for years," Bodie stated. "Although, now he wants my blessing on his upcoming marriage to Lilian."

"You don't want to give it?" she asked.

"I'm not sure what value there is in it," Bodie said. "I gave my blessing to my mother's last four husbands and each of those unions ended in divorce."

"But this is your father," she countered. "Maybe his marriage will be different."

Or maybe it would end the same as his mother's.

"Perhaps you just need to spend time with your father and Lilian," Sarah suggested. "Get to know them as a couple and see if what they share can last."

He wanted this to last. His farmer beside him. Her hand in his. Her words challenging him to change his perspective. He conceded, "Perhaps you are right."

"Obviously, I am." She chuckled, then said, "So, I'm thinking you didn't go into law enforcement to follow in your father's footsteps?"

"I vowed never to be like my dad."

Sarah shifted and her bewildered gaze met his.

"I was ten when my mom and dad divorced," he explained, putting into words what he hadn't shared with anyone. He smoothed his thumb over Sarah's palm, tracing a small soothing circle and continued, "It seemed like whenever I needed my dad, he was always working. Eventually, I stopped trying to call him."

"But you didn't stop needing him," Sarah said softly and all too wisely.

And to be fair, his dad hadn't stopped trying to keep a father-son connection, despite the obstacles. The biggest one being Bodie's stubborn resistance. Bodie shrugged, trying to keep that truth from settling too close to home. "I was pretty busy looking after my little sister and younger brother. And

I was already changing into someone he no longer recognized."

"So, you were supposed to go along to get along," Bodie assessed.

She lifted her head and arched an eyebrow at him. "Do you have a book that you keep handy so you can recite a perfectly placed witty expression at the appropriate time?"

"No, but I appreciate the compliment about my wit." He chuckled. "I should probably start jotting all these sayings down for easier reference."

"Words matter," she replied cheekily, then laughed and said, "Okay. Last question for the night." At his frown, she pushed his shoulder lightly. "This is my bonus one."

Yes. I want to kiss you. Here. Under the stars. Please let that be the question. Bodie held his breath.

Finally, Sarah said, "What are your feelings on good-morning and good-night texts?"

"I've always been partial to good-morning and good-night kisses," he said, then asked, "What about you?" *If I asked you to kiss me, would you?*

"Unfortunately, that's all we have time for tonight," she said, playfully echoing his words from the other day in the truck.

"You really aren't going to tell me, are you?" he asked.

"I'm going to sleep on it." She made a show of stretching and yawning, as if she was suddenly exhausted. "Maybe I'll even text you my answer in the morning." With that, she snuggled up against his side, rested her head on his shoulder and reminded him to wake her up to take over the watch.

Bodie fiddled with the blanket around her shoulders, ensured she was covered down to her boots, and listened to her breaths even out. Soon enough, she was asleep and Bodie was left to his own thoughts.

His gaze slid to the wisp of a cowgirl beside him in her butterfly-bright overalls with her sunshine-drenched laugh and her obvious affection for her animals, her farm and her grandmother. And right there under that tree, he might have reconsidered shunning all love had to offer.

Only, his life was his work, and he did not have room for more.

Besides, even he knew a breath-of-fresh-air farmer like her could not withstand a dark cloud like him for long. Eventually, it would be a washout.

CHAPTER TEN

THE STARS WERE fading in the sky when Sarah woke up, stiff from the hard ground, but surprisingly warm thanks to the blanket still covering her. She scrambled to her feet when she noticed Bodie wasn't beside her and his arms weren't around her. Falling asleep with her cowboy holding her had perhaps been the best part of her evening.

"Sorry if I woke you," Bodie said behind her.

Sarah turned around and noted two things. First, both horses were saddled and ready. Second, her cowboy looked wide-awake and totally refreshed, as if he'd slept in a plush room at a luxury five-star resort, not an uneven grassy glade in the forest. Sarah brushed her hair off her face and grumbled, "You were supposed to wake me so I could keep watch, and you could sleep."

"I'll get caught up tonight." He took the blanket from her, then folded and repacked it into a saddlebag. "It's okay. I'm used to pulling an all-nighter."

But that didn't make it right. Sarah unraveled her braids, finger-combed her hair, then retied the long strands into a ponytail. The way her cowboy watched her as if riveted almost made her reconsider the appeal of campout hair. Flustered, she tightened her ponytail and her focus. "What else needs to be done?"

"Well, you're in charge now." Bodie handed her Twilight's reins. His grin was adorably lopsided. "Herding a flock of sheep is outside of my skill set. You need to tell me what to do."

First, she was going to tell her heart to stand down. Sure, they had shared some truths last night. On the get-to-know-you-better scale, her cowboy had not disappointed. But where did that leave her? More intrigued than ever and more convinced falling for her cowboy might break her heart beyond recognition. It was best to stick to putting the farm back together and keeping her heart in one piece.

Besides, Bodie was investigating her. So, serious damage to her heart was out of the question. If she'd fallen a little bit for her cowboy already, well, she would simply *pay it no mind*. Surely then what she thought she felt for her cowboy would soon pass, right?

Sarah mounted Twilight and got back to the business of farming and not falling for a cowboy.

Bodie might not have worked livestock ever, but he proved to be a quick learner and more than capable on a horse. The sun was up when the sheep were finally secured back in the south pasture. After a bison head count and a corn crop check, they treated both Twilight and Calvin to an extra-long groom and rubdown.

Bodie closed the gate on Calvin's stall and joined Sarah in the center aisle of the stable. He ran a hand over his head and asked, "Don't suppose you've got another ten stalls that need cleaning?"

Sarah took in Bodie's reserved expression. It bothered her that he would choose mucking stalls over seeing his own family. Unfortunately, she couldn't stop the impending reunion between father and son. That had been put into motion last night. Thanks to her cowboy coming to her aid.

She shook her head. "It wouldn't matter anyway. Mav went straight to the sliding door on the porch when we got back. They know we're home."

"So, you're telling me my time is up." He plucked his cowboy hat off his head and scrubbed a hand through his hair, tousling the dark blond strands. "No more stalling."

"You need to talk to your dad. And I need to arrange for the corn harvest." Sarah picked up the empty lunch sack from the floor where she'd dropped it, rather than reach for Bodie's hand as if to soothe him. Still, she asked, "Are you okay?"

"Still haven't found those words," he admitted and set his hat back on his head.

"They'll come to you," she said.

His gaze searched hers as if he sought comfort from her after all.

And that made her want to shout yahoo to the skies.

Finally, he asked, "And if I can't find those words?"

I'll be right there with you. Of course she would. This was her home. Yet, she knew she wanted to be beside her cowboy in a different sort of way. In the sort of way that spoke of partners and deep affection and a reliance on each other that stuck through thick and thin. Sarah turned away from her cowboy. Surely a decent night's sleep would course correct her reckless thoughts.

"Don't worry." She started for the door and kept her words cheerful. "Grandma Rose will know what to say."

"I'm quite sure Rose will have something to say about this whole situation." Bodie held the door open. Uncertainty flashed across his face. "How do you think your grandmother is going to take it?"

"There is only one way to find out," Sarah said. "One thing I know for certain. Good or bad, Grandma Rose won't hold back her feelings."

Unlike Sarah.

Her awareness of her cowboy was ever present. If only her pay-it-no-mind approach was not proving to be slow to catch on. Still, she was quite certain she could manage her feelings for her cowboy. She just needed to be diligent. The walk from the stables to the farmhouse was silent except for the crunch of the gravel underneath their boots.

Rounding the corner of the farmhouse, Sarah took in the lone figure in the rocking chair on the front porch and picked up her pace. When she was close enough for her grandmother to hear her, she called out, "Good morning, Grandma. Where are Lilian and Sheriff Wells?"

Grandma Rose shushed Sarah and motioned them onto the porch. She waited until Sarah sat in the rocking chair beside her and Bodie stood at the railing in front of her. "Don't be shouting. Someone might hear you."

Bodie leaned against the railing and whispered, "Rose, is anyone else here?"

"Just me." Grandma Rose toasted Bodie with her teacup.

Confused, Sarah slid back into the rocking chair and pitched her voice lower. "But Lilian and Wells were here, right?"

"All night long. Such a darling couple." Grandma Rose blew into her hot tea before speaking again. "They promised me a VIP invite to all their wedding festivities too. I'm allowed a plus-one." Her gaze brightened. The wrinkles around her weathered face faded. "What do you think of that?"

"I think you're going to enjoy yourself thoroughly," Bodie offered, his words kind and seemingly genuine.

But he was the cowboy who claimed not to like the pomp and spectacle of a wedding. And he'd been less than enthusiastic about giving his blessing to the couple. Not that she was paying any mind to his feelings on weddings and all that. Still, Sarah gaped at him.

Grandma Rose's finger tapped silently against

her teacup. She looked deep in thought. "I just need to figure out who my plus-one will be."

Sarah raised her hand. "Why wouldn't I be your plus-one?"

Grandma Rose lifted her cup to hide her mouth, yet her words were loud enough to hear out in the driveway. "Play your cards right, and you might be someone else's plus-one, my dear."

Sarah's gaze connected with Bodie's. His eyes widened, revealing a mischievous and very compelling glint in the blue depths that captivated Sarah. *What if I wanted to be your plus-one, cowboy?* So much for paying him no mind. The heat in her cheeks was instantly dialed up to blazing.

One corner of Bodie's mouth lifted. He asked mildly, "So, Rose, where is the happy couple now?"

"I fixed them an early breakfast and sent them on their way." Grandma Rose set her cup on the table between the rocking chairs and grinned. "It wasn't long after sunrise."

Sarah watched Bodie relax against the railing and chewed on her bottom lip. "That's too bad. I was hoping to thank them in person." And learn exactly what they'd told her grandmother and what they'd withheld about the Bodie situation.

"There'll be time enough for that," Grandma Rose assured her, and leaned forward in her chair as if imparting a secret. Her volume lowered again. "I told them they had to leave, otherwise Bodie's cover would be ruined. They said they would be in touch, Bodie."

Bodie propped his hands on the railing behind him and arched an eyebrow at Sarah. He looked anything but irritated.

Sarah asked casually, "What did they tell you exactly, Grandma?"

"Everything," Grandma Rose chided. "There was nothing for it. I took one look at the distinguished sheriff and knew Bodie belonged to him." Grandma Rose tapped the corner of her eye and watched Bodie. "It's those baby blues. They give you away instantly."

Sarah glanced at Bodie. It was his baby blues that gave Sarah butterflies and had her considering sharing more than truths with him. Sharing something like her heart and forever. Surely that idea would pass soon enough. She just had to wait it out. Sarah crossed her arms over her chest.

Grandma Rose wrapped the tea bag string around the handle on her cup and tipped her head toward Bodie. Both of her eyebrows lifted knowingly. "As long as we are on the subject, we should also mention the elephant in the room." Her grandmother glanced from Sarah to Bodie and back, then added, "It's Bodie's face."

Sarah exhaled, pleased her grandmother hadn't caught on to Sarah's interest in her cowboy, which was becoming more and more unstoppable.

Bodie coughed.

"What's wrong with his face?" Sarah blurted. She was rather fond of her cowboy's brooding good looks.

"Bodie, you've a very handsome face," Grandma Rose said, her words soothing. Then she quickly turned no-nonsense and added, "We must hide it though. Bodie is a ringer for his father. He can't just show his face around town." Grandma Rose paused and fluttered her hand. "Worse, if our bandit sees Bodie with his father, he'll know Bodie isn't a farmhand, same as I did."

"Grandma," Sarah chided.

"It's fine. We all know I'm more of an apprentice around here." Bodie chuckled. "Do you have something in mind for my face, Rose?"

Sarah pinched the bridge of her nose and peered at Bodie. How was he keeping a straight face?

"I do." Grandma Rose dunked her tea bag into her cup and looked quite pleased with herself. "But we need to discuss our partnership first and decide our roles."

Bodie ran his hand over his mouth and asked, "What partnership is that?"

"The one where we partner with you to find our bison bandit," Grandma Rose explained. "Before you think to deny me, understand this is my family legacy and farm at stake. I cannot sit back and do nothing. And I raised my granddaughter in the same manner."

Sarah was glad her grandmother's grit was front and center. Yet, she also felt a strange urge to apologize too.

Bodie nodded and asked, "Did you mention to

my father that you wanted to assist in the investigation?"

Grandma Rose's smile was wise, her gaze shrewd, as if she was staring down her opponent at the poker table and refusing to fold. "The sheriff's department is assisting you. Your father is not the one I need to seek approval from."

Bodie dipped his chin, as if conceding the round to her.

"We are farmers," Sarah stated, because it felt like the blunt reminder was required. "We are not like those amateur sleuths you watch on TV, Grandma."

And while Sarah was tempted to join Bodie, it was not for an investigation. She wanted it to be for things like a starlit stroll or a picnic at the grotto or a walk down the aisle. Sarah blanched.

Not only was she in date territory, she'd skipped straight ahead to the big, life-changing stuff. It was as if *pay it no mind* meant *pay it every mind* in excruciating detail. Sarah snatched a cinnamon-apple biscotti from her grandmother's assorted pastry plate and snapped it in half.

"But Bodie is a professional sleuth," Grandma countered, and sipped her tea. "We just need to help him see what he has been missing."

Like fun and midnight dances and good-night kisses. Or rather, none of those things. Because Sarah and her cowboy were not an item and that was how she preferred it. Sarah frowned and brushed the biscotti crumbs off her jeans.

Bodie asked mildly, "Rose, what have I been missing?"

"The clues that will remove Sarah from your suspect list," Grandma Rose replied and then eyed Sarah over the rim of her teacup. "You, my dear, are a suspect. You realize that, don't you?"

"You don't have to sound so cheerful about it," Sarah grumbled.

"You have to admit there's a certain thrill to all this." Grandma Rose waggled her eyebrows. "Come on. Admit it. It's quite thrilling."

Thrilling? There was a certain thrill to the way Bodie looked at her last night during their twenty questions. As if he saw her and liked all he saw. Even more delightful was the way he held her. As if he cherished her just as she was. Sarah crunched down on her biscotti and stayed silent.

"I haven't felt this youthful in a long while." Grandma Rose broke the corner off her fig scone and popped it in her mouth. Enthusiasm coated her words like powdered sugar. "Perhaps I need to live on the edge more than I knew."

Sarah's head snapped up and she focused on her grandma. "What does that mean?"

"Well, you've got me reconsidering." Her grandma's words were smooth and sweet like her favorite honey.

Sarah held her breath, sensing her grandma was about to set them into another sticky situation.

Bodie was still against the railing, waiting too.

"A partnership is typically between two people,"

her grandma started, her smile big and all too satisfied. "Since my granddaughter isn't interested, it seems I will have to be your partner, Bodie."

Bodie's eyebrows climbed up his forehead.

Sarah shook her head. "I don't think."

"I always knew I was meant for something like this." Her grandmother shimmied in her rocking chair, then added, "I really do have the steadiest of nerves. I will show you. Bodie, you can count on me."

Sarah shook her head again. "Grandma."

Grandma Rose ignored Sarah's protest and rambled on. "It's going to be great. This works better. No one will suspect me, and I have been known to get people talking."

Sarah smoothed her palm over her face and conceded. "I'll do it."

"Do what, dear?" Grandma Rose asked.

"Partner with Bodie," Sarah replied.

"I thought we just decided I'm more suitable as his partner." Grandma Rose emptied her teacup and set it on the side table.

"I don't think *we* decided anything," Sarah said.

"You think we should let Bodie choose his partner, don't you? You do make a good point," Grandma Rose mused, and glanced at Bodie as if to make her case. "I have very good ideas about how to keep your cover and how to do a proper pasture stakeout."

"A pasture stakeout," Bodie said, his words sounded strained.

Sarah intervened. "Bodie is not making a choice." And if he did want to make a choice for something like a life partner, well, Sarah might just be tempted to raise her hand. Talk about foolish. Yet, now was not the time to get distracted. She forced herself back to her grandma. "There isn't going to be a pasture stakeout."

"Not that you know about," Grandma Rose muttered. "Bodie and I can't be revealing our plans to just anyone."

Sarah looked at Bodie, silently pleading for backup as if they were already partners on the same team.

Bodie gave Sarah a reassuring grin, then pushed away from the railing and dropped down in front of her grandmother until they were eye level. He set his hand over his heart and said, "Rose, you have my word. I'm going to do everything I can to make sure your legacy and farm are not harmed."

"I sense a *but* coming my way." Grandma Rose frowned, yet appreciation was in her gaze.

"But you need to let me handle this," Bodie said gently. "It's my job. And I'm pretty good at it."

And he was pretty good at letting people down gently too. *Please be careful with my heart, cowboy.*

"Are you better at spotting bison bandits than you are at spotting barn animals?" Grandma Rose countered.

Bodie chuckled, not looking the least offended. "Much better. That I can promise you."

What about promising to set her heart down softly so she could recover? Sarah gripped the rocking chair armrests.

"I'll give you forty-eight hours before I start poking around." Grandma Rose eyed him. "And you really need to hear me out about your face."

Before Sarah could protest, Bodie stuck his hand out and said, "Deal."

Grandma Rose brushed his arm aside and pushed out of her chair. "Around here, we seal our deals with a hug."

Sarah wondered when that tradition started. She couldn't remember ever sealing a deal with a hug. However, watching Bodie embrace her grandmother, Sarah suddenly wanted the same kind of embrace from him. Although, she feared hugging her cowboy would require a deal she wasn't prepared to make.

"We have to take this discussion offline, as they say." Grandma Rose released Bodie and patted his shoulder. "There's someone coming up the drive."

Sarah watched the familiar silver truck zooming along the road. "It's only Sawyer."

"Can't be too careful," Grandma Rose warned and wrapped her arm around Bodie's. "Bodie, you should question Sawyer and see what he might know."

"No." Sarah rose and insisted, "Bodie should not question Sawyer. What would he think?" It was bad enough Bodie was investigating Sarah. She didn't need her friends drawn into the case too.

"Sarah is right. We must act natural." Grandma Rose nodded, then shouted, "Sawyer, where were you every night this past week?"

Sawyer shut his truck door and removed his sunglasses. Confusion washed over his face. "What was that?"

Sarah frowned at her grandmother, then rushed down the porch stairs. Sawyer embraced her and lifted her off her feet. It was the perfect kind of all-encompassing welcome.

Only there were no butterflies. No jolts of awareness. And it was the wrong cowboy sweeping her off her boots. That realization caused an undeniable uptick in her pulse. And a pinch of disloyalty toward her friend.

Her words fell out rapidly. "Grandma Rose is practicing her sleuthing skills for one of those murder-mystery dinners the Baker sisters are taking her to." As for Sarah, she was supposed to be practicing paying her cowboy no mind.

"That sounds fun." Sawyer set Sarah back on the ground, released her and smiled. Then he called out, "I'm good at those mystery dinners, Rose. I would be more than happy to give you some tips."

"Would you now?" Grandma Rose murmured.

Sarah covered her wince and tried to sound cheerful. "I'm glad you're here, Sawyer. I was going to call you."

"Well, if you're looking for a chocolate fix, I have the perfect solution." Sawyer opened his back passenger door and took out two potted plants.

Sarah accepted one of the plants. "What are they?"

"That's the really cool part." Sawyer grinned. "They are cacao plants. Now you can grow your own chocolate beans."

"Seriously?" Sarah marveled at the long green leaves and smiled at Sawyer. "They're perfect."

Same as her good friend. Sawyer wasn't investigating her. Nor would he ever believe she could be guilty. Plus, he brought her great gifts. Yet, he didn't make her pulse race, or those butterflies flutter. Did that really matter?

Sawyer walked onto the porch, shook Bodie's hand, then said, "There's something different."

"It's the hat." Bodie took off the cowboy hat and grinned. "Artie gave me one of his. I'm sure you recognize it."

"That must be it." Sawyer's expression cleared and his smile returned. "We still need to have those drinks and dinner. How about I cash in that rain check for tonight?"

She wanted a dinner date. Just not with Sawyer. Sarah said, "We need your combine, Sawyer. The corn is ready to harvest."

"That's why I came by." Sawyer gave Sarah the other cacao plant and frowned. "It's going to be another week before the combine is fixed."

"Another week?" Sarah said. "It's practically new. How can it have so many issues?"

"You know how high-tech that computer system

is in the cab," Sawyer said. "There's always an update for something or other."

"You should ask for an upgrade," her grandmother said.

"It's already one of the newest models on the market," Sarah said.

"Goes to show sometimes you don't need fancy things," her grandmother mused. "Simple and basic might seem dull, but if it's reliable, who cares."

Sawyer asked, "Can't you just hold the crop, Sarah-Belle?"

There was no holding over two-hundred acres of corn. Sarah tightened her arms around the plants, but that panic simmered. Her grandmother had warned her to get a backup plan, but she'd been chasing sheep.

"Rain is coming too," her grandmother announced, as if she always reported the weather correctly. Everyone glanced at her.

Bodie pulled out his cell phone and tapped on the screen. Then he winced and said, "Rain is in the forecast later this weekend."

"We have no choice then," Sarah said. "We have to harvest this afternoon."

"How are you going to harvest without the combine?" Sawyer scratched his chin.

"Looks like Maizey is coming out of the shed." Her grandmother grinned and rubbed her hands together. "I'm sure she's got one more good run left in her. She's vintage, but with a proper tune-up that old tractor should run like new."

Sarah hoped so. She didn't have any other option.

"Let me check on Dad's old tractor. Two will be better than one." Sawyer headed down the steps. "I'll be in touch if I can get it started." Goodbyes all around, Sawyer jumped in his truck and drove off.

Sarah glanced at Bodie. "How do you feel about a tractor tune-up?"

"If you can give me a few hours of sleep, I guarantee I can get the tractor running," he said.

"You guarantee it." Sarah arched an eyebrow.

"Everyone knows a good nap resets the mind and restores the body," Bodie said. His expression was serious, yet amusement flashed in his eyes.

Sarah swallowed her chuckle.

"Very true." Grandma Rose hummed her agreement. "After all, you can't achieve your dreams with a tired mind."

Heat flashed through Bodie's gaze. He considered Sarah as if she could be his dream.

Sarah concentrated on keeping the blush she felt from spreading.

Bodie's grin slipped out and he drawled, "So, are we napping or not?"

There was no *we* in napping. Besides, her mind was far from tired. She had to secure a grain elevator for the corn. Keep her grandmother from plotting a pasture stakeout. And cut off her cowboy curiosity.

"Let's meet at the storage barn at noon." Sarah followed her grandmother and Bodie to the front door and added, "That gives us four hours to sleep or whatever."

"That works for me." Bodie held the door open and guided her grandmother inside.

Sarah moved to step by him, but his hand on her arm stalled her. She raised her gaze to his.

One corner of his mouth lifted when he said, "Sweet dreams, Sarah."

Could you be my dream, cowboy? Sarah nodded and walked inside.

"Bodie, your dad left you a duffel of clean clothes." Her grandmother pointed to the dark bag in the foyer. "That's it right there."

"Thanks." Bodie explained, "I needed more clothes than what I originally crammed in my motorcycle saddlebags."

"You didn't plan to stay long, did you?" she asked. At his small head shake, Sarah finished her thought and busted any chance of a misplaced cowboy dream. "Because you thought I was guilty before you even met me."

"I'm sorry." He had the grace to wince and look anything but comfortable. "I was going off the information I had in front of me."

"You need new information," Sarah stated flatly and headed down the hall. "The correct information."

"Bodie already promised he's going to find our

bandit," Grandma Rose said. "We need to give him the chance to do just that."

Fine. But Sarah was not giving her cowboy a chance to ride off with her heart.

CHAPTER ELEVEN

Bodie woke up two hours later from his nap feeling—dare he say it—restored. Worse, he slept as if he hadn't a care in the world. His mind hadn't been racing, leaving him to toss and turn or study the textured ceiling for the first hour. Instead, he had simply drifted off to sleep as if the countryside silence was his personal lullaby.

Now, he feared he was one catnap away from losing his edge. Then where would he be? He relied on his edge to keep him sharp and on top of his investigative game.

Frowning, he stuck his head under the shower spray in the quaint yet well-appointed bathroom. Even the water was the right temperature and the water pressure invigorating. Lingering was all too tempting. Clearly, he needed to move into the apartment over Pearl and Artie's garage soon, power or no power, before he got too comfortable. He belonged at the agency fighting crime, not a cozy farmhouse with an enchanting farmer.

One almost-perfect nap aside—*because let's be clear*—his perfect nap would be a blanket spread out in a sunflower field under the fall sun. With his farmer beside him. Her hand in his. And nowhere else they wanted to be.

All the rainbow and sappy fluff aside, Bodie had a job to do and a case that would not solve itself. Bodie checked the time on the nightstand clock. He wasn't due to meet Sarah in the storage barn for another couple of hours. Time enough for coffee and a work call.

Out in the hallway, Bodie passed by Sarah's closed bedroom door and headed downstairs before he wondered if she had slept as peacefully as him. He shook his head. If he wasn't careful, the next thing he knew he would be inviting Sarah into his dreams too. Good thing he spent his days immersed in facts and skipped the daydreams.

Only the soft thump of Mav's tail on the hardwood floor greeted him in the quiet family room. Bodie draped a blanket carefully over Rose, who was snoozing in her recliner, then checked the temperature of the heat lamp over the pigpen.

Coffee cup in hand, he walked outside with Mav at his side and called his chief for a debrief. Because his mind was back on what mattered most— his work.

The call was short and informative. If Bodie hadn't already set aside his insurance-fraud theory, his chief's update would have forced him to. One of Bodie's counterparts came across a pop-up livestock auction across the border in Oklahoma the day before. And a Rickelle farm bison was believed to have been run through the auction. The information was being sent to Sheriff Hopson for Bodie to review.

Bodie stepped inside the storage barn just as a shout rattled up to the rafters. Perched in the metal seat of the vintage tractor was his farmer. Her straw cowboy hat was gone. Her expression was fierce. And it was a toss-up whether her grip was tighter on the wrench in her left hand or the steering wheel in her right.

"Work." She banged the wrench on the tractor. Her frustration was obvious. "I need one thing to work. One thing." She swung the wrench again and grumbled, "It's not too much to ask, is it?" *Bang. Bang. Bang.* Then she hollered, "Well, is it?"

Bodie asked his chief to hold, then said, "No." He lifted his voice loud enough to get his farmer's attention and added, "It isn't too much to ask."

His farmer's wide-eyed gaze clashed with his. Her mouth formed a dismayed O.

Bodie told his chief he needed to go and would check in later after he'd spoken to his father and reviewed the new information. Then he ended the call, slid his phone in his pocket and approached the tractor.

"Sorry, if I disrupted your phone call." Sarah dropped her head on the metal steering wheel. The wrench dangled from her hand.

"It was nothing." At least nothing he wanted to unload onto his already clearly stressed cowgirl.

He eased the wrench from her fingers and tossed it into the toolbox on the floor. "You okay?"

"I couldn't sleep." She clutched the steering wheel in both hands and looked as if she was at the starting line for a tractor race. "My mind wouldn't rest."

He nodded and ran his hand over the worn fender on the tractor.

"I came in here while I coordinated drivers and trucks to transport the corn to the nearest grain elevator tonight." She paused, then chuckled, but her laugh was stiff. "Then I got the fun idea to text Lacey a tractor picture and let her know we can't make it to the Owl tonight. I captioned it We Got a Better Offer. Date night with a tractor and a cornfield. So silly."

You should know I really want that date. And that was even more silly. Because there were things he was not telling her right now. Surely, that was for the best.

"I hoped by some miracle this tractor would just start right up. The harvest must happen." Sarah shifted her attention to him. Her gaze—usually so expressive—was bleak. "I expanded the corn against my grandmother's and other people's advice. The corn and bison were supposed to be the main revenue. Without the corn, my grandmother won't be able to stay here, and the property will be sold."

Now he knew what she was fighting for—not herself, but her grandmother. True to her nature.

Bodie propped his arm on the tractor instead of gathering her into his arms and pledging to fight for her. But she was fighting for a home and roots and the long haul. It wasn't in his nature to want those things, let alone fight for them for himself. Except when he looked at her...

"Now, everything is riding on an old tractor from 1952. Sounds absurd." Defeat and dismay were clear. "What was I thinking?"

"You were thinking you wanted your grandmother to keep the only home she's ever known," he said. "It's admirable." Fitting, too, for such a generous cowgirl.

"I tell everyone that I came here so my grandma would not be alone anymore," she confessed. "The truth is, I didn't want to be alone either."

"There's nothing wrong with not wanting to be alone." Recently, even he was reevaluating his go-it-alone mindset.

"Well, if this harvest doesn't happen, alone is what both Grandma Rose and I will be." She stood up.

"That's not happening." He moved over to her.

She set her hands on his shoulders and let him swing her down. Hope seeped back into her gaze. "You think you can really get this tractor running?"

"I think we can try," he said, then added, "But you should know. I'm not a mechanic by trade. I only tinker with my motorcycles on occasion."

Still, that hope brightened.

But he wasn't her knight in shining armor. He

wasn't staying. He wasn't meant for the long haul. Yet, despite all the reasons he shouldn't, he still wanted to kiss her. Instead, he rambled, "When I was a kid, my dad was always fixing something around the house or out in the garage. I was his right hand." It meant he fetched tools and cold water on the hot days until his parents divorced. But those days trailing after his dad were some of his favorite memories growing up.

Sarah eyed him. "Then your dad was the one who taught you how to fix things?"

His dad would have, if Bodie had taken the time to ask him. But when Bodie was old enough to truly learn, he had stopped following his dad around and started following his own path. Now, he wished he had paid closer attention. He very much wanted to be the one to save his farmer's harvest and home. He admitted, "He did teach me the importance of reading an instruction manual."

She chuckled. "As it happens, I found one of those online for the tractor."

"Then we have a place to start." He lowered his arm, took her hand in his, and squeezed. "Ready?"

Sarah nodded. "We totally got this."

We. There was a certain appeal there to be sure, although, it was nothing Bodie could afford to get used to. After all, he had new leads and once his case was wrapped up, he would be on his way. Was he anxious to hit the road? Not so much. But sticking around hadn't ever been part of the discussion.

Worse, an hour and no rumbling of the tractor

engine later, they were back at the beginning. With a harvest looming and no feasible way to complete it. Bodie paged through the owner's manual they'd pulled up on Sarah's phone again. "We need to pull out the engine."

"That sounds complicated." Sarah wrinkled her nose. "Not to mention greasy and messy."

"Getting my hands greasy was always my favorite part with my dad." He grinned.

"Then he should be here for this," she countered. "He would certainly enjoy it more than me."

"You're right." Bodie gave her phone back to her. "I need to call him."

Sarah searched his face. "Are you sure?"

And that right there was what made her special. Despite her own worry and stress, she was concerned about him. He nodded and said, "We need backup."

Her smile was full of delight and approval.

But this wasn't a reconciliation between father and son. Bodie intended to talk about *his* investigation and *her* tractor only. Some might call that misaligned priorities. Bodie preferred to call it just doing his job.

Several rings later, Bodie returned his father's greeting and said, "Dad, I have Sarah here too. We wanted to thank you for staying with Rose last night."

Sarah added, "I plan to thank you and Lilian properly with dinner one night soon."

"That's not necessary," his father replied readily, then added, his words amused, "But you can do me a favor and convince Lilian we don't need miniature donkeys. Seems she's taken quite a liking to Tansy and Pepper."

Sarah pressed her hand over her mouth and caught her laugh. "I'll be sure to tell Lilian she can visit my donkeys whenever she wants."

Bodie wondered if Sarah would extend the same invitation to him when he left. He frowned. He hadn't even left yet and already he was plotting his return. First things first. He had to give his farmer a reason to offer him a come-back-soon invite. He said, "Dad, I could sure use your help. When was the last time you got your hands greasy?"

To pass the time until Bodie's dad arrived with his tools and know-how, Sarah and Bodie shared a chicken-salad sandwich and read through the owner's manual for the tractor.

The door to the storage barn slammed open then shut.

"Uncle Bodie!" That excited shout ricocheted up to the rafters inside the barn. "Uncle Bodie!"

Bodie turned from the workbench in time to see a young girl wearing a sparkly pink cowgirl hat and matching boots running toward him. Her long braids swung down her back.

The spirited girl came up to Bodie in a rush of barely contained energy and announced, "Uncle Bodie, Mom says if we all help with the harvest tonight, you and Ms. Sarah can go to the rodeo with us tomorrow." One audible inhale and her words tumbled free again. "I'm in the parade. You gotta be there. My dad and Mama-Beth are coming and you can meet baby Dylan. He's really my half-brother, but mom says all that matters is that Dylan is my brother, and I love him cause he's family."

That sounded like his stepsister. Lacey had only ever referred to Bodie as her big brother and her family. And he was forever grateful for that.

Bodie caught sight of Lilian and his father coming inside the storage barn. Then he rubbed his chin, smoothed out his smile, and considered his Aspen. "Who are you?"

"Uncle Bodie." His stepniece rolled her eyes and said, "It's me. Aspen."

He kept his expression somber and his words thoughtful. "I don't think so."

Aspen's eyebrows sank together, and her nose wrinkled.

"No. You can't be Aspen." Bodie picked up his phone from the workbench and opened his photo app then said, "You see. I've got a picture of the *real* Aspen." He tapped on his phone screen and continued casually, "You're a bit too tall. And besides, the Aspen that I know doesn't wear cowboy boots or the colors of the rainbow."

"Pink isn't in the rainbow." Aspen set her hands on her hips. "So, what does the *real* Aspen wear?"

"Well, I'll show you." Bodie flashed his phone at his stepniece and kept his expression blank. "See. This is the *real* Aspen."

Aspen's laughter erupted like a sugar rush. She

clutched her stomach. "Uncle Bodie, that's me on Halloween last year. I was dressed up like a scarecrow." She pointed her thumbs into her chest. "I'm the real me. Right here."

"I don't know," Bodie mused. "Because the *real* Aspen told me when she met me, she was gonna hug me so hard even my toes would be happy."

Giggling, Aspen launched herself at him with so much enthusiasm her cowgirl hat tumbled to the floor.

Bodie caught her and lifted her up.

Aspen laughed louder and squeezed him tight then whispered, "Don't let go until your toes are super happy, okay?"

His gaze collided with Sarah's. His farmer held Aspen's bold-colored cowboy hat. Her expression was tender and her grin full of affection. Right then, there wasn't a part of him that wasn't happy. He gave Aspen one more squeeze, set her down, and said, "What's this about helping with the harvest?"

"Well, I'm helping with the donkeys, ducklings, and piglets," Aspen explained. "If Ms. Sarah says it's okay. And Uncle Carter is doing the harvest because he's got the big giant machine thing."

Sarah wiped the dust from Aspen's hat and handed it to her. "Do you mean a combine?"

"Yeah. It's parked outside." Aspen propped her hat on her head and giggled. "Everyone is arguing about who gets to drive it first."

Surprise splashed across Sarah's face.

"It seems my sons have not harvested corn yet." Lilian greeted both Sarah and Bodie with quick embraces, then said, "They are quite excited."

"To put it mildly." His father gave Sarah a hug, then he turned and shook Bodie's hand.

Bodie said, "But, Dad, I called you for tractor help, not a combine rescue."

Just then, Lacey came inside. "Sarah sent me a picture of the tractor here and I showed it to everyone else." Her words were mild and all too confident. "And we all agreed Sarah's tractor is good for hayrides next month, not harvesting hundreds of acres."

His sister wasn't wrong. Still, Bodie said, "It's all we've got."

"Wrong." Lacey speared her arms out. "You've got family here, big brother. And it is way past time you remember that."

Here was another challenge to his go-it-alone policy. Bodie crossed his arms over his chest.

"Are you seriously telling me there is a combine in my driveway?" Sarah pointed to the door. "Like outside. Right now."

"Yes." Lacey grinned, then frowned. "I should warn you, there are a number of arguing Sloan cowboys out there too, but we can work around them."

Sarah squeezed Bodie's arm. "I love your family."

And he adored his farmer's smile. He hadn't seen it all day and he was quite thrilled to be even remotely responsible for its return. And he was even more grateful to his family's unexpected arrival.

"Come on then," Lacey urged. "You've never seen cowboys so enthused about corn."

"I don't know," his father mused. "I'm sort of excited about that tractor over there. It's practically begging for another chance to prove itself in the fields. And I would very much like to give it that opportunity."

And perhaps this was Bodie and his father's opportunity too. For a second chance that was about more than tractor repairs and his case.

"Let's get Sarah sorted and you two can work on the tractor all night long if you want." Lacey linked her arm through Sarah's and led her outside.

Aspen slipped her hand in Bodie's, as if afraid he meant to wander away, and tugged him toward the door. "Come on, Uncle Bodie. The rest of our family is here. They've been waiting to meet you."

Sure enough, there was a combine in Sarah's driveway and a collection of cowboys and cowgirls gathered outside. Aspen handled the introductions as if she was a seasoned hostess, then sprinted off when Rose came out and invited her inside to meet the piglets.

Elsie Sloan worked her way over to Sarah's side. The cowgirl was petite. Her words were bold and dipped in resolve. "It's been decided the cowgirls are going to show the cowboys how the corn harvest is done."

"I'm going to be in the grain tractor out there

with you, wife," Ryan Sloan said. His lopsided grin gave away his good humor.

"Stop pouting, Mr. Sloan," Elsie chided, yet her gaze sparkled at her husband. "You'll get a turn in the combine. I promise."

Ryan took his wife's hand and pressed a kiss on the inside of Elsie's wrist. "Stop distracting me." Elsie laughed and waggled her eyebrows at Sarah. "I highly recommend grabbing your cowboy and going for a midnight combine ride."

Yes. Where did he sign up for that portion of the evening harvest?

Sarah slanted her gaze at Bodie.

Bodie held her stare until her cheeks flushed a pretty pink and she looked away.

"I'm going with Elsie and Sarah too." Tess pressed a kiss to Carter's cheek.

"Fine by me." Carter wrapped his arm around Tess's waist, pulled her in close and kissed her properly and unapologetically.

Bodie marveled at the easy and open affection. There was nothing pretentious about their actions. It felt very natural and genuine. His mother's public displays of attention always seemed to be for show. And Bodie's ex had refrained from what she'd called putting their love on display for just anyone to see. Yet, there was something refreshing about the Sloan family, as if they simply could not express their love enough. He supposed there was something freeing about it as well.

His gaze tracked back to Sarah. There was certainly something refreshing about his farmer that drew him to her again and again.

Carter grinned wide. "I'm hoping I can talk Sarah into a tractor race if we get her old one in the shed up and running."

"Who am I racing?" Sarah chuckled.

Bodie was more than pleased to see his farmer happy again. There was still a harvest to complete and his case to solve, but that spark in her gaze flickered once more. And that suited him just fine.

"My grandpa Sam and uncle Roy claim their 1951 tractor is the fastest in the Panhandle," Carter said. "We want to prove them wrong."

Sarah laughed. "I can guarantee Grandma Rose is going to want to be in the driver's seat if you get her Maizey running again."

"That's what I'm talking about." Carter rubbed his hands together. "A race of the original great old-timers."

"You in, son?" Bodie's father smiled at him and sounded as excited as Aspen had earlier. "Feel like getting your hands greasy after all?"

Bodie couldn't help but smile back. Twice now in a matter of days, his father had come to his aid when Bodie had needed him. It was time for Bodie to do the same. The past was there to be dealt with later. Right now, it was about taking a step forward for himself and his farmer. Bodie nodded and said, "I'll be right there."

"Come on, Carter, let's see what tools we need." The pair headed toward the storage shed.

Bodie set his hand on Sarah's lower back, drawing her attention to him and asked, "You good?"

"Better than that." She smiled, tipped her head, and eyed him. "Remember, you don't have to have the right words with your dad. Sometimes just being together is enough."

His cowgirl certainly knew what to say. Those feelings inside him expanded, yet he fought back the words. Instead, he pressed a kiss on her temple and said, "Have fun and save that midnight ride for me."

"Come on, Sarah." Elsie clutched Sarah's arm before she could respond. Then Elsie grabbed Tess's hand and said, "It's time to get our combine on, ladies. The corn isn't going to harvest itself."

The trio rushed off in a flurry of laughter and chatter.

Lacey and Caleb carried the food inside the farmhouse. It seemed there was a rule about no harvesting on empty stomachs. Once Caleb rattled off the menu of three-bean chili, baked mac and cheese, cheddar biscuits, and homemade brownies, everyone agreed it was a rule not to be broken.

The driveway cleared in mere seconds.

Bodie took his hat off and scrubbed his hand over his head. He slanted his gaze to Lilian and knew his words sounded more than a little bewildered. "Is it always like this?"

"Worse." Lilian chuckled. "The Sloan family isn't all here. The rest are at the Owl for the rodeo kickoff. Maggie, my daughter-in-law, oversees the whole rodeo."

Bodie whistled and said, "I'm looking forward to meeting everyone else." And he meant it.

"I know I said it the other day, but it bears repeating." Lilian's smile was sincere. Her words earnest. "Welcome to the family."

Bodie said, "Thanks, but it's not quite the dinner table."

"It's a start and that's all that matters." Lilian turned and walked toward the house.

Welcome to the family. And just like that, Bodie collected another reason to come back to Three Springs.

CHAPTER TWELVE

SARAH WAS QUITE certain she had not talked or laughed so much, well, ever. She connected instantly with Tess and Elsie Sloan. The women had already started a group chat and coordinated calendars for a cowgirl night out the following week. And Sarah was already looking forward to it.

She walked beside Tess into the backyard. Ryan and Elsie were making another run in the combine and ordered Tess and Sarah to take a break.

Up on the patio, Bodie, Carter, and Wells sat around the fire pit, their expressions reserved as if their discussion was more serious than who got the last brownie. Sarah frowned and glanced at Tess.

Aspen came around the corner, framed by Tansy and Pepper. Her joyful greeting rolled across the backyard before she sprinted over to them. The cowboys on the porch stood and headed their way too.

"Don't worry, Ms. Sarah." Aspen slipped her hand into Sarah's and pulled Sarah's attention to her. "The donkeys and Mav and me made sure everyone is tucked in for the night. It was good-night kisses and sweet-dream wishes all around."

Sarah thanked the adorable young girl. Her gaze connected with Bodie's over Aspen's head and those sweet-dream wishes circled through Sarah all over again. Same as they had when she'd watched Bodie embrace Aspen earlier. For the first time in a long while, Sarah pictured her life beyond just a farmer. Beyond her grandmother's caretaker. But dreams about a cowboy by her side and a family of her own, while sweet, were just that—wishes.

"We were sent in for food." Tess wrapped her arm around Carter's waist and leaned her head against his chest.

"Elsie is driving the combine, and Ryan is still pulling the grain cart," Sarah explained. "They're convinced we can finish tonight if we don't stop."

Wells yawned. "Sounds ambitious."

And selfish on her part. Sarah frowned. "I can't ask you all to stay up the entire night. You've done so much for me already."

Lacey and Caleb strolled over. Lacey handed Sarah and Tess bottles of water and grinned. "You didn't ask us. We volunteered."

"But—" Sarah started.

Carter cut her off. "But we will happily accept a home-cooked meal in return."

Tess shoved her husband's shoulder playfully and said, "No. We will not. We're happy to help."

"And happy to eat," Carter added, his words good-natured.

"A meal hardly feels like enough," Sarah argued.

"Trust me," Lacey stated. "You will be exhausted after feeding this group."

"I can't thank you enough," Sarah said, and looked at Carter and Tess.

"You're family," Carter said, and his gaze slid over to Bodie. "And even if you weren't, we would be here. This community sticks together and looks after each other."

For the first time since she'd moved back, Sarah felt as if she just might be part of something bigger. The thought warmed her and touched her heart. She cleared her throat. "I'm still making that dinner for everyone. And if you ever need anything from me, please ask."

Caleb rubbed his chin and lifted his hand. "I took a peek into your garden greenhouse and noticed you have chives and thyme."

"Take whatever." Sarah laughed. "It's yours."

Caleb grinned. "I make a mean sweet potato hash and fried eggs."

"That will be on the breakfast menu in the morning," Lacey said. "We're staying over tonight. Rose and I worked it all out earlier."

"Gran Rose and I are watching a movie with the piglets," Aspen said. "Gran Rose says the piglets like to fall asleep to movies about princesses and princes. I get to pick one."

Sarah swallowed her laughter and nodded.

"That sounds fun." Carter smiled at Aspen, then considered the others. "But I still say there's nothing like a night run in the combine to clear your mind."

"I like the movie option with Aspen better." Caleb's brow wrinkled. "The combine is just not that fun, big brother. At all."

"Then you're doing it wrong," Carter countered. His words dry.

"There's a right way?" Caleb argued.

Carter squeezed Tess and she smiled at him. "Next time, combine with your fiancée, little brother, and then get back to me."

Caleb rubbed his chin and smiled at Lacey. "How about it? Want to kick Ryan out of the grain tractor and take a turn with me?"

Lacey set her hand in his and said, "I thought you'd never ask."

Sarah looked at Bodie. "Any chance I could convince you to join me?"

"Consider me convinced," her cowboy said. His gaze warmed. His expression softened. "Count me in for the rest of the night too."

That declaration led to a disagreement over who stayed up all night with Sarah and Bodie. Finally, Lacey and Caleb won out, given they were both used to working nights. Tess and Carter's claims about being well-versed in overnights, thanks to their toddler twins, backfired and earned them the opportunity to head home and get some well-deserved rest. Especially since Tess and Carter's twins were spending the night at Tess's cousin's house. Wells and Lilian headed out too, after Lilian declared her retired status granted her immunity from working the night shift, and she tugged Wells along with her.

Bodie joined Sarah inside the combine cab and handed her a paper bag. "Rose and I decided you would not stop to eat dinner. So, I packed you something and figured a meal on the go would be better than nothing."

It was perfect. Sarah polished off the flask of chili and the cheddar biscuit while explaining the combine to Bodie. Soon enough, they were back to the harvest. Sarah was in the captain's chair, watching the computer screen and control board. And Bodie was beside her in the second seat that looked much smaller with her cowboy in it.

They passed the first few hours with a country combine karaoke. Thanks to the music streaming app Carter had installed. Then they traded places with Lacey and Caleb. Bodie drove the grain tractor for the next hour and Sarah rested her eyes. Now her grain bin was full, and the trucks were on their way to the grain elevator with the rest of the corn. They were waiting for the last semitruck to arrive. Lacey and Caleb had already gone into the house to finally get some sleep.

"You look wide-awake." Bodie stretched his arms over his head and eyed her. "How is that possible?"

"I'm too excited to sleep. This is my first official corn harvest where it counted." Sarah ran her hands over the steering wheel and marveled,

"When we finish these last rows of corn, I can say I did it. I did this."

Bodie shifted in his chair and said, "Corn is your passion."

"Don't laugh," she said.

"I wasn't going to," he said quietly. "I think it's special. I think it matters."

That drew her gaze to him, and she said, "I think so too. It's the direction I would take the farm."

"Why don't you?" he asked.

"It's not what's been done." She shrugged and added, "And I was given other advice along the way." From well-meaning people and even her family. How could she not listen to them?

"Perhaps you should take your own advice," he suggested. "Follow your passion."

"Perhaps one day." And only if she managed to turn the farm around soon. Sarah's gaze drifted out over the harvested fields. She couldn't deny the beat of pride right now. She had taken her corn crop from seed to harvest like a true farmer. Bodie wasn't wrong. It mattered. A lot.

Bodie stacked his hands behind his head, his gaze fixed out the front window "Well, now I know what a farmer's night shift looks like."

Sarah opened the container of grapes Bodie had packed for her and asked, "Do you hate it?"

"Not even a little bit." He never hesitated.

His words both thrilled and instantly calmed her. Loving the farm life was not a requirement for her partner. But having a partner who understood her and didn't mind sharing her lifestyle was. She said, "Now that we know what keeps me up at night." She popped a grape in her mouth and slanted her gaze at him. "Tell me what keeps you up at night."

"Is this that twenty questions thing again?" Bodie tipped his hat up and grinned. "I would have thought you ran out of questions the other night."

"Hardly," she said, and laughed at his bemused expression and continued, "Seriously, I want to know more about you."

"Like what?" he asked.

"Anything." She shrugged and ate another grape. "Tell me what you dream about. Tell me what you want in life."

Bodie's eyebrows lifted.

But Sarah rolled on. "Tell me something that leaves you restless. Or what makes you sleepless. Or gets you out of bed in the morning." *Let me know I'm not alone in seeing something more here. Something beyond corn crops and bison bandits. Something worth reaching for.*

Bodie opened and closed his mouth.

"Tell me what makes your heart race. Or what makes it stop." Sarah set the grape container on the dash, then leaned over and rested her palm against his chest. She held his stare and said softly, "Give me a truth. Your truth." *Something. Anything.*

Because I cannot be falling alone.

Please, please don't let me fall alone.

He covered her hand with his own, anchoring her against him, and said simply, "You."

Maybe it was the soothing warmth of his touch. Or the aching tenderness in his gaze. But her thoughts scattered like so many seeds in the wind and she saw only him. She whispered, "What?"

"You leave me restless. You steal my sleep. You get me out of bed in the morning." He reached up and traced his fingers across her cheek. "You're my first thought and my last."

Had she ever been that for someone before? Sarah could not look away.

"You make my pulse race," he continued.

Hers raced too. Because her cowboy of few words chose the perfect ones now, drawing her to him.

He leaned forward and brushed his lips over hers. The softest caress. The barest connection. Nothing more than a hint. But enough to make the attraction flare. The awareness spark.

This was something after all and she wasn't in it alone.

Only he eased back, far enough to capture her gaze in his again. "If I kiss you, I fear you will leave me more than breathless."

She was already there. And she hadn't truly kissed him yet. She held herself still, heard the rasp in her words. "You make it sound like that's a bad thing."

A flash of a grin crossed his face, hardly creasing his one cheek. "I was taught to avoid things that are bad for me."

Her turn to smile. "I have an idea."

"Is it a good one?" One eyebrow arched.

"I think so." She cupped his cheek in her palm and ran her thumb over his bottom lip. Grinning at his soft audible inhale, she asked, "What if I kissed you instead?"

The soft glare from the computer screen illuminated his face. His ice-blue eyes flared.

"And if it's bad," she said, and shrugged, "you don't have to kiss me back."

He gathered her closer.

"What do you think?" Her words barely registered as a whisper. She was already breathless.

His gaze traveled slowly over her face, as if memorizing her, then he met her gaze. He traced his fingers over her cheek. One corner of his mouth lifted. "I think if you kiss me, there is no way I'm not participating."

"Good answer." Sarah sealed her lips to his and was about to give herself over to the moment.

But twin lights flooded the entire combine cab like spotlights. Sarah jumped back, shaded her eyes, and squinted out the windshield. "I think that might be our truck driver for the last haul of corn."

"Talk about timing," Bodie muttered, then opened the cab door. "I'll go speak to him." He was out and on the ground before Sarah could pull him back to her.

She wanted to finish what they'd started. She wanted a real kiss from her cowboy. Sarah sank into the captain's chair. Her pulse continued in a quick staccato. But combines weren't for getting lost in a cowboy's arms and forgetting herself. There was work to do and a farm to save.

Sarah shoved her hat on her head, climbed out to meet the late truck driver and finally get back to the business of harvesting.

The last of the corn was headed to the grain elevator located just outside Amarillo, and the sun was rising when Bodie and Sarah finally walked inside the quiet farmhouse. Hand in hand, they made their way upstairs in search of showers, a change of clothes, and well-earned shut-eye as her grandmother called it.

Bodie stopped outside Sarah's bedroom door and turned toward her. His words were slow, as if he had all day to linger. "You know. I just realized you never did answer the question from the other night."

Sarah eyed him, feeling tired yet intrigued at the same time. "What one was that?"

He braced his arm on the doorframe near her head and grinned. "Do you prefer good-night or good-morning kisses, or was it texts?"

I'm starting to prefer you. More than I should. She said, "I'm feeling rather partial to good-morning sleep-tight kisses."

"I'm not sure I know that one." He tucked a strand of her hair behind her ear.

"Here. I'll show you." She stepped forward and curved her arms around his neck.

He wasted no time, anchoring his arms around her waist and pulling her against him. They met halfway.

This time, there were no spotlights. No interruptions. But there was knee-buckling and her being swept off her boots. This kiss was more than she expected. More compelling. More giving. More breathless. And so much more revealing.

Finally, she eased back.

Bodie pressed the softest of kisses to her lips and said, "I think this is the part where I wish you sweet-dream wishes."

Sarah reluctantly released him and whispered, "Same to you."

She waited until he disappeared down the hallway, then escaped into her room and leaned back against the closed bedroom door.

Suddenly, she knew more than his truth. She knew her own now too.

It was too late to fear falling for her cowboy. She had already fallen.

And now she had to brace herself for the impact.

CHAPTER THIRTEEN

BODIE DRIED HIS hair with a towel, then changed into clean clothes. He'd taken a shower to recharge his mind. Sleep was not in the cards. His gut was pushing him to action, and he'd learned over the years to pay attention to his hunches.

Last night around the fire pit, Carter had informed Wells about a farmer he knew in Llyne who had livestock go missing this past week, and he wasn't the only farmer in the county. That, coupled with the pop-up auction Bodie's counterpart across the border in Oklahoma had encountered, did not bode well.

But Bodie could not quite shake loose the conversation he had with the final truck driver to arrive earlier. The truck driver told Bodie he was late due to making a wrong turn, and claimed he'd gotten his trees mixed up. That sounded all too familiar. Bodie had used the same excuse the first day he met Sarah. However, according to the truck driver, there was a neighbor on the road who had been more than happy to set him straight and get him on his way.

Bodie grabbed his boots and headed out of the guest bedroom. He checked Sarah's door, noted it was closed, and went downstairs. He didn't wake Sarah. There was no sense alarming his farmer if his hunch proved to be nothing more than a sleep-deprived short circuit.

In the kitchen, Bodie found Lacey and Caleb hugging in front of the stove and wished them good morning.

Lacey greeted him. "Last night was a lot of work but we had a good time, didn't we?"

Caleb agreed.

Bodie had a very good evening with Sarah in the combine. Those were words he never thought he'd put in a sentence: a combine harvester and a good time. Then there was the kiss he and Sarah had shared outside her bedroom door. Talk about mesmerizing. Not to mention exhilarating and any number of other enchanting things. But now was definitely not the time to dwell on their kiss or when they might find time for another.

He eased his foot into his boot, looked at his stepsister, and asked, "Do you mind coming out for a ride?"

Lacey turned and eyed him. "That sounds very official."

Caleb kept his attention on Bodie and said, "I think it is."

Caleb was the only one besides Lacey and Wells who knew about Bodie's investigation. If the rest of the Sloan family had been told, they were keeping the information to themselves. Bodie appreciated their discretion. Bodie nodded. "I hope I'm wrong."

Lacey shook her head and said, "You're not usually wrong."

Caleb kissed her cheek and said, "Be careful. You too, Bodie."

"Caleb, I didn't tell Sarah." Bodie set his hat on his head and continued, "I didn't want to worry her if this turns out to be nothing."

"My mom and I take early-morning rides at least once a week." Caleb stirred the potatoes on the stove. "It's our way of connecting. It seems to me that you and Lacey are due for the same kind of reconnection yourselves."

That sealed it for Bodie. He stepped forward and shook Caleb's hand. "I'm glad my sister has you and your family."

"The feeling is mutual." Caleb grinned and added, "Welcome to the family, Bodie."

There it was again. The welcome was simple. The acceptance straightforward and seeming without any catches. Yet the joining, well, that set him back still. Bodie had siblings he called family in an offhand, blood-relative kind of way.

Here, there was a choice to join in, and it wasn't to be taken lightly. There was nothing casual about the bond among them and family meant something. But Bodie had mastered being on his own. He worried it was all he knew how to do.

It wasn't long before Bodie and Lacey had Calvin

and Twilight saddled. After warming up the horses, they rode out to the far pasture and the bison.

"You and Swells seem to be getting along rather well," Lacey commented. "Dare I say you've turned a corner in your father-son relationship."

"Nothing that dramatic." Bodie shifted in the saddle. "We worked on a tractor together and discussed the case a bit." His father had also given Bodie the file of information his chief had sent over.

"Why would it be so bad to turn that corner?" Lacey glanced at him. "He is your dad after all."

Because Bodie had been wrong about Sarah, and now he worried he was wrong about his dad too. That would make him two for two on things he was convinced he knew before arriving in Three Springs. It seemed as if this small town wanted to turn everything he thought he knew inside out. That made him uncomfortable and more than a little uptight. All of which were not good for keeping his horse calm, obviously. Bodie said, "I'm pressing a conversational Pause on this topic."

"Fine. What should we talk about then?" Lacey eyed him. Her gaze flashed in the early morning light. "Oh, I know. Let's talk about you and Sarah."

"What about us?" he countered.

Now, if he wanted a beginning to their story—to the start of them—his near-perfect kiss with Sarah would be it. But *us* only worked if both people were present and accounted for in the relationship. Bodie knew that much firsthand. How many times had his ex-fiancée accused him of not being available? When it came to balancing work and love, well, love always lost. *Nice fast-forward, Hopson*. After all, it was just one kiss, not love.

Bodie frowned and said, "There is no *us* between Sarah and me, by the way."

"Are you trying to fool me or yourself?" Lacey chuckled and adjusted her hold on the reins.

"I'm serious." His near-perfect kiss with his farmer aside, he argued, "Sarah is meant for a cowboy."

"What does that even mean?" Lacey's brow furrowed.

Bodie was not a farmer by trade. He was barely a farmer in progress. He could not herd livestock or drive tractors. He could not even spot simple barn animals. He wasn't sure what he could possibly give Sarah. Well, if he was still in fast-forward, it would be something like love. As if he believed that was enough. He blurted, "I'm not a cowboy."

Lacey shook her head. "That's what you are going with."

Well, he sure wasn't going with his feelings. "Look," he said, "I'm not the cowboy to her cowgirl."

"Or—" Lacey stressed the word and knocked the brim of her hat higher to meet his gaze "—maybe you are Sarah's ideal cowboy, and you just don't want to admit it."

Bodie shifted in the saddle again and countered, "Why would I do that?"

"Because if you called yourself a cowboy, you might be tempted to call Three Springs home." Lacey lifted her eyebrows and gave him a pointed look.

Home. Another word that had been floated out there a lot recently. It was not quite so elusive to him now. But *home* came with roots and the long haul and perhaps even his farmer. But grabbing it meant giving up too. He loosened his grip on the reins and said, "It doesn't matter if I call myself a cowboy or not. You know my work is focused elsewhere."

"There is important law enforcement work to be done around here too," Lacey stated. "Besides, your family is here. That should matter too."

It was starting to. More than he ever thought it would. He said, "Look, Dad and I worked on a tractor and spent an entire evening together. For the first time in years, it was good between us. Let that be enough."

"Only if it's enough for you," Lacey said, a stubborn lift to her chin.

"It is." *Not enough.* Bodie's frown deepened.

But what it was *was* starting to feel like was a big deal. All of it. *Home. Family. The idea of an us.* He'd come back to work a case and tie up loose ends. He hadn't come back to build something he was scared he might one day ruin. And that was why go-it-alone worked. He urged Calvin into a run.

His mood declined even more when the bison

count came up two short. His gut had been spot-on. Too bad he didn't feel like celebrating. He called his father and asked him to locate the truck driver for more questioning.

Now, Lacey and Bodie were at the gate where the friendly neighbor had turned around the lost truck driver last night. Their horses were grazing in the pasture. Lacey leaned against the fence and watched him.

Bodie walked the dirt road and followed the truck tire marks. "It's obvious the grain truck turned around here last night after the driver made the wrong turn."

"Well, the lock is intact," Lacey said and pointed to the red bubble light on the gate. "Even your makeshift alarm is still attached and wired properly."

"Still, the driver spoke to someone here." Bodie set his hands on his hips. And more bison were gone.

"It's logical to think it was Sawyer out here." Lacey propped her boot on the bottom rung. "He's friendly and a neighbor."

And he was Sarah's best friend. If Sawyer had helped the truck driver last night, why hide it?

"Sawyer should be questioned," Lacey mused.

Bodie frowned.

"As a potential witness," Lacey clarified.

It still did not sit well. All Bodie saw in his mind was Sarah's face. She wouldn't understand. And if her friend was involved somehow, she would be hurt. The last thing Bodie wanted was his farmer hurt.

He swallowed around a sudden bad taste in his mouth then said, "I'll talk to Sawyer after we get a description of the friendly neighbor from the truck driver. Dad should have that today."

And Bodie would have his case back in the forefront and his feelings in the distance.

"We should head back." Lacey pushed off the fence. "Sarah is going to start wondering about us."

Bodie nodded and hopped over the fence. They mounted the horses and then rode single file down the trail through the forest.

When they reached the prairie, Lacey reined her horse in beside Bodie. "You need to tell Sarah what is going on."

Bodie shook his head. "We don't know what is going on." Not yet anyway. But he would.

"You don't have to like it," Lacey countered. "But you have to tell her."

He struggled with the idea. Against all reason. He had delivered much more devastating news to people before. It was part of his job. Now, he wrestled with telling his farmer two more of her bison were missing and her best friend may or may not be involved and possibly responsible for putting her farm in financial harm. He'd watched her lose hope yesterday over the corn. He didn't want to give her a repeat today. He said, "I'm not telling her yet."

"When will you tell her?" Lacey pressed.

How about after it was finished? *Nice, Hopson.*

If Sawyer was guilty, his farmer would be devastated, and Bodie would be on his way out of town. Now he hurt too. Bodie clamped his teeth together and remained silent.

"You have no intention of telling her, do you?" Lacey glared at him. "I don't agree with this."

"You don't have to like it," he said with regret. "But it's my case."

Bodie urged Calvin into another run, although he wasn't in any particular hurry to return to the farmhouse.

The sibling stalemate followed them into the stables and continued while they rubbed down the horses. Lacey tried one last time to change his mind about telling Sarah when they walked outside the stable barn. Bodie simply shook his head and shut her down.

Sarah came around the corner from the direction of the grain bin and smiled. "Thanks for taking care of the horses. I was just coming to do that. Lacey, Aspen is inside with the piglets and Caleb is waiting on his peanut-butter banana muffins to come out of the oven."

"Those are a favorite at our house. I'll be sure to leave some here." Lacey hugged Sarah. "Thanks for letting us stay over. I'm going to collect my crew and head out. We need to get Aspen ready for the rodeo parade today."

"I'm the one who should be thanking you," Sarah said.

Lacey gave Bodie a tight squeeze, then followed

that up with a hard, disgruntled look before she headed inside the farmhouse.

Sarah studied Bodie. "What did I miss?"

"Nothing but a sibling dispute." One that made Bodie feel all kinds of bad for doing his job and not wanting to loop his farmer in. It was just that he didn't want to worry her. Sarah had enough to deal with. *Stop kidding yourself, Hopson. You want to protect her anyway you can, even from yourself.*

"Want to talk about it?" Sarah bumped her shoulder against his.

And nudged at his guilt. Still, he grumbled, "Not really in the mood for talking."

Her face fell. Hurt flashed through her hazel eyes before she turned away and gave him her back.

This was why he never really got into his feelings. He took a second before following her onto the back porch. He set his hand on her shoulder and waited for her to turn around. When she faced him, he confessed, "Lacey and I are disagreeing about you."

"Me?" Confusion colored her words.

"Yeah." Bodie took off his cowboy hat and tugged on his hair. "Lacey thinks I need to tell you the truth."

She crossed her arms over her chest, tipped her head, and finally met his stare. "What truth is that?"

That I like you more than I should. No. Too soon. Too complicated. He tucked his feelings away.

That I'm leaving soon. But he wasn't opening that up for discussion.

How about that I want to kiss you again. Call me selfish and greedy. Now was not the time to get distracted, even if she looked fetching in the morning sun and her brightly colored overalls.

The truth was, he was going to hurt her. And he wasn't sure there was any way to stop it. He exhaled and finally said, "Lacey and I were not only in the stables this morning. We rode out to check on the bison."

She froze, as if bracing herself. "Why?"

"Call it a hunch." He hedged, then he filled her in on his conversation with the truck driver, omitting the part about the friendly neighbor, and finished with, "Two bison are missing."

Her exhale was short. Her words were brisk. "You think the driver ran into the bison bandit."

"I think it's possible," he said slowly. Whoever was out there had information Bodie wanted.

She paced around him and turned back. "What now?"

"We wait while my dad finds the driver and questions him," Bodie explained. "When we get a description of the person the driver spoke to, we can go from there."

"You expect me to just stand by." She set her hands on her hips and frowned at him. "You want me to be patient when my livelihood and my grandmother's home are at stake."

I want you to trust me. He considered her. "I want you to let me do my job."

"Fine." She pointed at him. "But you have to tell my grandmother."

"We should do that now," he said and turned to go inside.

The back door swung open. Aspen came out and wrapped him in a warm hug, then she rushed over to Sarah to treat her to the same. She wouldn't get into the truck until both Sarah and Bodie vowed to be at the rodeo that afternoon.

Caleb shook Bodie's hand then gave him a pair of yellow-tinted safety glasses. Amusement shifted across Caleb's face. "Got these from my truck earlier. Rose told me you need them, and that you would understand."

Bodie held back a grin and tucked the safety glasses into his shirt pocket. Then got another hug from Aspen and his family was gone. He followed Sarah inside to the kitchen, where Rose was seated at the island, an assortment of hats and shirts spread across the counter.

"Grandma, what is all this?" Sarah picked up a muffin from the tray on the island and peeled off the wrapper. "Are you cleaning out your closet?"

"We'll get to this." Rose fiddled with the knob on the vintage radio sitting on the counter and settled on an up-tempo country tune. She tapped her fingers on her leg and waggled her eyebrows. "Now listen up, you two. You need to practice your rhythm for the dance after the rodeo tonight."

Sarah popped a piece of muffin into her mouth and spoke around the bite. "I'm not sure we will be going."

"Of course you will," Rose challenged. "The harvest is done. You've no excuses." Rose paused and considered Bodie. "Unless."

Bodie saw the shrewd glint in the older cowgirl's gaze, and again held back his smile. Rose was nothing if not enterprising and entertaining.

"Unless what?" Sarah took another bite of her muffin.

"Unless you're worried about his face." Rose wrinkled her nose and peered closer at Bodie. "That's it, isn't it?"

Sarah sputtered, then coughed and set her muffin on the counter.

Bodie filled a water glass and handed it to Sarah. His laughter slipped out. "I did promise we were going to discuss my face, didn't I?"

"No time like the present." Rose's mouth quirked and she held up her hands as if she was framing him for a picture. "For starters, I don't recommend shaving. And you can't wear a fake mustache." She tipped her hands, as if seeing him from another angle, then added, "If you start sweating when you're dancing—and you're not doing it right if you don't—well, the mustache will slide off."

"Grandma, how do you know this?" Sarah sipped her water, then wiped her mouth and hands on a paper towel.

"I know things," Rose claimed.

Bodie appreciated Rose's insight, touched the stubble covering his cheek, and nodded. "Anything else?"

"Don't suppose we could get colored contacts at the general store on our way to the rodeo," Rose mused. At Sarah's flat *no*, Rose shrugged and said, "Maybe shaping your eyebrows will do."

Sarah groaned.

Bodie chuckled.

Rose rattled on, "It's a toss-up whether we want to shave all your hair off or dye it."

"I vote neither," Sarah said flatly and refilled her water glass.

Bodie was a *no* vote too.

Rose drummed her fingers on the counter and asked, "What's the shape of your head?"

Bodie resisted the urge to remove his cowboy hat and instead replied, "Normal."

"There's only one solution then," Rose stated, seemingly satisfied. "We need hair dye. If we don't like it, we shave it all off."

Bodie crossed his arms over his chest.

"Or we don't go out dancing," Sarah suggested, and set the glass lid over the muffins. "We stay home. No one will recognize him here."

Stay home. With his farmer. Bodie voted yes.

"How will you dance the night away then?" Rose looked put out.

Bodie had a few ideas. The back porch. The music app on his phone. The moonlight turned up.

But he was already otherwise engaged. With his case, not a cowgirl.

"Well, I've got your wardrobe changes for the rodeo today," Rose declared and motioned to the collection of clothes on the counter. "We can discuss our evening plans later."

His included following those leads, not twirling a cowgirl across a dance floor. Although he couldn't deny it sounded fun.

"Wardrobe changes?" Sarah moved over to the kitchen island and touched a neon yellow parking vest.

"So Bodie can maintain his cover," Rose whisper-talked then added, "If he changes his T-shirts and hats on the hour, it'll be hard for anyone to place him."

Bodie nodded and appreciated Rose's ingenuity. At least one of them was putting the case first. Bodie needed to follow Rose's example.

"You're just going to need to keep your face turned away," Rose continued. "Avoid direct eye contact. And don't talk to anyone. It's the best we can do." Rose glanced at him and asked in a hushed tone, "Did you get the glasses from Caleb?"

Bodie patted his pocket. "Got them right here."

"Those are for our pasture stakeout." Rose beamed. "Tonight, we catch our bison bandit by surprise and take him down."

Sarah's eyes widened.

Bodie rubbed the back of his neck. Time to quit

stalling and get back to the business of bison. He started, "About that—"

Sarah interrupted, "I have a Chance Blackwell T-shirt. Bodie could wear it at the rodeo. Then, there won't be so many plaid shirts for him to be seen in." Sarah backed out of the kitchen toward the stairs and blurted, "Grandma, you must have an extra bucket hat for him to use too."

"Why didn't I think of that? It's a very good idea." Rose slid off the stool and walked toward her bedroom. "I'm sure I've got an extra one in my closet."

Bodie leaned against the counter and waited for his farmer to return. She came back quickly, and she wasn't empty-handed. Bodie asked, "What just happened?"

"We can't tell her about the bison." Sarah kept her voice low. "She's already plotting a pasture stakeout. Who knows what she'll do if she learns two more have disappeared. She might head out there now with a tent and her cane."

He wouldn't put it past her.

"We can't let her out of our sight," Sarah said. "We have to keep an extra-close eye on her from now on."

Bodie eyed his farmer. He wanted to keep both Rose and Sarah close and for longer than his investigation. More of those truths he wasn't spilling.

"Be careful with this." Sarah suddenly looked flustered. She handed him the dark T-shirt and added, "I know it sounds ridiculous. It's just a T-shirt, but it's one of my favorites."

She was becoming his favorite. Bodie accepted the T-shirt and decided there was absolutely nothing ridiculous about that revelation.

CHAPTER FOURTEEN

SARAH PARKED HER truck in the dirt lot outside the Three Springs Rodeo Arena and left her sunglasses on the dash. The afternoon sun was hidden behind the clouds and would be setting soon enough. Bodie hopped out, then leaned back inside to offer his hand to Grandma Rose. Sarah met the pair near the truck's tailgate.

"You remember the order of your wardrobe changes, right?" Grandma Rose faced Bodie and recited the order using her fingers. "First is the event-staff smock. Then the plaid shirt when you go backstage with Aspen. Then it's the medical-staff shirt."

"Got it." Bodie tugged on the cuff of his plaid button-down.

"Is this really necessary?" Sarah stuck her hands in her overall pockets and considered Bodie's layered look, with the final exclamation point being the neon yellow event-staff vest, courtesy of Maggie Sloan, the rodeo director.

Her grandmother ignored Sarah and kept her gaze fixed on Bodie. "Pay attention in the medical tent," her grandmother told him. "Everybody talks when they are injured and in pain."

"Grandma, I don't know about that," Sarah said.

"They can't help it." Her grandmother straightened the collar of Bodie's event-staff vest and explained. "I've seen it on TV hundreds of times. Pain turns 'em into chatterboxes every single time."

Bodie nodded and rolled his lips together, as if catching his smile. Then he said all too seriously, "Any other helpful tips, Rose?"

Sarah had one—stop encouraging her grandmother. Or rather, stop being so kind as to include her grandmother. And then perhaps Sarah would not find one more thing to appreciate about him. From his kisses to his chivalry, Sarah being sweet on her cowboy was practically a given. What she intended to do about it was not so certain.

"One last thing," Grandma Rose instructed and thrust a pair of tinted sunglasses at Bodie. "Don't aim those blue moon eyes at Sarah. Or everybody's gonna know you two have a thing for each other."

Sarah blanched. "Grandma."

"What?" Grandma Rose countered. "Anybody can see it."

Bodie aimed his one-sided grin at Sarah over her grandmother's head, not seeming the least bit worried about their apparent thing for each other or anyone taking notice. Then he took her grandmother's arm in his and said, "You'll have to explain what blue moon eyes are, Rose. I can't stop it if I don't know what I'm doing."

"You can't help yourself." Her grandmother patted Bodie's shoulder and added, "I know my granddaughter is quite the catch."

Sarah appreciated her grandmother's compliment.

Bodie met Sarah's gaze and held it. "I couldn't agree more."

Sarah felt her sigh down to her toes.

"I knew you were hooked on her," Grandma Rose said. Pleasure spread across her grandmother's face before she frowned. "And that is why you must wear sunglasses. We can't have everyone knowing it and asking questions about you."

It was enough Sarah knew that Bodie and she were a bit hooked on each other. She wasn't falling alone after all.

"Good point, Rose." Bodie slipped on the sunglasses and asked, "Better?"

"For now." Rose tapped the large tote bag she'd given to Sarah. "Don't forget. I've got extra hats and glasses to switch out too when you change shirts. Nobody will remember you."

It hardly mattered what hat, sunglasses, or shirt Bodie wore. Sarah spotted her cowboy around the arena all afternoon. Whether he was chatting with other rodeo volunteers or beaming with pride when Aspen rode in the parade or leaning against the fence post during the main event with Grant Sloan, the on-site rodeo doctor. It was as if even in a crowded arena, they were undeniably aware of each other.

Her cowboy kept his presence low-key and appropriately under the radar, according to Grandma Rose. If only Sarah could say the same for her grandmother. There wasn't a local in attendance Grandma Rose didn't stop to greet and talk to. And she ended each conversation the same with a promise to see them later at the dance. Sarah finally decided an evening at the Owl was better for her grandmother than a pasture stakeout. As for Sarah, the more locals she reconnected with, the more she was looking forward to extending her evening.

"We've got our winners." Her grandmother motioned to Aspen at her side.

The young girl held up three horseshoes. "Now we get to decorate them and take them home."

"Give those to Sarah to paint for us," her grandmother instructed. Once Aspen transferred the horseshoes to Sarah, her grandmother took Aspen's hand. "We must go pick our pig for the pig races and scout out our competition."

Aspen cheered. "Gran Rose says we're on a winning streak because we got good game plans."

Sarah laughed and pointed to the horseshoes. "What is your plan for these?"

"Paint mine green for the luck of the Irish," her grandmother decided.

"Pink." Aspen's mouth twisted to the side then she grinned. "Add lots and lots of glitter, please."

"One dazzled horseshoe and a lucky one coming up," Sarah said and watched the pair beeline for the pigpens. Then she made her way over to a picnic table and found herself happily stopping to chat with more locals along the way.

She had her paint colors selected and her paintbrushes ready when Sawyer sank onto the bench across from her. Sarah slid a horseshoe across the table. "Here, paint this one green for Grandma Rose. We're celebrating their win in the horseshoe tournament."

Sawyer dipped a paintbrush into the green paint and said, "I didn't think you'd be here and having so much fun after your all-night harvesting and the stress of the missing bison."

Neither did she. But she was enjoying herself and the break from her worry. Sarah swirled pink over Aspen's horseshoe and said, "I'm hoping everything will be resolved soon, now that the authorities are involved."

"I didn't know you went to the police." Sawyer squeezed more paint on the plate and glanced at her. "I thought you were just filing insurance claims with Jonah."

"Well, I am friends with a deputy and her stepdad is the sheriff," she said lightly. *Not to mention, I kissed the sheriff's son this morning. I can't stop thinking about him. And I want to kiss him again. So not relevant.* She added, "I didn't have far to go."

"Right." Sawyer chuckled, but it was slightly off-key. "What did they say?"

Sarah caught sight of Aspen and her grandmother. The pair appeared to be having a rather animated conversation with Bodie near the medical office. Then her grandmother plucked Bodie's cowboy hat off his head and swapped it out for a fire engine–red bucket hat. Bodie, good sport that he was, tightened the strap right under his chin and kept chatting with the pair. Sarah swallowed her laughter and looked at Sawyer. "I'm sorry. What?"

Sawyer glanced over his shoulder as if to see who caught her attention, then turned back to her and said, "I don't think I've seen Bodie in the same shirt all day. That is him over there, isn't it?"

That was definitely her cowboy over there. Where she wanted to be. Joining in on their fun. Now she sounded disloyal to her friend. Sarah waved her paintbrush in the air and said, "Bodie is learning the rodeo ropes. They needed extra volunteers."

"He seems to be fitting right in," Sawyer mused.

Her cowboy was fitting in so well, Sarah wasn't exactly sure what she would do when Bodie was not right down the hall in her guest bedroom. What she was not going to do was let her heart take the leap and fall head over boots for him. Satisfied she had a sound game plan, she said, "Bodie was really helpful with last night's harvest. So was the entire Sloan family. I owe them."

"I heard Carter brought over his combine," Sawyer said. "You'll owe the sheriff, too, I suppose. What did he say about the missing bison anyway?"

Suddenly inspired, Sarah dipped her paintbrush into the canary yellow paint and started on her horseshoe. She said, "They're following up on some leads now."

"That's fast work." A shadow passed over Sawyer's face but cleared so quickly Sarah wasn't certain it had been there. He said, "They are good at what they do, I suppose."

"I sure hope so." Sarah waved her hand over the yellow paint to help it dry and decided on a second coat for her sunflower theme.

"Maybe I should go talk to the sheriff." Sawyer finished her grandmother's horseshoe and grinned easily. "See if I can help in any way."

"That would be great." Sarah tipped her head and considered him. "Thanks for looking out for me."

"We're friends. It's what we do." Sawyer reached across the table and took her hand in his. "That and we always forgive each other."

"Please tell me you don't have another rescue stashed someplace around here." Sarah eyed him.

He shook his head and chuckled. "I can go find one if you want."

"Please don't." Sarah squeezed his hand and said, "Grandma Rose is coming back over. I haven't told her the police are involved."

"She won't hear it from me." Sawyer released her hand. His smile stayed in place. "Remember, I'm here for you anytime."

Sarah grinned at him. "I know, and I appreciate it."

Grandma Rose and Aspen scooted onto the bench with Sarah. Aspen picked up the glitter Sarah had found on the art table and got to work on her horseshoe.

Grandma Rose wore Bodie's cowboy hat and waggled her eyebrows at Sarah. "If you're wanting to get a bandage from the medical tent, now is the time to do it. Aspen and I can finish up here and discuss our strategy for the pig race."

Sarah set her paintbrush down and arched an eyebrow at her grandmother.

Her grandmother nudged her elbow into Sarah's side and added, "You know, a bandage for that cut on your hand."

"You cut yourself?" Concern covered Sawyer's words.

"It's nothing." Sarah touched the back of her hand and explained, "I hit my hand on the stake when I was collecting the horseshoes for Grandma and Aspen."

"You could use a bandage," her grandmother said. "Keep the dirt out."

"I can get you one," Sawyer offered.

"No," her grandmother insisted. "It's best for the medical team to examine it first. It might be deeper than it looks."

"Rose is right," Sawyer conceded. "If you cut yourself, you should have it checked out. At the very least, get a bandage."

Not him too. Sarah frowned and noted the stubborn glint in her grandmother's gaze. She stood up. "Fine. I'll head over there and come right back."

"Meet us at the stands," her grandmother stated,

then added, "The barrel racing is coming up and we don't want to miss Vivian Sloan."

"I'll be there," Sarah said. "I always wanted to learn how to barrel race."

Sawyer went to stand, but her grandmother said, "Stay a minute, Sawyer. I wanted to talk to you about when your parents are due to return. I heard they went from Amarillo down to the gulf."

Sarah headed for the medical tent. When she caught sight of a familiar blue-eyed cowboy in a medical-staff T-shirt, leaning against the arena gate, talking to Dr. Grant Sloan, Sarah realized what her grandmother was on about.

Smiling, she approached the men and said, "Any chance I could get a Band-Aid?"

Grant Sloan glanced between Bodie and Sarah, then motioned to a door behind him. "I'm going to let my assistant handle this one and sneak over to see my wife."

Bodie opened the door and followed Sarah into a small exam room. She spun around, took in her cowboy, and burst out laughing. "You do know you can take off Grandma Rose's hat."

"It's quite comfortable." Bodie's grin stretched wide. His gaze gleamed. "I'm kind of partial to it actually."

I'm kinda partial to you, cowboy. Sarah raised her arm and said, "I really do have a cut on my hand." And she was glad for it. Now she had her cowboy all to herself.

He was quick to respond. He had her cut cleaned

and bandaged in no time. Yet, he kept her hand in his. His thumb smoothed over her palm.

"Grandma Rose promised most of the arena that we would be at the dance this evening." Even Sarah had made a few of those promises herself. She asked, "Is that okay with you?"

He grinned and said, "Only if you save a dance for me."

"I can do that," she said.

He adjusted his hold, raised her fingers to his lips, and pressed a kiss on her knuckles. Then he eyed her. "Are you okay?"

She could get used to her cowboy caring for her. She replied, "I am now."

And before she could stop it, her heart took that leap.

CHAPTER FIFTEEN

"Why did I know you would be in some corner brooding?" Lacey dropped into the cushioned chair beside Bodie on the outdoor patio at the Feisty Owl Bar and Grille. She held her full drink aloft to keep her cocktail from splashing over the sides.

"I've got a good view from here of the band and the stage." And more specifically of his farmer dancing and laughing on the dance floor. "And I can stretch my legs without worrying about getting my toes stomped on." He extended his legs and stacked his ankles one over the other to prove his point. "See? Totally not brooding."

"Fine, I stand corrected." Lacey settled back into the chair and sipped her cocktail, which looked to be stuffed with mint leaves and ice. "What are you doing then?"

Considering all the impossibilities of a farmer and a ranger and a lifetime together, he answered, "Waiting to hear back from Dad."

Lacey swirled her straw and stirred the ice around in her glass. "No news on the truck driver then?"

"The truck was located at the driver's residence just north of Amarillo," Bodie explained. "According to his wife, her husband parked and was gone in under an hour. He had an overnight fishing trip with his brother at their family's camp at the lake. He'd been looking forward to it for months."

"Let me guess," Lacey said and frowned. "The camp is somewhere remote."

Bodie nodded. "So, we wait."

"Have you talked to Sawyer yet?" Lacey asked, her words mildly curious.

He shook his head. "Haven't found the right time."

Like take now, for instance. Sawyer was in his sights. But the cowboy was otherwise occupied, twirling Sarah around the dance floor in perfect time to the beat of the music and making them look like the perfect cowboy couple. Just like at the rodeo arena, the bar was not the place to talk to Sawyer, either. Mostly, Bodie did not want to ruin his farmer's good time. And just like at the rodeo earlier, Bodie wished it was him with his farmer, not Sawyer.

And that made him perhaps not the most unobjective person to question Sawyer. Until Bodie got his feelings for his farmer sorted and appropriately tucked away, he decided to wait and watch from the sidelines. However, all bets were off if Bodie got proof of Sawyer's involvement.

"I keep going back to the friendly neighbor who helped out our truck driver," Lacey argued. "The only neighbor Sarah has is the McGowans. And Pearl and Artie are in the gulf."

Sawyer spun Sarah into view again. She practically sparkled from her smile to her boots. He argued, "Whoever the driver spoke to could have been lying about being a neighbor." He very much wanted that to be the case. If only for his farmer's sake.

"I know one thing," Lacey said, a tease in her words. She waved her hand in front of his face and chuckled. "Rose wasn't kidding about those moon eyes of yours. You haven't been able to take them off Sarah since I sat down."

To be clear, he hadn't been able to take them off his farmer all day.

"You could make this easy on both of you and just ask her to dance," Lacey suggested.

But that was the problem. If Bodie finally got his farmer in his arms, he was not going to let her go. He had trouble earlier in the medical office. But a bull rider with a dislocated shoulder was brought in and Sarah fled the exam room. He said, "She's having too much fun to interrupt her."

"You're allowed to have fun too." Lacey poked his shoulder. "Dancing is a good way to pass the time while we wait for information and can make our next move."

"You should be taking your own advice," Bodie said and tipped his head toward the door leading to the patio, where Caleb emerged.

"You do make a good point." Lacey stood and

said, "Let me know when you hear something." And then she was off, grabbing Caleb's arm and guiding him onto the crowded dance floor for a slow dance, despite the upbeat song.

Sarah finished up another line dance and wiped her forehead. Then she linked arms with Elsie Sloan and the two cowgirls headed inside. And that left Bodie to his own thoughts once again. He heard his cowgirl's laughter before he saw her. Heard her claim her boots were tired and she needed a breather before she hit the dance floor again. Bodie waited and if he held his breath to see if she would find him, he wasn't telling.

Seconds later, Sarah plopped right down beside Bodie on the sofa.

He finally exhaled. Delighted his farmer was right where he wanted her.

"That was odd." Sarah unwrapped a straw and stuck it in her soda. "Trey Ramsey didn't know Sawyer's combine wasn't working. Trey is the go-to mechanic for heavy equipment in this county and the surrounding ones."

"Perhaps Sawyer took it someplace else to get it repaired," Bodie mused. "Sawyer works out of town often, doesn't he?" There, he defended Sawyer. There should be points for that.

"Maybe. It's just…" Sarah brushed her hand in the air, then said, "You know what? I probably misheard. It's really loud inside. It doesn't matter." She set her drink on the table and smiled at Bodie. "I didn't come over here to talk about Sawyer."

That was a relief. He now had another piece of information he wanted to chase down. Yet, he wanted to believe Sawyer's combine was simply someplace else. And he really wanted to focus on his cowgirl. He asked, "What do you want to talk about?"

"I was not thinking about talking exactly," she said, and suddenly looked both shy and slightly unsure. "I was thinking more about dancing. With you."

He didn't respond fast enough. She rattled on, rather adorably and rapidly. "Or if it's too crowded out there, we can dance here."

Bodie stood and extended his arm toward her. "You decide."

Her smile lit up her face and made him believe it was only for him. And wasn't that heady and all too captivating.

Sarah slid her hand into his. He pulled her up and straight into him. Her breath came out in a soft whoosh.

Then she curved her arms around his neck and said, "Right here works really well."

For him too. He finally had her in his embrace and all to himself. He gathered her closer and lost himself in the music and the moment.

Two slow songs and a dip later, he righted her and pulled her back into his arms. She laughed and said, "You've got some serious dance moves."

"You sound surprised," he teased, then explained, "My ex-fiancée made us take dance lessons before we were even engaged."

"That's thinking ahead." She leaned away until she looked into his eyes and said, "You never did tell me what happened with you and your ex."

"Nothing all that unusual." He shrugged one shoulder. "We had different expectations for our relationship."

"What were those?" she asked.

"She told me I gave more to work than to her," he explained. "I wasn't present enough. And she didn't want to be a team of one anymore."

Sarah tipped her head and watched him.

"Since I was obviously dedicated to what she called my solo life mission, she handed back the ring and wished me well." And walked out of his life. No chance for a conversation. Or a compromise. Or for him to change. He tucked a piece of hair behind Sarah's ear and added, "She moved and married. The last we spoke she told me she was living her best life."

Sarah's smile was wistful. She asked, "That is the goal, isn't it? To live our best lives."

"I think the goal is to enjoy the good moments." Like the one right now with her.

"Today was good." Her words were simple and honest.

"You looked like you were having fun whenever I saw you." He pulled her in closer.

"I've had fun all day," Sarah admitted.

"You sound surprised," he said.

"I am," she replied. "I know that sounds strange. It's just the first time I've really gotten involved in the community. It makes me want to do it more often."

"That doesn't sound strange," he said. It sounded appealing, especially with her.

"How about you?" she asked. "Did you enjoy today?"

"Well, Grant told me I could be his medical assistant anytime." Bodie grinned. "Apparently, his last rodeo assistant vomited all over a bull rider when he saw the guy's broken wrist."

"Definitely not the bedside manner you want."

Silence surrounded them for a beat, then Bodie said, "I would've had more fun today with you."

"Yeah," Sarah said. "I would've liked that too."

"I did manage to learn a few things," Bodie said.

Sarah shifted and pressed her fingers over his mouth. "Can we not talk about missing livestock and bison bandits and all that?"

He reached up and curved his fingers around hers. "Absolutely."

"Thanks," she said. "It's not that I don't want to know. It's just that I want…"

He pressed a kiss against her palm and finished for her. "It's just that you want to enjoy this moment."

Sarah nodded.

He spun her out, then twirled her back into his arms. "Then let's do just that."

A modified two-step due to space constraints

and three slow dances in, and Bodie was about to claim this as his best night ever. Yet he should have known his best life was on the job, not in a corner on a patio in the local bar and grill.

Bodie saw Lacey and Elsie rush outside. He knew before Lacey met his gaze across the patio that the women were looking for them. He instantly stilled.

"Everything ok?" Sarah asked.

Definitely not. Bodie braced his arm around Sarah's waist and watched the women hurry toward them.

"Sorry to interrupt." Alarm was there in Elsie's expression and words. "Sarah, it's your grandmother."

Sarah stiffened and swayed into Bodie's side. "What happened?"

"She fell in the parking lot," Lacey explained. "The paramedics are on their way."

Sarah gasped and was gone before he could stop her. Racing inside with Elsie right beside her.

Lacey and Bodie followed the two women through the Owl, out the front entrance, and into the parking lot. A crowd had already formed around Rose, who lay on the sidewalk near the stairs. The EMTs pulled in and removed a gurney from the back of the ambulance. Sawyer was beside Sarah, escorting her through the worried onlookers and straight to her grandmother. Caleb and Ryan moved the onlookers away to give the EMTs room to work on Rose.

Bodie caught sight of Sarah. Her cheeks were damp. Her skin much too pale. He stepped forward, intent on shoving anyone in his path aside. All he wanted was to get to his farmer and her grandmother.

Lacey set her hand on Bodie's arm and said lowly, "Don't. You'll start up talk about a love triangle and blow your cover if you charge over there now."

Bodie stilled and watched Sawyer thread his arm around a clearly distraught Sarah. She sagged against her friend as Sawyer helped her stand up. Then the pair followed the gurney into the ambulance and the EMTs shut the doors, blocking Bodie out. Seconds later, the ambulance drove out of the parking lot and took his farmer with it.

But that should be Bodie's arm around Sarah. His words comforting her. Bodie should be in that ambulance beside her. Bodie was her…what was he really? Other than temporary. His farmer deserved more than short-term. She deserved a cowboy who would stick. One who could promise to always be by her side. One who was a present partner. But what did Bodie really know about that?

Bodie spun on his boot heels, slipped around the side of the building, and yanked his phone out. It was time to connect with his father and his peer who was tracking down leads across the border in Oklahoma. He'd put it off long enough, selfishly extending his time with his farmer on the back patio.

Greedy. That was what he'd been. Now, Rose was injured and his farmer in an ambulance.

And Bodie knew what his worst life was.

CHAPTER SIXTEEN

SARAH SAT IN the recliner next to her grandmother's hospital bed and tried not to fuss over her too much. She was grateful they had gotten through the emergency room at Belleridge Regional Hospital swiftly and efficiently. Her grandmother's forehead had been stitched and bandaged in the emergency room. Then her grandmother had been sent for scans of her head and X-rays of her body. And finally admitted into her fourth-floor hospital room.

Although Sarah still hadn't quite shaken off the fright and panic of seeing her grandmother bleeding on the sidewalk. She suspected her grandmother might be on the mend before Sarah completely recovered.

Sawyer returned with a large plastic drink tumbler that he had filled with ice and water. He put the tumbler beside her grandmother and began to pace, as if he too was still processing her grandmother's accident.

"You have to find Bodie." Her grandmother fiddled with the buttons on the hospital bed control pad. The head of the bed started raising and she continued, "I got us a solid lead."

"Grandma, you need to take it easy." Sarah nudged her grandmother's fingers off the control pad and stopped the bed. The results from her grandmother's X-rays were not back yet and Sarah wasn't certain sitting up was the best angle for her injured limbs.

"No time for that," Grandma Rose insisted. Her pale face and bandaged temple tempered the resolve in her words. "We got a lead to follow."

"You hit your head," Sarah said, and tried to sound soothing. "And injured your hip."

"Because I was chasing our lead out into the parking lot," Rose declared and frowned. "What'd you think I was doing?"

Sarah had no idea what she thought her grandmother was up to when she'd slipped on the curb outside. Sarah had left her grandmother with the Baker sisters, certain if her grandma was sitting at the bar with her friends, she couldn't get herself into trouble. Clearly, she'd been wrong.

She pulled the covers up under her grandmother's chin, but nothing softened the hit of guilt. If Sarah had been inside, watching over her grandma like she'd promised she would do, and not dancing in the corner with her cowboy, her grandma would not be in a hospital bed right now.

Worse than all that, Sarah wanted her grandmother to have found a solid lead. The loss of two more bison was pushing the farm and its limited finances into that unrecoverable territory.

"How many fingers am I holding up, Rose?" Sawyer hovered at the foot of the bed. Worry on his face. "I think Rose definitely has a concussion."

"I don't have a concussion," Rose harrumphed. "I knocked my noggin harder than this at the farm and still got my work done." Rose skimmed her fingers over her bandage. "This won't stop me. I've got a lead."

"Yes, we've heard." Sawyer set his hand on the footrail of the bed. His words were encouraging, as if he was content to humor Rose for now. He asked, "Why don't you tell us about this lead? Maybe we can follow up on it for you."

"I've got to talk to my partner first," Rose said, back to insistent and resolved. "You can fetch Bodie for me."

Sawyer's eyebrows lifted. "Bodie is your partner, Rose?"

"There's a lot you don't know about me, Sawyer," Grandma Rose exclaimed and waved her fingers in front of her face. "But there's no time for stories now. Bodie will want to hear what I learned about our bison bandit."

Sarah gripped her hands together in her lap and worked hard to keep her cool. She hadn't confided in Sawyer about who Bodie really was. It was a secret she intended to keep, if only because she didn't want to answer questions about Bodie that might lead to more questions about her and her cowboy.

Yet now the question was how to stop her grandmother from talking.

Sawyer's gaze connected with Sarah's. Confusion filled his face. "I don't follow."

"Am I slurring my words?" Grandma Rose tapped her mouth, then tugged on her earlobe. "My words sound fine to me." Her grandmother said slowly, "*H-e-l-l-o.*"

Sarah sighed and looked at Sawyer. "The thief stealing our bison. Grandma calls him our bison bandit."

Sawyer nodded. "What about him?"

"We are hoping he will be found soon," Sarah explained.

Again, Sawyer nodded. "I'm still confused." He paused and asked mildly, "How does Bodie fit into all this?"

"Sawyer, seeing as you're not my partner, it is mum's the word for now." Grandma Rose stretched her mouth wide open, then pulled on her other ear as if checking her right side for reception. Then she nodded and added, "At least until Bodie comes in."

Sawyer frowned.

Sarah gave Sawyer an apologetic look, then took her grandmother's hand and drew her attention to her and said, "Grandma, Bodie is back at the Owl. He didn't ride with us." But Sarah wanted him here. Right beside her, holding her hand.

"Good thinking on his part. He can't be giving himself away now." Her grandmother's face cleared and brightened. "I'm sure he's on the way."

Sarah hoped he was. She could use his steady presence and strength.

"You should call him just in case," Grandma Rose urged then added, "Tell him to hurry. If they give me pain meds, I might fall asleep and forget what I know."

Sarah scanned her grandmother's face. "Are you in pain?"

"Of course," Grandma Rose replied, a touch of indignation in her words. "I hit my head and busted my hip. You would be in pain too."

Just then, the door swung open, and a familiar cowboy doctor strode in, a smile on his face. Dr. Grant Sloan had traded his cowboy hat and jeans from earlier at the rodeo for a long white coat and scrubs.

Relief rushed through Sarah. Her grandmother's care would be in the best hands possible with Grant Sloan.

Grant nodded to Sarah, shook Sawyer's hand, then the skilled, well-known orthopedic surgeon approached her grandmother's bed. His manner was easygoing and good-natured. "Looks like you've gotten yourself in a bit of a scrape, Rose. I hope your opponent fared worse."

"You'd have to ask the sidewalk, doc." Her grandmother grinned wide and asked sweetly, "Are you springing me out of here then?"

"Not quite." Dr. Sloan tapped on the computer attached to the wall and added, "We've got to discuss the few parts that didn't fare so well in your sidewalk scrape."

Sawyer's phone chimed. He mouthed an apology to Sarah and stepped outside to take the call.

Sarah returned her attention to Dr. Sloan and prepared herself. Her parents would want a detailed report when she called them to let them know what had happened. The prognosis was better than expected. Her grandmother had suffered bruised ribs and a hairline hip fracture that would require surgery. However, she showed no signs of a concussion. Dr. Sloan promised to return in the morning with the details about the surgery in the next forty-eight hours.

Sarah urged her grandmother to rest and only got her to agree once she promised to go out and look for Bodie. Sarah stepped into the hallway and leaned against the railing on the wall.

Sawyer shoved his phone into his pocket and came toward her. There was something almost frantic and slightly panicked about him. Sarah chalked it up to being inside the hospital. She knew they made some people nervous, and she guessed her friend was one of them.

Sawyer approached her, dropped to one knee and blurted, "Sarah-Belle, marry me."

Sarah blinked. She really did not have time for her friend to fall apart now.

But Sawyer never moved. Simply stayed on one knee and stared at her imploringly.

"What are you doing?" Sarah shoved away from

the wall and tugged on Sawyer's arm until he was standing again. "Did you hit your head too?"

"I'm asking you to be my wife." Sawyer rushed on, his words more like nervous chatter. "I'm tired of waiting. We're meant to be together."

"Where is this coming from?" Sarah pressed a hand to her forehead. Perhaps she was the one with the concussion. She shook her head. "What is wrong with you?"

"Nothing is wrong," Sawyer said. That imploring expression was back on his face. "I just don't want to hide my feelings for you anymore. I know you feel something for me too."

What she felt for her friend hardly compared to what she felt for her cowboy. Sarah stammered, "I can't marry you." *Won't* was more like it.

"Yes, you can," Sawyer pleaded and latched onto her hand. "And you should. We need each other. We're good for each other."

Sarah yanked her arm free and retreated a step.

Sawyer took her silence as a *please proceed* and continued, "We can look after each other. Build something together. I know you've thought about it. Thought about us as a family."

Once again, she had those thoughts, but they involved her cowboy. She crossed her arms over her chest. "Have you thought about us like that?"

"Sure," Sawyer said, although he hardly sounded convincing. "We've been friends for a long time. It's the next logical step."

Sarah wasn't certain she wanted logical in a marriage proposal. Romance and her favorite flowers. A declaration of love perhaps. A spark. Like the one she felt when she kissed Bodie. Or danced with Bodie. Or laughed with Bodie. Yes, her cowboy caused her to spark. Sarah cleared her throat. "We can't get married, Sawyer."

"Not right now," Sawyer said, as if purposely misunderstanding her. "Rose needs to heal first. But we can get engaged. Right here. Right now."

Sarah took another step back. "We are not getting engaged. Now or any time."

"You're distracted," he said, his words soothing. "Just think it over. Give me that much." He took his phone out again and fumbled with it. Then he said, "We can talk about it when I get back."

"Where are you going?" she asked.

"I've got a job," Sawyer explained. "Then I can come back with a ring, and you'll have to say yes."

With that pronouncement, her friend disappeared inside the elevator. Sarah checked on her grandma but was too restless and worried about her friend to sit. She decided on coffee and hoped it might bring her some much-needed clarity.

The night had certainly taken a strange turn, and she sensed it wasn't finished twisting her up yet.

THE WAIT WAS OVER. While Bodie bedded down Sarah's farm for the evening, despite the rain that moved in, the pieces for his case had started to fall into place.

In part thanks to his farmer and her offhand

comment about Sawyer's combine not in fact being at the local repair shop. A quick internet search and a half dozen phone calls later, Bodie's hunch paid off and he located a fairly new model combine at an impound yard in the neighboring county that matched the description of Sawyer's harvester. According to the impound yard manager, the combine owner had missed over six months of loan payments, and the bank had decided to recoup its losses and had the harvester repossessed, where it was now waiting to go to auction.

Unfortunately, Bodie now had motive for Sawyer to steal and sell Sarah's bison. He wanted to believe Sawyer was not involved, if only for his farmer's sake. However, the argument was becoming more and more difficult to maintain.

The doorbell rang. Bodie opened the front door and Mav raced onto the front porch to greet Lacey and his father. Both were in full uniform and looking more serious than social.

"Finally got a positive ID from the trucker," his father said, wasting no time getting to the point. "It was Sawyer McGowan who turned the trucker around the night of the harvest."

That put Sawyer at the pasture the same night two of Sarah's bison disappeared. Yeah, it was definitely getting harder to defend his farmer's friend. Bodie finished the last of his coffee, ignored the bitter aftertaste, and walked back to the kitchen. "Where is Sawyer?"

"Not at his family's house." Lacey followed him.

"We just did a house call and perimeter check. No one is there."

Sawyer was everywhere when Bodie didn't want to find him and nowhere when he did. That left Sawyer's last known location—with Bodie's farmer at the hospital. Bodie rinsed the coffee cup in the sink and dried his hands. "Can one of you follow me to the hospital? I told Sarah I would drop off her truck for her."

"I'll go with you," his father said.

Lacey said, "I'll be out at the back pasture gate in case our thief decides to help himself to another bison this evening while Rose and Sarah are otherwise occupied."

"It would certainly be an opportune time." Bodie frowned and grabbed the bag he had packed, then said, "I'll relieve you, Lacey, when I finish at the hospital."

It was inside the lobby of Belleridge Regional Hospital that his case got much clearer and everything else more complicated. Bodie waited for his father to join him and quickly updated him. "Just received word from my peer in Oklahoma. Another pop-up auction is set for the morning."

His father nodded. "Do we have a location?"

"State line." Bodie watched the elevator bay and added, "Five a.m."

His father smoothed his fingers through his beard. "If Sawyer hasn't off-loaded those bison, he will be needing to, and soon."

Bodie agreed. The elevator doors slid open, and

a couple walked out. No sign of Sawyer. Too bad that. Then Bodie would have saved himself a run-in with his farmer.

Bodie shook his head and said, "I really want Sawyer to be upstairs with Sarah." And at the same time, Bodie wanted to be the one comforting his farmer and Rose. He wanted to be the one who was there for them. He slanted his gaze toward his dad and asked, "Have you ever been on a case where you wanted to be wrong?"

"More than once." His father set his hand on Bodie's shoulder and continued, "But I didn't let it stop me from doing my job."

Nor would Bodie. He started for the elevator bay. "I'll meet you outside."

"Give Rose and Sarah my regards," his father said, then he added, "And son, don't forget to tread lightly. You've got a cowgirl's heart on the line."

Bodie nodded, his only acknowledgment to his father's wise words, then he stepped into the elevator. His dad wasn't wrong. A cowgirl's heart was on the line.

But Bodie was not known for stepping softly. Especially now, when he could not afford to. Justice was within reach and Bodie would stop at nothing to get it. Only this time, he feared he could end up with nothing in return.

CHAPTER SEVENTEEN

HER SECOND CUP of coffee in hand, Sarah turned the corner to walk back to her grandmother's room and came face-to-face with her cowboy. He wore dark jeans and a dark T-shirt. Only there was something darker in his gaze—a shadow like that of regret. Or perhaps that was simply Sarah, seeing her own reflection in her cowboy's blue eyes.

He did a slow sweep from her head to her toes in a clinical manner, as if reassuring himself she was okay. Then he asked bluntly, "Where is Sawyer?"

Sarah lifted her coffee cup to her lips and watched Bodie through the steam, then said, "Sawyer left a little while ago."

"Did he say where he was going?" Bodie pressed.

"No." Sarah lowered her arm and considered him. There was an urgency in his words, yet he appeared composed. "Is there something going on I should know about?"

More of that steady composure. He lifted one shoulder and said, "I just need to talk to him."

That wasn't all of it. She sensed that in her gut. Sarah tipped her head and eyed him. "What is going on?" For a minute, she was convinced he was going to shut her out, the same as Sawyer.

His jaw clenched, then released as if he'd worked through his response. Finally, he said, "The truck driver positively identified Sawyer at your pasture gate the other night."

His words were matter-of-fact, almost methodical. Was he testing her? Her response? Sarah curved her hands around her coffee cup and forced herself to stay as composed as her cowboy. But her insides were knotted. "I'm sure Sawyer has a good explanation."

Bodie dipped his chin in a clipped acknowledgment and said, "That is why I want to talk to him. To hear his explanation."

But that was not all. It was the precision in his words and his carefully maintained expression that gave him away. Bodie did not believe there was a good reason for Sawyer's presence at her pastures. But he was wrong. She argued, "Sawyer is not stealing from me."

That muscle in his jaw flexed again. The only break in his otherwise well-maintained composure. "That remains to be proven."

Surprise splashed through her like ice water. How could he believe her friend would do that to her? "Sawyer did not take my bison," she repeated, and kept the sharp bite in her words. "He wants to marry me."

His eyebrows flexed, a quick arch up, then settled back into place. "Is that so?"

So cool and unaffected. Where was the cowboy who had held her and danced with her, as if he never wanted to let her go, only hours ago? She countered, "It's not hard to believe someone would want to marry me."

"No, it isn't. Not at all," he conceded, his gaze softened for an instant. Just the smallest fracture in his ice-blue eyes. Then his words were wrapped in that cool calm once again. "It's just interesting he wants to marry you now."

Sarah clenched her coffee cup. "Don't make it into something it isn't." She would be wise to take her own advice.

He watched her and asked, "What is it then?"

"I don't know." Sarah winced. "But Sawyer is innocent." He had to be. He was her friend. He was one of the few people Sarah trusted, other than her grandmother.

"Like I said, I want to talk to Sawyer." Bodie took his phone out and glanced at the screen. "My dad is waiting downstairs for me. I should go."

But you will be back, right? For me. Sarah nodded. "I'll text you if I hear from Sawyer."

Bodie tipped his head toward the door. "Mind if I talk to Rose before I take off?"

"I'm sure she would like that," Sarah said, and followed him into her grandmother's room.

Her grandmother's smile stretched wide at seeing Bodie, wiping away any traces of pain and weariness from her weathered face. Bodie too transformed before Sarah's eyes, back to the considerate cowboy she'd come to know. And Sarah felt a pinch of guilt for doubting his intentions.

He took a plush blanket from the bag he carried and draped it with a flourish over her grandmother. "I thought you might like something from home to keep you warm."

"You brought my favorite blanket." Her grandmother tucked the blanket under her chin and clutched his hand. "Got any sweet treats hidden in that bag?"

Bodie slanted his gaze at Sarah, amusement sparked in his eyes, then he whispered, "I wasn't sure what the doctor's orders were."

"Dr. Sloan gave me one of his lollipops from his personal stash earlier," her grandmother whispered back. "I'm certain he would approve sweet treats."

"Well, I'm going to leave this on the table." Bodie set the bag on the rolling table within easy reach for her grandmother and added, "If you get bored later, you might consider taking a peek inside."

"You're a good one, Bodie," her grandmother said. "A real keeper."

Sarah wanted him to be a good one. She wanted the same for Sawyer.

"Right back at you," Bodie said, then he kissed her grandmother's cheek. "Now you need to rest up so I can get my partner back."

Sarah wanted her cowboy back, not the distant version she'd met in the hall just now.

Her grandmother beamed, then her brow wrinkled. "Chasing a lead is what landed me here."

"How about you let me do the chasing from here on out," Bodie said, his words light and easy.

"That'll be fine." Her grandmother smoothed her hands over her blanket and yawned. Her eyes looked heavy. "Now I'm going to take a little intermission. Then we can discuss our plans for my lead."

"Get some sleep now," Bodie encouraged her. "We'll talk again tomorrow."

Her grandmother's eyes drifted shut.

Bodie fussed with her grandmother's blanket. He turned and caught Sarah watching him. He walked closer to her and kept his voice low. "There's a sandwich and fruit in there for you too. I thought you might be hungry."

There you are. There was the cowboy she recognized. She smiled and said, "Thanks. I appreciate it." *Or rather, you.*

He reached up, set his hand on her cheek. His thumb smooth on her skin. His gaze traveled over her face as if memorizing her. Softly, he said, "I am on your side. Please don't forget that."

He leaned in and kissed her, then he was gone. All before she could pull him to her. Hold onto him. Or participate. Sarah reached up and touched her bottom lip.

As far as kisses went, it wasn't reassuring or encouraging or even a heat-filled exploration that was made for lingering.

No. It felt nothing like that.

But it did feel exactly like goodbye.

Sarah was still puzzling over her last kiss with her cowboy when her grandmother mumbled, "I see the light."

"Sorry, Grandma," Sarah said and hit the lock screen on her cell phone. "It's only my phone."

"Oh, that's a relief." Her grandmother rubbed her eyes. "Now put it away before I get up and follow it."

Sarah flipped her phone over, set it on the rolling table and stood up. "I can't sleep."

"You won't get any rest if you keep checking your phone every other minute," her grandmother grumbled.

She was waiting for Sawyer to return her calls or texts. It had been radio silence since he'd proposed and split a few hours ago. The same could be said for Bodie. If he'd located Sawyer, he hadn't let Sarah know. And that left her restless and more than a little fidgety.

"You need to go find him." Her grandmother adjusted the pillow behind her head. "And stop pacing around the room. You're making me dizzy."

"Your eyes are closed." Sarah stepped over to the side of the bed.

"Your shoes are squeaking on the tile floor." Her grandmother tapped her ear. "It's my honey badger ears you're bothering."

Sarah sank back onto the recliner and purposely sat on her hands to keep from checking her phone.

"My dear, you know I love you, right?" her grandmother mumbled.

"Yes." Sarah smiled into the darkness. Her fingers flexed underneath her legs. Her gaze was stuck on her cell phone. "I love you too."

"If that was true, you would leave," her grandmother countered. "And let me have some quiet so my body can do its healing."

"I can't leave you here all by yourself," Sarah argued.

"I'm begging you," her grandmother said. "I can order you if you'd like. I'm still your elder. You have to respect my wishes."

"But Grandma," Sarah stressed.

"Even the nurses are quieter than you and they are working." Her grandmother sighed and added, "I really must insist."

"I just want to find Sawyer." If only to hear his explanation and know that he valued their friendship as much as she did all these years. Sarah added, "And talk to Bodie." If only to have him hold her and tell her that trusting people was her strength, not her biggest flaw.

"Don't come back until you've done both." Her grandmother pointed to the door.

Sarah gathered her truck keys and still hesitated. "I wouldn't leave if it wasn't important."

"I wouldn't kick you out if my sleep wasn't important." Her grandmother opened one eye and said, "Now you're hovering and making it worse."

"I'm going. I'm going." Sarah fussed with her grandmother's blanket, kissed her cheek, then headed out.

At the door, her grandmother's words stopped her. "Remember, dear, it's not about who has known you the longest. It's about the time they've taken to get to know you and what's really in your heart."

That was all fine and well. But Sarah worried she didn't know what was in her own heart. "Good night, Grandma. I'll be back as soon as I can."

"Don't hurry on my account," her grandmother said.

Sarah stopped at the nurses' station to ensure they had her cell phone number, then she stepped onto the elevator and decided on her first stop in her search for Sawyer.

It was the middle of the night and raining when Sarah pulled into the McGowans' drive and considered the dark ranch house. Only the dim porch lights were on. Sawyer's truck was not in the driveway.

Sarah parked, got the spare key from underneath the planter on the porch and unlocked the front door.

She wiped her boots on the welcome mat, then stepped into the foyer and called out a greeting. No answer, which was to be expected. She wasn't even certain what she was looking for or what she expected to find. Still, she walked the main rooms of the ranch house from the kitchen to the dining room to the family room.

All she encountered was more quiet and a collection of family photographs on the walls and every available shelf. One was Sawyer and Sarah on their high school prom night. They'd skipped the dance and gone to a bonfire with their friends in the countryside where there was an abandoned Airstream and no parents.

What she did not find was her friend or a livestock trailer or her bison. All good signs.

Why then was she still feeling uneasy, even after she had locked up and climbed back into her truck?

She should let the professionals do their job. That included letting Bodie do his job and question Sawyer.

Sarah wanted to believe Bodie only wanted to talk to Sawyer. But she needed to believe her friend was innocent. She needed to hear Sawyer's explanation.

Sarah drove past her house and kept on going.

It took another hour for Sarah to circle every public parking lot in downtown Three Springs. Sawyer's truck was nowhere to be found.

Sarah squeezed the steering wheel and pulled out of the parking lot at Five Star Grocery Depot.

Where are you, Sawyer?

When Sarah wanted time alone, she saddled Twilight and rode across her land. Sawyer had never been much for trail riding or horses. But he had always liked country campfires and long back road drives.

Sarah drummed her fingers on the steering wheel.

And he had always been the first one to suggest

hanging out at the abandoned Airstream out on the county line.

Sarah hadn't been out there since she had moved back. She wasn't even certain the Airstream would still be there. But if Sawyer wanted a hideout, it would certainly offer privacy. Still, it was a long shot, but the only idea she had. Vowing to go home if this last search came up empty, Sarah headed for the countryside and the abandoned Airstream that had served as the backdrop for more than one teenage gathering over the years.

Too many miles and more than one opportunity to turn around and head home, Sarah finally pulled her truck over to the side of the dirt road, grabbed a flashlight, and backtracked to find the turn she'd missed. Just as in high school, the drive she wanted was marked with the same three red reflectors in the shape of a triangle that some enterprising student had nailed to a tree trunk so many years ago.

It was a short walk around two deep tree-lined curves in the overgrown dirt road and a few jumps over puddles, and the Airstream came into view. Fortunately, the rain had finally blown through. Now, the moon shone bright enough to highlight the old aluminum camper. It should have had broken windows and weeds growing out of its tires.

Sarah traced the beam of her flashlight across the camper from one end to the other and marveled at its condition. Someone was looking after it. And from one glance at the ground, there hadn't been a campfire, bonfire, or gathering there in quite some time. It was no longer a teenage hangout, but it certainly seemed to be used by someone.

Just like that, she was out of her element. What had started as a noble mission to prove the innocence of her good friend now looked more like very bad judgment on her part. Time to call it. Sarah spun around and froze. She was not alone. Her heart climbed into her throat.

"Sarah." The shadowy figure stepped into view.

She took in the familiar chiseled jawline and strong build, then whispered, "Bodie."

"Yeah, it's me." He moved closer and looked her over, as if to make sure she was okay.

He wore the same dark denim jeans and T-shirt, but had added a pair of heavy-duty steel-toed boots and a windbreaker marked Special Ops. He looked every inch the confident law enforcement officer and serious-minded investigator. He also looked anything but thrilled to see her.

"What are you doing here?" She clicked off the flashlight, lowered her arm, and acted as if they'd bumped into each other at one of those merrymaking bonfires.

"I could ask the same of you." His gaze scanned the area in one sweep before landing back on her. He hadn't softened.

"We used to come here as kids," Sarah explained, then cleared her throat. "I thought if Sawyer was hiding out, he might be here."

"I got a similar tip." Bodie started for the Airstream.

Sarah reached for him, her fingers brushed over the arm of his jacket. But it was enough to get his attention. She asked, "You aren't going inside, are you?"

"If the door is open, I am," he said and walked by her. He glanced back only to ask, "You coming?"

Sarah fidgeted with her flashlight and considered which answer might annoy him the least.

"You've come all this way," he called back. "Don't you want to know who's right?"

"It's not about being…" Sarah stopped arguing when he opened the door and disappeared inside the camper. A crunch in the forest behind her sent her hurrying across the damp grass toward the Airstream. The door swung open on seemingly freshly oiled hinges. Inside, the camper was cluttered but not dirty. She spotted a familiar leather jacket and a sweatshirt with her friend's favorite sports team. So she had found Sawyer's hideout after all.

Bodie was in the back part of the camper, working his way around an air mattress.

Sarah moved to the front and picked up several papers scattered on the only old cushion remaining on the wood-plank couch. She skimmed over several bills marked Past Due and then gasped at a bill of sale. Angling the paperwork toward the window, she read it slowly. Top to bottom, then again. Her fingers crinkled the paper. The sound crackled in the predawn quiet.

Bodie returned and said, "Please tell me you're not destroying evidence."

"I'm not." Sarah lost her voice, then stammered, "I don't understand."

Something like regret flashed through Bodie's gaze before his expression returned to contained, and he took the paper from her stiff fingers.

"It's a bill of sale. From me," she whispered as if the softer she spoke the less chance there was of this being true. Then she added, "I never signed that paper. That's not even my signature."

Bodie remained silent. His expression became even more remote.

"But there is no trailer here," she rattled on, still searching for that explanation. "So, Sawyer couldn't have taken those last two bison. He couldn't transport them."

Bodie flinched and tipped his head toward the opposite window. "Look behind you."

"What?" Sarah twisted and leaned toward the window over the compact sink. There, parked on the back side of the Airstream, was a livestock trailer. Sarah braced her arms on the counter and blinked several times. Nothing changed the view or the facts.

"I'm sorry," Bodie said. "This isn't how I wanted this to go."

"There has to be an explanation." She rounded on Bodie and shook her head. "Sawyer wouldn't do this. We've been friends for too long."

Bodie let her go on.

And she did, getting more desperate for that explanation. "Sawyer is being framed. That happens all the time." At least she thought it did. What did she know really? It seemed she didn't even know her friend.

Suddenly, headlights illuminated the interior of the Airstream. A truck engine rumbled in the stillness.

Bodie grabbed her arm and tugged her down into a crouch in front of the cabinets. Then he motioned for her to work her way toward the back room. Bodie guided her into the open closet, then positioned himself in front of her and peered out the crooked blinds of the bedroom window.

The truck pulled around to the side of the Airstream. A door opened and slammed shut while the truck idled. Sarah held her breath until Bodie whispered, "It's Sawyer."

Sarah stood and tried to look around Bodie.

"He's hitching up the trailer now," Bodie said quietly, then added, "And he's got your bison too."

Sarah pushed herself under Bodie's arm and gasped. There was Sawyer guiding her pair of bison from a makeshift lean-to with a bucket of treats that he shook. Not only had he stolen her livestock, he had copied her herding trick too. Her bison had always been pushovers for treats.

She tried to push Bodie aside and whispered harshly, "We've got to go out there and stop him."

Bodie never moved, not even an inch. "I'm going to follow him."

"But if we stop him, we can get back my bison."

Sarah shoved his shoulder. "And he can tell us what is going on."

"When I follow him, I will see exactly what is going on," Bodie countered.

"When we follow him, we will learn who is framing him and putting him up to this," she stated and stopped poking at him. "Then, you can arrest them."

"Look, Sarah. I promise to get to the bottom of this. But you can't come with me."

She held his gaze and said, "You have to take me with you. Otherwise, I'm just going to follow you."

"We don't know exactly what we are walking into," he argued.

"You'll make sure I'm safe," she said.

He searched her face, then finally sighed and said, "You'll do everything I ask? I can't do my job if I'm worried about where you are at any given moment."

"I'll stay in the truck," she assured him.

"Let's go then." Bodie turned and started for the door. "Sawyer is leaving."

Sarah shoved her hands in the pockets of her jeans and suddenly worried she was about to lose more than her friend.

CHAPTER EIGHTEEN

BODIE WANTED TO turn his stepsister's truck around. Or, better yet, turn back time to the moment earlier on the outdoor patio when he'd first pulled Sarah into his arms. Or, still better, a full twenty-four-hour rewind to the combine harvester. When it had been just him and his farmer and a moonlit cornfield. He would happily trade another all-night twenty questions session over what was about to unfold.

But he had set things into motion before Sarah had shown up at the Airstream camp. It didn't matter how much he disliked having her beside him now. Or that he disliked even more everything she was about to get exposed to. The time to press Pause had long since passed. Nothing came before the job he had to do, not even his heart-of-gold farmer and her tender feelings. And that was what he hated the most.

Bodie slowed and turned into the designated rendezvous point. It was what Rose would most likely call: game on.

"But Sawyer kept going. Why are we here?"

Sarah straightened in the passenger seat and pointed out the window. "You have to keep going that way. Or you're going to lose him."

Bodie would not be the one losing tonight, at least not when it came to his case. He drove behind the industrial warehouse complex and kept silent. Unfortunately, sometimes seeing was believing.

There was a flurry of activity in the back parking lot of the business complex. A collection of marked and unmarked cars and an assortment of uniformed and plainclothes law enforcement officers filled the area.

"That looks like Lacey in her full uniform." Sarah lowered her arm. Her words were hesitant. "And that's your father."

Bodie cut the engine and let Sarah take in the scene unfolding right before her.

"Those people over there are in vests," Sarah said, then continued, "And everyone is in full gear."

Now she was getting the full picture. Bodie said, "Stay here. I'll be right back."

"Wait." Her fingers curled around the sleeve of his jacket and held on. "Where's Sawyer?"

"Most likely pulling into the pop-up livestock auction not a half mile from here to sell your bison," he replied and set his hand on the door. "Don't move please. I'll be back."

"Wait." She kept her tight grip on his jacket. There was an urgency to her words. "You promised I could talk to him first."

"No," Bodie corrected her. "I promised I was

going to get to the bottom of this." And that was exactly what he was about to do.

She released him and sat back. Her words were tentative, as if he hadn't quite doused all her hope yet. "You were never going to let me talk to Sawyer, were you?"

"Don't expect an apology. I won't ever apologize for trying to keep you safe."

"From my friend. Who, I might add, I've known most of my life," she retorted, but her bottom lip trembled before she tipped her chin up and rallied on. "Did you need all this? It seems a bit much for a handful of stolen bison."

"You weren't the only one with stolen livestock, Sarah." *But you are the one who matters the most. To me.* Now wasn't the time for a deep dive into his feelings. He cleared his throat and continued, "This is about more than Sawyer. It's about an illegal rustling ring running across multiple state lines."

She paled. Tears pooled in her suddenly wide eyes. "Maybe Sawyer doesn't know. Maybe if I…"

"Like it or not, Sawyer has broken the law." And her friend was most likely going to do it again in a matter of minutes. Bodie added, "There is no conversation that can change what he has done."

There it was. Her hazel eyes finally dulled. Bodie extinguished the last bit of her hope. Her faith was most likely broken now as well. Perhaps even her heart. He was just the messenger. Still, the damage was done.

"That's just it, isn't it?" she said in a charged

voice. "There was no conversation between you and me either. You didn't trust me with the full truth."

"Don't toss trust out there," he countered. "You didn't come to me. You went alone to the Airstream to find Sawyer yourself. Did you think you could protect him from the law?"

"He's my friend." Her voice cracked. Her hazel eyes filled again.

"And who am I?" he asked.

"I don't know," she said and shook her head. "I thought you were..." She paused, then exhaled a shaky breath and whispered, "Never mind. It doesn't matter."

Because there was no *us*. Like he had known all along. Bodie knew his objective like always. And like always, he would finish the job and see justice served. Unfortunately, whatever this might have been with Sarah was now collateral damage. And that was on him. He never should have started what he knew he couldn't finish. He opened his door and said, "I have to go."

She sprang forward and grabbed his hand. "Are you going in there with the others?"

He was leading it. He left that out and nodded. "It's my case. They're here to assist."

She paled. Her fingers went slack. "Be careful."

Bodie nodded and got out. Then scanned the officers gathered around the parking lot, found a deputy standing in the background, introduced himself, and said, "Deputy Byatt, I've got a special assignment for you."

The young deputy straightened and followed Bodie back to the truck. He motioned for Sarah to get out, introduced the pair, then added, "Deputy Byatt, don't let her out of your sight."

Deputy Byatt nodded. "Yes, sir."

Bodie glanced at Sarah and tipped his chin toward the young deputy. "He's in charge until I get back. What Deputy Byatt says goes."

Sarah frowned at him. "I know what to do."

That made one of them. He didn't know what to do about his farmer. Though now was not the time to deal with his feelings. Still, he gave in, pressed a kiss to her forehead. "I really am sorry. Please be careful."

He eyed the deputy one last time and went over to his team for a briefing. He needed to get in position and hope the rustlers gave them enough evidence for full arrests. Then at least he would have done his job well.

SARAH WAS BACK inside the truck. Her feet were propped on the seat. Her arms linked around her legs. Her forehead rested on her raised knees. Tears soaked through her jeans.

Deputy Byatt, otherwise known as just Kyle, had been more than happy to give Sarah a play-by-play of the action unfolding less than a block away. All thanks to the comms in his earpiece.

Livestock had been unloaded into pens. Money had exchanged hands. Then weapons had been drawn and arms thrown up in surrender. It was slightly uneventful and nothing quite as dramatic as the TV shows her grandmother watched. It was over rather swiftly and with little fanfare.

The last Sarah had seen Sawyer, he was handcuffed and being led to a sheriff's car parked not ten feet from where she sat in the truck.

Sawyer had caught sight of her and yelled about it all being a setup while proclaiming his innocence and pleading for her to hear him out.

When she had not reacted, he declared they were even. He had given her all those rescues in exchange for the bison. *Let's call it even, Sarah-Belle. Just tell them we agreed. No harm. No foul.*

Stunned, her mouth had dropped open, yet still no words came out.

Then Sawyer had volleyed his final shot before he was assisted into the back seat of the sheriff's car. He had shouted he knew she would forgive him. She had to. His Sarah-Belle always did.

But what Sarah always did didn't feel quite so good anymore. She rubbed her chest.

What must Bodie think of her? She'd been defending Sawyer to Bodie the entire drive to the illegal pop-up auction. Despite everything, she had been the loyal and faithful friend to the end.

Look where that got her. She looked the fool for sure. Naive. Silly. Gullible too.

All because she'd been invested in a friendship that proved to be nothing more than a farce. What she expected from a friend—things like loyalty, integrity, and honesty—had turned out to be not so important to Sawyer. Lesson learned.

The driver's side door opened. Sarah never lifted her head. Yet she knew it was Bodie. A jacket was draped over her shoulders—courtesy was ingrained in her cowboy. He was just built that way—cowboy chivalry as much a part of him as his blue eyes and his confidence.

His warmth suddenly surrounded her. His cologne filled her every inhale. And no judgment came from his side of the truck. Her tears fell all over again.

The truck engine rumbled. Bodie's words were steady and simple. "Home or hospital?"

"Neither." *Save your tears for later, cowgirl.* Falling apart would not help her grandmother or rescue the farm. Sarah wiped her cheeks, lifted her head, and stepped into the practical. "I need to pick up my truck back at the Airstream camp and get to the hospital."

"Are you sure?" He started to reach for her, then set his hand on the center console instead. "We could get it later. Tomorrow or something."

"It's fine." She sniffed and buckled her seat belt. "I'm fine." She focused on the action items, not her *feels*, and added, "I'm sure you have reports to fill out and all that."

"There's paperwork waiting for me," he allowed, then glanced over at her. "But I've got time for you. Whatever you need."

She needed to stand on her own. Rely on herself. "I appreciate that. I'm okay though." And she would repeat it until she believed it. She added, "Grandma Rose will worry if I'm not there soon. It'll be easier if I have my own vehicle."

"You got it." He backed out of the parking space, drove around the industrial warehouses, and turned onto the main road.

The silence stretched as far as the flat two-way highway did in both directions. Seemingly endless in the morning sunshine that only served to highlight her confusion, disappointment, and doubts. They all tumbled inside her as if set on the spin cycle. She tried to sleep. Tried to close her eyes and quiet her mind. Tried to turn up the radio and drown out everything else. Nothing worked.

Finally, she broke the silence, wanting only to press Mute on her own thoughts, and said, "I suppose you're going to tell me this could have happened to anybody."

Bodie shook his head and said, "Not just anybody."

"Of course, not you." She shoved the air vent away from her face to keep the air from chilling her still-damp cheeks. "You're much too smart for something like this."

"Or too heartless," he replied, his face set, and his words blunt.

"So, that's your advice." She eased her arms into the sleeves of his jacket and zipped it up under her chin, trying to trap more of his warmth. "I'm supposed to become heartless like you, so this doesn't happen to me again."

"Please don't. You're perfect just the way you are." He sounded sincere and unwavering. "I don't ever want to see you lose your light."

She crossed her arms over her chest and mumbled, "I think it is too late for that."

"I never wanted this for you," he countered, frustration skimmed across his words.

"But you got what you wanted." Oh, those feels were gaining traction along with the daylight. "A case closed. Justice served. I watched everyone shaking your hand back there. Congratulating you."

"The last thing I wanted was to see you get hurt," he said, still sounding determined and earnest. "You have to know that."

She knew she was deeply hurt. Betrayal tended to leave a mark. She knew she was unsure what to believe. Who to believe in. That was foundation shifting for sure and it left her on edge and wanting to lash out. Maybe it was unfair. Maybe she was allowed. Maybe she earned this.

Right or wrong, she refused to get burned again. She refused to throw her heart into something—someone—unless he was invested the same as her.

Call her demanding. Call her expectations too high.

But if cutting and running now kept her from heartbreak, she would be a fool no more.

She twisted in her seat and leaned against the

passenger door. "What do you see happening between us?"

Bodie slanted his gaze at her. His expression was guarded.

"Don't be shy," she goaded. Suddenly, she wanted something honest, even if it was brutal and hard to swallow. She wanted someone to respect her enough to cut to the chase. Not lie to her face like Sawyer had. "This is the day for full truths and revelations. So, let's air it all out. Right here. Right now."

Bodie tossed his cowboy hat on the back bench seat and asked, "You really want to talk about us now."

"There's no better time than now," she said. Her heart was already bruised and aching. How much worse could she feel? She flicked her wrist between them. "What are we doing?"

"I only promised to solve the bison disappearances," he stated, and turned off onto one of those back country roads, then added, "Nothing more."

Her cowboy wasn't into making promises. The truck hit a pothole. Her chest thumped. She asked, "Is that all this was then—a case?" *Is that all I was?*

"No. It's just," Bodie said, then paused. The uncomfortable kind of silence skittered inside the cab. Finally, he exhaled low and slow then said, "It's just my work—my life—is down south."

"And you don't want me to be a part of your life," she said. Any minute she would feel satisfied they were getting somewhere. Any minute she would feel something other than immensely sad.

"Is that what you want?" He dodged a pothole and glanced at her. "To go with me."

What did she have left here? It was time to stop kidding herself. Her parents would not let her grandmother return to her farmhouse with a busted hip. And Sarah lacked the funds to keep the farm afloat. She eyed her cowboy. "Are you asking me to go with you?"

"That's not fair," he challenged, his words curt. Then he continued, as if unfazed by her stony silence. "I know what you are doing. You know I won't ask you to give up your life here for me and when I don't, you will be proven right."

She shifted in the seat, as if dodging his words the same way he avoided the potholes. Still, she asked, "Proven right about what?"

"That your heart is always wrong," he said, quietly and all too knowingly.

"Ask me or don't. It doesn't matter. It's true either way," she lashed out. "I followed my heart here and look where that got me." A floundering farm. Betrayed by her long-time friend. Her grandma in the hospital, waiting for surgery.

"Your heart is in the right place," he insisted. "You belong here."

"And if I wanted you to stay?" *With me. To give us a chance.*

He frowned. "I can't."

"You won't," she countered.

"To what end," he said. His frustration filled the space between them.

A chill spread over her. "You don't believe in what we have. What this is between us."

"What is it really?" he asked. His words were cool. His expression detached.

She thought—or rather, hoped—what they felt for each other could be something like…she cut off the thought. He wasn't invested. She would return the favor and excuse her heart too. If only that icy chill in her core would numb her completely. Then it would be proof she really had cut and run after all.

She stammered, "I thought if nothing else, that this between us was real." Something she could count on.

"Look, I care about you." He slowed around a bend, then added, "A lot."

She cared about her greenhouse garden. A lot. So what? That numbness spread like a welcome blessing. Taking her to a place where she no longer cared. No longer felt anything. Where his words weren't supposed to hurt her. She charged on. "But you won't love me." And that was the nuts and bolts.

Regret filled his face. He said, "I don't know how to love you like you deserve."

"That's a cop-out," she countered.

He eyed her and remained silent.

Nothing to lose now. She didn't have his love, and it was unlikely she ever would. She said, "You just won't let yourself fall in love. You'd have to open your heart for that, and you already claimed not to have one."

"Don't lecture me on love and hearts." He pulled the truck next to hers on the back country road and continued, "Only minutes ago, you wanted me to ask you to go with me." He threw the truck in Park, faced her, and added, "So, you could follow my heart, not your own."

A shiver skated over her skin, then sank deep into her bones.

"That's what you did in the past. You followed someone else's heart instead of your own," he said, seemingly more than ready to give her what she demanded—unchecked truths. He added, "Even at the farm, you're doing everything everyone else has suggested. Rather than being true to yourself."

He was wrong. And she was more than ready to meet his challenge. "Is that what you're doing? Being true to yourself." At his stoic silence, she continued, "I watched you with Aspen and your family. With your dad too." No, she would not back down, either. "You need them. They need you." *I need you.*

"I'm doing what is best."

Stubborn cowboy. "You're doing what is easy." The words were clear and succinct inside the truck cab.

"The work I do is not easy," he said.

"This isn't about your job," she countered. "And

no one is asking you to give it up. We're just asking you not to do it alone anymore."

His gaze was distant. His words flat. "It's all I know how to do."

It was all he wanted to do. She should be happy now. She got what she asked for and it was hard to swallow. She cleared her throat, tackled back those tears, and said, "Then if you're not willing to even try, alone is all you will ever be."

He never responded. Never reached for her. Never even flinched. Stoic and stubborn to the end.

Sarah opened the truck door and climbed out.

Her boots hit the gravel, and she locked her knees to steady herself, as if she was making some grand entrance, not a hasty heartbreak of an exit. She twisted and shut the passenger door so very softly. Yet, the sound of her heart shattering was deafening in her own ears.

Still, she kept her chin and her shoulders back.

Because one foolish cowboy would not be her downfall.

CHAPTER NINETEEN

SIX DAYS HAD passed since his farmer got out of his truck and never looked back. Six days since Bodie had watched his farmer walk out of his life. Six days since he hadn't done a thing about it. Not that he was counting or anything.

He was simply marking the days same as a child marked off the days until Christmas. Only he wasn't looking forward to presents and Christmas morning joy. He was waiting for the day he stopped missing his farmer. Stopped looking for her. Stopping thinking about her. And the day he finally stopped hurting. He feared Christmas morning would be there and gone and he would still want her.

But there was nothing for it now. They had said it all in the truck cab. He was leaving. She was staying. And no amount of missing her changed those facts.

Inside the Silver Penny General Store, Bodie walked beside Aspen from the Halloween aisle back to the confectionary section where Lacey and Tess Sloan were already chatting. Bodie promised

Aspen he would get her whatever Halloween item she wanted.

Aspen chose a fluffy ghost-shaped pillow, which she was now hugging to her chest. She asked, "Uncle, do you think Sarah would want to be a witch or a wizard with us for Halloween? Or we could be the three little pigs."

Bodie cleared his expression before his too-perceptive niece noticed she'd taken him off-guard and said, "Don't you have costume plans with your friends?"

Lacey's eyebrows lifted. Tess watched them intently from the other side of the counter.

"Well, it'll be your first Halloween here." Aspen fiddled with the price tag on her ghost pillow and considered him. "We gotta celebrate it together."

How exactly was he supposed to tell his niece he was disappearing from her life again? Just as soon as he got around to checking in with his chief and getting his new orders. His chief had given Bodie what he had claimed was a well-earned week off to spend with his family. Then told Bodie to call him when Bodie was ready for his next assignment. But Bodie wasn't exactly making that call right this minute, so he kept silent and put it off a little while longer.

"Mama-Beth has a Halloween party. I think we should have one too." Aspen took his hand and swung their arms back and forth. "Then everyone gets to celebrate together at our boo bash."

Bodie smiled. "What's a boo bash?"

"Halloween games, apple bobbing, and pumpkin carving for sure," Aspen said, as if making up the details on the spot. "And hayrides."

"Aspen, your stepmom and dad live in downtown Belleridge." Lacey laughed. "They do not have hayrides at their Halloween party."

"But we could." Aspen shrugged and tugged on Bodie's arm. His niece sounded so earnest. "I heard Grandpa Swells bragging that he and Uncle Bodie got Sarah's old tractor running better than ever."

Aspen wasn't wrong. Thanks to Carter and his brother Josh's help with parts, they'd gotten it running before Bodie jumped into the combine with Sarah. Bodie had wanted to show Sarah, but work had gotten in the way. Not that he needed the reminder. It was always work first.

Lacey frowned and opened the bag of chocolate-covered almonds Tess gave her.

"And besides Mom, you told Ms. Sarah her tractor is made for hayrides," Aspen continued.

Lacey plopped an almond in her mouth and conceded. "I did say that, didn't I?"

"I bet a boo bash would cheer up Gran Rose too." Aspen seemed to warm to her argument. "Gran Rose told me she would be boogying real soon. Uncle Grant said she would too. She could boogie at the boo bash, if we had one."

Bodie had gone to see Rose the day after her surgery. He'd been both relieved and disappointed Rose had been asleep when he arrived. He'd left her favorite truffles and flowers on the nightstand, then snuck out. Fortunately, Grant was keeping him up to date on Rose's recovery. Bodie considered trying again in the daytime but worried he might run into Sarah. Coward that he was, he stayed away during typical visiting hours.

Aspen wrapped her arm around Bodie's waist and said, "And besides, Mom, Uncle Bodie needs cheering up too."

"I'm very happy," Bodie argued and forced himself to grin, but gave up when he caught his reflection in the mirror on the wall behind the counter. Not a convincing look.

"You aren't happy, Uncle." Aspen scrunched her face and frowned at him. "You've been sitting on the porch all alone at night. Without any sweet treats."

True and true. Apparently, he needed to work on his situational awareness skills. He hadn't known his niece was spying on him. Surely, once he left town and his emotions behind, his head would clear.

"Aspen, how do you know your uncle is awake?" Lacey asked, as if she too was concerned about Bodie losing his edge. Then she added, "You're supposed to be sleeping, Aspen."

"Because I see Uncle Bodie when I check on him," Aspen explained. "You know, Mom. You and Caleb always check on me. So, I figured I should check on Uncle Bodie. Cause no one else is."

Affection filled Lacey's face and smile.

Bodie lifted his niece up and into a bear hug. "Thank you for checking on me."

"You're welcome." Aspen squeezed him, then leaned back to look at him. "Now can we ask Ms. Sarah about a boo bash? Pretty please."

Now they were right back to the tricky part. Rather than ruin his niece's sparkle, Bodie paused. "We'll talk about it."

"But we just did talk." Aspen's eyebrows drew down. "Now it's your turn. You gotta ask Ms. Sarah."

But he already had his turn. And he broke Sarah's heart and his own. There wasn't anything left to ask his farmer. Bodie said, "I'll see what I can do."

"Promise," Aspen said.

Bodie nodded.

Delight swept over Aspen's face. Excitement rushed her words. "You're the best, Uncle Bodie."

Bodie hugged her, aware she might not be thinking that soon. She might be thinking he was the worst ever. He set his niece down, albeit reluctantly. As if she was the last bit of good he had to hold onto.

"Hey, Aspen, want to come help me take the chocolates out of the molds?" Tess asked and smiled. "You can even taste the broken ones."

"Yes." Aspen cheered and hurried around the counter with Tess. The pair disappeared through a door marked Private.

"Now you've done it," Lacey said, although she

didn't appear all that put out. She sounded more gleeful than anything.

"What?" Bodie reached into the almond bag and took a few.

"You promised you'd talk to Sarah." Lacey popped several almonds into her mouth. Her grin was all too satisfied. "Now you have to, or you will crush your niece."

"Can't you tell Aspen I tried, and Sarah never responded?"

"Oh no, big brother." Lacey shook her head and patted his shoulder, as if consoling him. "This one is all on you to make right."

"I won't be here," Bodie announced. For Halloween or any other upcoming holiday. The almonds and chocolate soured his stomach. As soon as he called his chief back, he would have his new orders. One phone call and he would be gone.

"Well, you should have shut down the boo bash talk from the start," Lacey said unhelpfully. Worse, there was no regret in her words, either.

"And disappoint Aspen right out of the gate." Bodie shook his head and tossed another chocolate almond in his mouth. Only, the dark chocolate added to the bitter taste already coating his mouth.

"She'll get over it." Lacey shrugged, as if unmoved.

But Bodie was not sure he would. As it was, he should have been over his farmer and that didn't seem to be happening. He still felt guilty about hurting Sarah. Still felt badly all around. Definitely not over it yet. But he would be. Walking away was the right decision. Bodie said, "A boo bash did sound fun."

"Aspen usually has good ideas." Lacey chuckled and then seemed to take pity on him. "And you know. Aspen isn't wrong. You should talk to Sarah."

"About a boo bash," Bodie said.

"And other things," Lacey shot back, not allowing him to deflect. "You are miserable. Even Aspen noticed it."

"Just restless." He wiped his palm on his jeans and resisted reaching for more almonds. Chocolate was proving not to be the mood lifter it claimed to be. "Nothing getting back to work won't solve."

"Keep telling yourself that," Lacey said.

He planned to. He said, "You know I've always put everything into my work." And he intended to do that again. Once he called his chief.

"What you've always done isn't what you always need to do," she argued.

But it was, if he couldn't have his farmer. "It's better this way."

"For who?" she asked.

"Come on, Lacey. Sarah and I left things where they were meant to be." There was no need to see her again and relive all that. Not to mention he wasn't sure he could manage a second goodbye with his farmer. The first had been awful. "It'll be hard enough saying goodbye to you and Aspen and everyone else."

"Good," she said. "Maybe you'll miss us enough to come back."

He already missed them, and he hadn't left yet. He cleared his throat and said, "I have to come back for Dad and Lilian's wedding." But that date wasn't even set yet.

"At least do me one favor before you go." Lacey walked with him toward the exit. "Come to family dinner tonight. The entire Sloan family will be there."

Lilian finished with a customer and smiled at them.

Bodie paused beside the register and asked, "Lilian. What can I bring to dinner tonight?"

Pleasure flashed in Lilian's eyes. "We tell our guests to bring wine and tell our family to have a date."

That he certainly did not have. Bodie said, "A date?"

"A date on the calendar they want to host family dinner," she explained.

"What if the family lives out of town?" Bodie asked.

"Then give us a date you will be back," Lilian said simply and succinctly. "And we'll let you use our kitchen. You've been working at our new house so much this week, you know the place better than we do. It's as much your home as ours."

Lilian and his dad had bought a fixer-upper and were in the process of turning it into their forever-together home. Bodie was glad he was able to pitch in, even for a little while. It wasn't his home, but he would be happy to visit. For now, he would be heading to Five Star and perusing the grocery store's wine section before he headed back to Lacey's house and finally made that call to his chief. He smiled. "I'll see you tonight then for dinner."

"Would you mind dropping this by our new house? I know you weren't supposed to help your dad today," Lilian said and handed Bodie a pint of white paint. "But your father decided to install closet organizers. After his last call, I fear there's going to be more than a little touch-up required."

"Sure thing." Bodie took the paint and headed out.

There was one conversation Bodie needed to have before he left town. It involved his father, not his farmer. It was long overdue. And Bodie had skirted around it, despite working side by side with his father every day for the past week.

In his defense, the first few days Bodie was too busy heading off his hurt and anger and regret over his farmer one nail at a time. His dad had never pressed for details. He'd simply offered Bodie a nail gun and indicated the stack of shiplap waiting to go up for Lilian's rustic accent wall in their dining room. That project complete, his father had simply walked Bodie to another room and explained their next DIY project. The pair had finished the week yesterday with a successful install of the stainless-steel sink and gas grill in the now-updated outdoor kitchen.

But they had not really talked. Time to fix that. And then perhaps Bodie would have gotten one thing right before he skipped town.

IT HAD TAKEN Sarah all week, but she finally made her way to the sheriff's department to review and sign the final copy of her witness testimony statement. Her grandmother's surgery and recovery had been her priority. Then there were numerous calls to her parents overseas, arranging a rehab facility for her grandmother to transfer to in the coming days, and the farm to look after. And if she'd wanted to arrive at the sheriff's offices when her eyes were no longer red-rimmed and puffy, well, that was her prerogative too.

Fortunately, she was escorted to a small conference room when she arrived by none other than the kind and friendly Deputy Kyle. Her witness statement was signed and her eyes still dry.

Deputy Kyle set a cup of coffee on the table beside her and said, "There's someone who wants to speak to you before you leave."

Bodie. Sarah's pulse slowed. She smoothed her expression into indifferent. "Sure. That's fine."

"I'll be right back." Deputy Kyle walked out.

Sarah touched her braids, then her overalls, but stopped. What she looked like wasn't important. What she was going to say to her cowboy was. Only she wasn't sure.

What took you so long?
Apology accepted.

I'm fine. Are you?

Nothing felt quite right. Sarah stood when the door opened behind her. Her breath stuck in her throat. Finally, she turned. It wasn't Bodie. She exhaled hard and said, "Sawyer."

"Hey, Sarah-Belle." Sawyer tipped his head toward the table. "Mind if we talk for a minute?"

"Fine." Sarah handed Deputy Kyle the signed witness testimony.

Then Deputy Kyle informed her he would be standing right outside the door if she needed anything. She needed…no, her cowboy wasn't there. He wasn't hers. She was on her own and going to be better for it. No doubt about it. Any day now she would be better.

She waited until the door closed, then turned back to the table. Sawyer wore a county-issued white polo shirt and navy pants, and wasn't quite as reserved as she would have expected, given he'd been arrested. Sarah sat in the chair across the table from him and folded her arms over her chest.

"I know you think you have the money for my bail, but you don't need to post it," Sawyer said, sounding nothing but magnanimous, then he explained, "My lawyer is working a plea deal with community service for my testimony."

Sarah reached for the coffee cup and eyed him. "Why would you think I'm here for that?"

"Because it's what you do," Sawyer said. His words were relaxed and confident. "It's who you are. You're the nice one."

"What are you?" she asked.

"Hopefully a lesson learned," he said.

"Have you learned a lesson then?" she asked.

"Sometimes, no matter what you do, you still fail. That's the lesson." He shrugged one shoulder. "And it's time we both face the facts. We both failed."

"How so?" she asked.

"You're not a farmer," he said simply. "And I'm not a good business owner."

"Of course I'm a farmer," she told him, and released the paper coffee cup before she crumpled it in her hand. "What do you think I've been doing all this time?"

"Come on, Sarah-Belle," he said, his words edged into cajoling. "You've been at it for several years. Have you turned a profit yet?"

"You stole my bison and ruined the chance," she said, keeping her words blunt.

"Sarah-Belle, you can't say no to anyone." He shook his head, as if regretting he was the one breaking this news to her and continued, "You do everything everyone suggests on the farm, no matter what it is. We both know you weren't going to turn a profit either way."

The joke was on him. She had earned more than projected on her corn crop. But that was her business. Hers alone to celebrate.

Sawyer slumped back in his chair and considered her. "Face it, Sarah-Belle. You're a follower, not a farmer."

Bodie had accused her of following the wrong hearts. Now Sawyer did the same. *Buck up, cowgirl, the truth hurts.* "That does not justify you stealing from me. Better I'm a follower than whatever you are."

She had a few appropriate words. A bad friend. A possible felon. And scared. That much she could see in the way he refused to look her in the eyes for too long.

"I'm not very lucky at the horse track for one," he said wryly. "If I hadn't bet away my business profits, I wouldn't have resorted to borrowing your bison."

"Stealing," she corrected.

"I was going to pay you back." He set his hands on the table and spread his fingers out. "I had it all worked out. I just needed a bit more time. Once I got my combine out of the repo yard, I would've started earning again." More fidgeting, and he said, "There would have been money to support us both."

"I never asked for your support," she said.

"But you needed it," he countered. "You're meant to look after people and animals, not crops."

"I like to believe I can do it all," she said, gathering her resolve.

"But it's not working out." He shifted again in his seat. "No one will think less of you for throwing in the towel."

What wasn't working out was Sarah expecting more from Sawyer than he could give. What wasn't working out was Sarah expecting her friend to value their relationship the same as she did. What wasn't working out was Sarah waiting for an apology that was not coming.

Open your eyes, cowgirl.

That was it, wasn't it? If she wanted someone to see her as capable of doing it all, she had to see herself the same. Time to prove who she was.

"You know what, Sawyer," she said, drawing his gaze to her and forcing him to hold it. "You were right. I have learned a lesson after all."

"Yeah?" Sawyer drawled, then asked, "What is that?"

"That I don't need to forgive you, Sawyer," she said. At his surprised expression, she continued, "But I will one day. Because that's who I am."

Yes, she wore her heart on her sleeve. Maybe she was too quick to forgive and too ready with second chances. But she was not fragile. Or weak. Or naive. She was a cowgirl with a big heart and a passion for farming. And she was through apologizing for who she was.

"But here's the thing." She held Sawyer's gaze and grinned. "I don't need to forgive you, Sawyer, because I've already forgiven myself."

Sawyer flinched and smoothed a hand over his cheek.

"Oh, and you could've just told me you were sorry." She motioned between them. "Maybe skipped all this. Just started and ended with an apology."

For the first time, his bravado faltered, and he whispered, "I don't know how."

"I might be nice and a follower as you claim," she said and stood. "But at least I'm not a coward. Take care, Sawyer."

And with that, she walked out. Ready to go all in and bet on herself.

CHAPTER TWENTY

BODIE FOUND HIS dad in the garage in what looked to be a standoff. His hands were on his hips and his stare fixed on pieces of what Bodie assumed were the closet organizer system Lilian had mentioned earlier. Only the sections were scattered haphazardly across the garage floor and seeming to be less than organized.

His father greeted him, then said, "Before you ask, there are no written instructions. Just a series of instructional pictures printed on a scale so small not even a mouse could read them."

Bodie picked up the paperwork from the workbench and scanned it. Grinning, he said, "We might have better luck asking a fly to translate for us."

His father chuckled and his shoulders relaxed. "Good to know it wasn't just me."

Bodie took out his phone and did a quick internet search for the closet organizer brand website. Several clicks later and he had the same pictural instructions, only slightly enlarged. He frowned. "I think we might be on our own with this one."

His dad glanced at him, relief evident when he said, "Then you can stay and help."

"Sure." Bodie tossed the instructions back on the workbench. "Why didn't you call me sooner?"

"Figured I took up enough of your time this week." His dad picked up a smaller wooden shelf and worked his way around the longer pieces and added, "I knew Aspen would want to spend time with you since she was in school all week and you'll be heading out soon."

"We went riding this morning. Aspen showed me her favorite trail near the lake." Bodie found a pencil, then looked for something to write on. "After our ride, we had lunch at Lily Moon and chocolates at the general store."

"That pretty much sums up Aspen's ideal day." His dad chuckled, set his shelf down as if giving up on finding its match.

Bodie's ideal day would have been all that and included his farmer. Or it would have, once upon a time. He gave up finding a piece of paper, tore the top flap off a cardboard box and stopped his dad from picking up yet another random shelf. "Okay, Dad. We need to organize your closet organizer."

His dad paused and considered him. "That's what I've been trying to do for the past few hours."

"Sorry, Dad." Bodie laughed. "But there's no system to your system."

"You have a better idea?" His dad grinned. "Please tell me that you do."

"We're going to take a step back," Bodie explained. "Let's inventory what we have. Draw out what we want in the closet. Then build it."

"That sounds very organized." His dad chuckled. "Where were you this morning when I decided to tackle this project? You could've saved me hours."

Hours ago, Bodie was trying to decide what would make him miss his farmer less. Turned out, there didn't seem to be anything that didn't make him think of Sarah. And as soon as he thought of her, he missed her. Take right now for example. There was nothing about standing in a garage and putting together closet shelves that should remind him of her. Yet, there he was, missing her all the same. Bodie got to work and hoped eventually he would work his farmer out of his system.

"Got a text from your chief this morning." His dad held one of the assembled wood panels they had carried into the primary bedroom closet, and added casually, "He told me he hasn't heard from you yet. Considering a change of pace perhaps?"

Bodie set a screw and drilled it into the wall. "I'm not sure I know how to change speeds."

"I was convinced of the same thing myself when your mom and I separated. When she took you, your brother and sister and moved as far away as the courts would let her, I threw myself into my career. When your summer visits got shorter as you got older, I convinced myself that my job was enough for me." His dad waited for Bodie to secure the piece with several more screws before he stepped back and added, "It took meeting Lacey's mom years after your mother and I divorced to realize I'd been lying to myself for a while."

But Bodie wasn't like his dad. Besides, Bodie had no one to slow down for, especially now. He placed the last of the screws and set the cordless drill down.

His dad said, "I'm considering slowing down even more."

Bodie shifted his attention from the new shelves to his dad. "Do you mean you're retiring?"

"You don't have to look quite so shocked." His dad frowned and motioned for him to pick up the bottom of the dresser unit they had assembled. "There comes a time when you start looking at more than the badge."

"It's just," Bodie started and lifted the dresser then eyed his father over the top. "It's just all you've ever done."

And every time Bodie pictured his father he was in a uniform. Except lately, he had been seeing more sides to his dad beside the law enforcement officer. Bodie was seeing a man he could relate to.

"I like to think I was a dad too," his father said, then added, "A good neighbor. A good friend."

Bodie nodded. They hefted the drawer unit into place and secured it.

"Or perhaps I want to make sure I can be those things now," his father admitted, his words wistful. "Round out my legacy, if you will."

Bodie's mentor had left that kind of legacy. He considered his dad, saw the thoughtful glint in his gaze, and wondered if his dad had regrets like him. He asked, "What does Lilian think?"

"Lilian is working on those same things too." His dad's smile was wry yet affectionate. "Let's just say Lilian also knows quite a bit about mending those family ties."

Bodie grinned. "It sounds like you and Lilian are well aligned."

"These shelves are well aligned." His dad laughed, set the level on the top shelf. "And these drawers." He opened and closed the top drawer of the dresser, then eyed Bodie. His expression amused and wise. "What Lilian and I are is in love, son."

In love. Sarah had accused Bodie of not even trying to love. Giving up before he even gave it a go. Bodie rubbed his chest.

"Never thought I'd find a love like this again," his dad mused, his smile bloomed. "I certainly wasn't looking for it."

Bodie hadn't been looking for someone like his farmer, either. He said, "Third time is the charm then."

"The third time is a gift," his dad corrected. "This time I plan to treasure every minute with Lilian. I didn't always do that in my relationships."

Bodie took the opening and finally stepped into the past. "Are you talking about you and Mom?"

"I know that neither of us valued our marriage like we should have," his father explained. "I poured my attention into work and providing for my children. I should've tended to my marriage and that's on me."

"But..." Bodie said, sensing there was more.

"But I wish your mother had given me a chance to make things right before she'd moved on with someone else," his father said, then held up his hands. His expression was thoughtful. "I'm not saying things wouldn't have ended the same between us. I just wasn't given an option to fight. She'd made the decision for us."

Bodie had made the decision not to love too. Then his farmer came along. Bodie picked up the tools and followed his father out of the closet. "Are you telling me that Mom was having an affair? That's why you left us?"

"She wanted to be with him," his father said. "He gave her the attention she craved."

"What about us?" Bodie asked, referring to himself and his siblings. He was not entirely surprised his mother had skimmed over the details of her affair all these years. After witnessing several of her divorces, Bodie had suspected his mother had jumped first. And Bodie had not been in a place where he could move beyond his resentment to hear his father out. That is, until his farmer came into his life and changed his perspective.

"I thought it would be best for you kids to be with your mom and stepdad since I was working all the time," he explained.

And perhaps grieving the loss of his marriage

and his family too. Bodie asked, "Why didn't you ever tell us?"

"I thought I was doing right by you and your brother and sister. You were all so young," his father explained. "Hardly seemed right to pull you into things that were meant to be handled by the adults."

Bodie realized his mother had been dragging him into her relationship conflicts since he was ten years old. One after the other. And each time, his mother placed blame on her partner and his faults. Bodie had sided with his mom and decided love wasn't worth the effort. Yet, perhaps his mother wasn't putting in the effort into her relationship—he couldn't answer for her. But he could answer for himself.

"I assumed one day you would come to me and want to hear the other side." His father opened the garage door. "I just never imagined it would take so long."

"I'm sorry about that." Bodie set his hand on his dad's shoulder. "Sorry it took so long for me to come here."

"What's important is that we're here now." His father embraced him and said, "Mending things between us."

"It feels really good," Bodie said.

"You'll feel even better when you mend things between you and Sarah," his dad stated. "You don't want to wait for too long with her."

"I'm not sure things can be fixed." Bodie scratched

his cheek. One thing was certain—they would not be if he did not even try.

"Here's what I know, son." His father arranged the tools on the workbench then said, "Love isn't one-sided. It requires participation by both sides to make the relationship a success."

Bodie was beginning to understand that.

"Your mother and I didn't put the work in," his father admitted. "That's on us. Maybe we didn't have the right kind of love."

Bodie propped his hip against the workbench and asked, "What kind is that?"

"The kind worth fighting for." His father eyed him. His gaze gleamed.

"How do you know if you have that kind?" Bodie asked.

"How much do you hurt?" his dad shot back.

He hurt more than he ever imagined possible. Not physically—that he would have managed. This was deeper and more intense. More insistent. So insistent, it seemed determined to drag him under. He countered, "Does it matter?"

"Sure does. It can make the difference between fighting or walking." His dad dropped his hand on Bodie's shoulder and squeezed. "And if it's a fierce enough love, well then, I think that's worth fighting for."

Fierce love. Bodie heard the phrase tossed about. Never gave it much consideration.

But his farmer, well, Sarah was fierce in her loyalty to Sawyer. She was even fiercer in the truck with Bodie. Calling Bodie out and challenging him to be better. To do better.

And Bodie had been fierce about his need to make sure no one dimmed that precious light inside her. Going so far as to step away from her to ensure he didn't ruin her sunshine.

Oh, the highs and lows he was feeling over his farmer were certainly something fierce.

But he had run. Just like his mom.

There was some irony for sure. Bodie had worked his whole adult life not to be like his father. Only to realize he had become just like his mother. His mom was out of a relationship before she could ever really get hurt and already moving on with someone new. His mom's string of broken romances and swift rebounds proved that. But where did that leave Bodie?

He had a decision to make, he supposed. Keep running or start fighting.

His smile started slow. He knew what he wanted. Who he wanted. In his heart he knew.

There never was a decision to be made. He only had to open his heart.

"Dad." His grin stretched wide. He said, "I have to go. But I'll see you at dinner tonight."

"Anything I can help with, son?" his dad asked.

"I'll let you know." Bodie hugged his father and added, "I've got some calls to make first." Details and a strategy to figure out.

After all, if he was going to fight, it was going to be for keeps.

SEVERAL HOURS LATER, when he parked outside the Sloan farmhouse, Bodie had parts of his plan in place. However, he was still puzzling through the largest piece of his playing-for-keeps strategy. After all, Bodie had broken hearts, but he'd never actually attempted to mend one. All he knew was he couldn't wait any longer. It was time to try something.

Bodie walked inside the Sloan farmhouse and shook hands with everyone. Then he set the wine bottle on the kitchen island and said, "Unfortunately, I can't stay. I've got to take care of something."

"You went and accepted another case already?" Lacey set her hands on her hips and frowned at him. "You just couldn't wait until tomorrow to leave."

"No, it's not that." Bodie brushed his hand over his head. "That would've been a lot easier to handle."

The room went quiet, and all eyes turned on him.

"It's just that. Well, I. You see." Bodie paused and lifted his gaze to the ceiling. The center of attention had never quite suited him. But his farmer suited him quite well. And if he couldn't admit what he'd done in front of his family, how would he handle things in front of his farmer? *Alone is all you'll ever be if you don't try.*

"You see." He exhaled and met their curious stares. "I broke a cowgirl's heart, and I sort of need to fix it. Right away." Before he lost her for good.

Sam Sloan, the patriarch of the family and soon to be Bodie's step-grandfather, chuckled. His white beard lifted and revealed his wide smile. "Well, son, you've come to the right place."

"We happen to know a bit about that kind of breaking and fixing." Carter pressed a tumbler with a splash of bourbon and ice into Bodie's hand and said, "This will help you get through what's coming."

Before Bodie could ask what that was, Caleb dropped his hand on Bodie's shoulder and squeezed. "Trust me. We've all been in your boots before."

"Fortunately, we found our way." Ryan tapped his glass against Bodie's and added, "You will too."

"Not without help," Lacey said, confidence in her words.

"Of course. That's what we're here for." Caleb grinned at Bodie and lifted his eyebrows up and down. "Bodie already knows that. Why do you think he's here, telling us what he did? He needs us."

That, Bodie realized, was one of those truths. And there was nothing uncomfortable about it now. He was not on his own anymore and he was glad for it.

"Better come and sit, son." Sam pulled out a chair at the large kitchen table. "We have figured out how to fix more than a few things around this table and we haven't failed yet."

"Even if it takes all night." Carter smiled. "No

one leaves until it's right. That's how we do things around here."

Nobody seemed the least bit put out or bothered by that fact. In fact, everyone went into motion at once, seeming to work like skilled staff in a commercial kitchen. Plates were filled, the extras set out in the middle of the table, drinks served, and everyone seated in what seemed like minutes.

Ryan dropped into the chair beside Bodie and announced, "I'm calling dibs on the mocha cream pie. I've been looking at it in the refrigerator since last night."

"You can't do that." Caleb aimed his fork at his brother and added, "In this family we share."

"Not Tess's pie we don't," Ryan said and nudged his elbow into Bodie's arm. "I come up with my best heartbreak solutions with chocolate and pie."

Laughter and grumbles rolled around the table.

"I made two pies." Tess laughed, then said, "But Ryan, you need to share with Bodie. He looks like he might need an extra boost of chocolate."

Ryan high-fived Bodie and said, "I've got your back, Bodie."

Glasses were lifted around the table. Lilian took his father's hand in hers, met Bodie's stare, and said, "We all do."

"Now that we're seated, we can get to the fixing." Sam's gaze gleamed. He smeared butter on a homemade biscuit and said, "Bodie, you best start from the beginning."

Bodie did what he was asked and filled them

all in. Along the way, he discovered this family returned to the table even when it was broken and did not give up until it was fixed. And he realized he would be forever grateful to have a seat among them.

CHAPTER TWENTY-ONE

SARAH WALKED INTO her grandmother's hospital room the morning after her Sawyer encounter. She had a container of fresh fruit and a new outlook. She might not have her cowboy, but that hardly meant she couldn't have a properly good life. She just needed to build it for herself. On her own terms.

"That does not look like a Double Dutch to-go box," her grandmother said. "Sunday mornings are doughnut mornings."

"We've never had Sunday doughnut mornings," Sarah said.

"Well, we should have," her grandmother replied and pointed to the door. Her gaze was hopeful. "Perhaps you could dash on over to Double Dutch and we can start now."

Sarah chuckled. "Doughnuts are not on your recovery diet."

Her grandmother blew a raspberry. "I'll recover faster with a sweet treat. Where's Bodie? He would agree."

Sarah had filled her grandmother in on the rustling ring and Sawyer's involvement. Her grandmother had wanted all the details from start to finish. When it came to Sawyer, her grandmother claimed he had done wrong and would need to make amends for that. With that settled, her grandmother had refused to let Sarah give her the abridged version of Sarah and Bodie's conversation in the truck. And every day, her grandmother was convinced Bodie would arrive so Sarah could make her own amends.

"I know Bodie has been leaving me sweet treats." Her grandmother grinned. "He's like the tooth fairy. Sneaking in and out while I'm sleeping, but I'm going to catch him."

"I'm fairly certain he does not want to be caught," Sarah mused. "Or he would come around during normal visiting hours."

Her grandmother harrumphed. "He isn't coming around on account of you. You broke his heart, you know."

"I did no such thing," she argued. He broke hers. And besides, she couldn't break something he didn't have. But her grandmother and she had been going round and round about Sarah's fallout with Bodie all week. She wasn't there for another bout of who broke whose heart. Sarah adjusted the recliner and sat down beside her grandmother's bed and said, "Grandma, we need to talk about the farm."

"I suppose it's time," her grandmother conceded. She peered at her. "Sure you don't want to get those doughnuts? This feels like a chocolate sort of conversation."

"We got the truffles from your secret admirer." Sarah opened the drawer in the nightstand and removed the box from the Silver Penny.

"You keep 'em. You're likely to need them more than me," her grandmother said. Sarah opened her mouth, but her grandmother spoke first. "Now, mind your elder and let me get this out."

Sarah closed her mouth and wound the purple ribbon on the box around her finger.

"I'm sorry, my dear, for burdening you," her grandmother said, regret in her eyes and face. "With me and the farm."

Sarah shook her head and took her grandmother's hand in hers. "You were never that, Grandma."

"You really are a gem." Her grandmother patted Sarah's arm. "Don't ever forget it. And remember, when someone tries to tarnish your shine, polish yourself off and always shine brighter. It's the best sort of payback."

Payback was all well and good, although perhaps not Sarah's style. Going forward, she wanted only to stay true to herself. She nodded to let her grandmother know she was paying attention.

"I've decided I'm going to shine too." Her grandmother released Sarah's hand and slid a folder out from under her pillow. "And I've decided to do that here."

Sarah took the folder and stared at the cover. It was a brochure for Harmony Heritage Senior Living Community. She glanced from the folder to her grandma and said, "I don't understand."

"I think I can be happy there," her grandmother explained and tapped her finger on the cover. "Look at page eight. They've got water aerobics in a heated indoor pool. Doc Sloan tells me it will do wonders for my joints."

"You're moving out of your home," Sarah said, her stomach churned. "Leaving the farm." Because Sarah failed.

"Don't look sad, my dear," her grandmother chided. "It's time for us to find our happy."

Sarah said, "But that's the farm. Your home. Your life. The place you've claimed made you the happiest."

Her grandmother tipped her head and studied her. Her words were pensive. "You know what I've been doing every night while I've been stuck in this bed?"

"Waiting to catch your sweet treat source," Sarah said dryly.

Her grandmother chuckled. "Yes. That, and I've been thinking and remembering," she said, and patted her heart. "All my good memories are on the farm and I cherish those like no one can imagine." Her grandmother dabbed the corner of her eye. "But I realized those memories travel. Why they came with me here and kept me company."

Sarah wiped her own eyes.

"It seems that I've been hanging around the farm because I was afraid to let go," her grandmother admitted. "I'm blessed for the life I had. But it has come time for me to find a different sort of happy."

"But this is a big decision," Sarah countered. "We should take some time. Maybe take a tour. Discuss it."

"I've had more than enough time," her grandmother said. "And if I wait too long, the pool might get cold before I get in."

Sarah searched her grandmother's face and noted the glint in her grandmother's gaze. She said, "You really want to do this?"

Her grandmother nodded. "It's time for you to do the same, my dear. It's time for you to dive in."

"I don't think they'll let me join you for water aerobics," Sarah said.

"More's the pity," her grandmother replied. Her gaze flashed brighter. "But I don't want you living your happy through me anymore."

Sarah stilled.

"It's past time you find your own personal happy," her grandmother said, then added, "And then be greedy and enjoy it. For you. For yourself." Her grandmother reached for her hand. "Don't be afraid. We can jump together."

Sarah held onto her grandmother and said, "What if I don't know what my happy is?" Or where to jump?

Her grandmother squeezed her fingers and looked her in the eye. "Your heart knows. You just need to let it speak."

Her cowboy. That was what her heart told her.

Where her heart wanted to go. Still, Sarah hesitated and said, "What if my happy is with someone who doesn't want me?"

Her grandmother harrumphed and snatched the chocolate box from Sarah, then waved her arm. "Look around you. It's more floral shop than hospital room in here."

Sarah took in the vibrant bouquets blooming on every bit of open counter space and the flowering potted plants on the windowsill. Everything from roses to orchids to brilliantly colored fall mums.

"Your cowboy hasn't only been delivering chocolates," her grandmother said, a satisfied grin on her face. "He's brought flowers too."

Sarah smiled. "He really cares about you."

Her grandmother pressed her palm on her forehead and sighed. "No, my dear, the flowers are for you. He can't bring 'em to you so he's showing you his heart here."

Sarah stood and touched the petal of a white rose surrounded by a dozen deep purple roses. The card attached read *Saw the moon. Thought of you.* Sarah blinked and reread the card. Sarah plucked the card from the bouquet of yellow roses and orange lilies. This one read simply *Another day. Another thought of you.*

Her grandmother chuckled behind her.

Sarah walked to the window and reached for the card in the burgundy mum plant. It read *Is there a season I won't think of you?*

Her grandmother's laughter spilled out, a delightful sound. She said, "Catching on yet?"

Sarah held the card and turned around to face her grandmother. "Why didn't you tell me?"

Her grandmother bit into a truffle. Her words held no remorse. "You weren't ready to listen."

"What am I supposed to do now?" Sarah asked.

"Tell him how you feel." Her grandmother polished off her truffle.

Was it that simple?

"And if you don't put him out of his misery soon, I'm afraid he's going to have a whole sunflower patch delivered here," her grandmother said with a chuckle. "We won't be able to move what for all the flowers in our way."

Her grandmother looked anything but put out by the idea.

"Although, I would like to see what he brings next," her grandmother mused and took out another truffle. "Perhaps one more night won't matter."

"But it won't matter if I tell him how I feel," Sarah argued. "He's leaving. I'm staying."

"How do you know it won't matter?" Her grandmother chewed slowly and eyed her. "Things might have changed since you two last spoke. Tell him again what's in your heart, if you must. Tell him a million times."

What was in her heart? Oh, she knew what she felt. But to say it out loud. To risk it all and put it into words and then give those words a voice. That was giving her heart the lead and all the power. She shook her head.

"Someone has to say it first," her grandmother argued. "Might as well be you. Love isn't a competition, you know. You don't get points for saying *I love you* last." Her grandmother waggled her eyebrows. "But you might get your very own cowgirl kind of fairy tale. To do that you have to start with the words."

I love you. Three little words that had changed the course of her life more than once. Every decision came after her partner had told her he loved her. Sarah's gaze drifted around the room, skipping from one vivid flower petal to the next. Bodie was right. She had been falling in line and following her partners.

But she had not held back with her cowboy. Bodie had not ever dared to tell her who she was. He only ever saw her as she was—happy, scared, carefree, worried. It hadn't mattered. He'd been there. Right beside her every step.

And that was the true power, wasn't it? Having someone beside her. Not to carry her or change her or fix her. But to hold her. To support her. To believe in her. It was having a partner who she could treat the same. It was giving everything she had and knowing she would have it in return.

It was something like a serious-minded cowboy and a sunshiny cowgirl and a lifetime together.

Sarah sank onto the recliner and knew her words sounded dazed. "Grandma, I think I'm in love."

Grandma hooted, then sobered. "That's all fine and well, my dear, but what are you going to do about it?"

"Tell him," Sarah said, although rather weakly.

"That's a sure place to start." Her grandmother nodded. "Now we need something to win him over."

"My love isn't enough?"

"Of course it is," her grandmother assured her. "But there's nothing like a grand declaration. The very thought makes my own heart sing."

"This is why people don't like to go first." Sarah frowned. "There's too much pressure."

Her grandmother waggled her eyebrows. "Oh, there is even more joy."

There was that. Sarah smiled wide. "Tell me you have ideas, Grandma."

"Of course I do," her grandmother stated.

Sarah exhaled.

Then her grandmother added, "But first we must discuss the farm."

"The farm," Sarah repeated.

"Yes, dear. We need to know if you're staying or going."

"Where would I go?" Sarah asked.

"With your cowboy, of course," her grandmother replied, as if it was obvious. "If that's what you want."

It was about so much more than love. Telling Bodie what was in her heart suddenly seemed like the easy part. Sarah buried her face in her hands and groaned. "This just got complicated. Really complicated."

"Well," her grandmother said. "To farm or not to farm. Or rather, are you a farmer or not?"

Sarah lowered her arms. "I want to be."

"Everyone wants to be something, dear," her grandmother said. "I want to be a synchronized swimmer. Remind me to ask my new water aerobics instructor about lessons." Her grandmother waved her hand. "Never mind about that. Back to you, dear. Are you a farmer or not?"

This was it. Time to be who she was. Sarah straightened. "Yes. I'm a farmer."

"Good. Try not to forget it." Her grandmother smoothed her hands over her blanket. "Now a farmer needs a farm and lucky for you, I happen to have one that needs a refresh to ensure it's here for the next generation. I have a legacy to preserve after all." Her grandmother grinned at her. "I've been thinking there's a future in corn."

That was her grandmother's blessing and approval to take the farm in the direction Sarah wanted. Her grandmother believed in her. Everything seemed to right itself. And Sarah knew if she stood up, she would feel more than steady and more than ready to step into the future.

"Now, I'll sell the farm to you at a friends-and-family discounted rate," her grandmother announced. "Can't just give it to you. You understand, right?"

Sarah nodded.

"It's not like I have a farm to give your brother

and sister too," her grandmother continued. "Or your parents, for that matter. Not that any of them want their own farms. Although I never understood why not."

Oh, how she adored her grandmother. Sarah burst out laughing. "I never understood them either."

"We're the sensible ones in the family," her grandmother said. "Now, where were we?"

"I believe I'm buying your farm," Sarah said. "And telling Bodie how I feel."

"Right." Her grandmother rubbed her hands together. "Now we know what you are doing, it's up to you to convince Bodie everything he wants is here too."

"That's a tall order," she said.

"I'm confident you can manage."

Sarah collapsed back in the recliner and drummed her fingers on the armrests and mused, "Grandma, how do I convince a cowboy that his heart is the best decision he will ever make?"

Her grandmother hummed and said, "I'm sure we'll think of something."

That was it. Sarah sprang forward and smiled. It wasn't about convincing him. Or a perfect grand gesture.

All she really had to do was get her cowboy to follow her lead. And she knew just what to do.

CHAPTER TWENTY-TWO

B℮DIE WALKED OUT of the law offices of Dalton and Buckner and spotted his sister's truck parked under the shade of an oak tree and headed her way. He opened the truck and climbed in.

Lacey started the engine, glanced at him, and said, "All set?"

He nodded. He was as ready as he would ever be. Less than forty-eight hours after family dinner at the Sloan farmhouse and Bodie had taken more than one big step toward the future he wanted. The biggest and the most important step was yet to come. But he couldn't take that step without a certain someone. He buckled his seat belt, but his nerves still rattled around inside him.

"Any second thoughts?" Lacey put her foot on the gas.

"No." Not a single one. He was certain about what he felt. How he felt about his farmer. The only part he was uncertain about was what exactly to say.

"Just speak from your heart," Lacey said into the silence. "And you'll be fine."

That was the problem. There was so much inside him that he wanted to get out. So much Bodie wanted to share. But his cowgirl deserved the perfect words. And Bodie had to get this right.

He spent the entire drive over to his cowgirl's farm silently rehearsing and revising his speech.

Only to have his carefully practiced words scattered like so many sunflower seeds in mere seconds. And he hadn't even greeted his cowgirl yet. But she was there. Right in his sight.

Bodie sat forward in the passenger seat and lifted his sunglasses off his eyes. The image in the middle of the road that led to his farmer's house was the same with or without his tinted lenses.

His cowgirl. His motorcycle. Thirteen ducklings and one dog were all blocking his way.

He felt his grin building and asked, "What is that?"

Lacey slowed her truck and smiled. "I believe that is Sarah and her cavalry."

Bodie felt a definite kick in his pulse and tried to temper the beat of anticipation in his words. "What are they doing?"

"Seems to me they are taking a stance." Lacey stopped her truck and eyed him.

Please be on my side, cowgirl. His pulse skipped another beat. His grin stretched and he asked, "Over what?"

"You won't know until you get out of my truck and talk to her." Lacey laughed and shoved him on the shoulder.

"Okay. I'm going." Bodie snatched his cowboy hat from the back seat and climbed out. *This was it*. Setting his hat on his head, he rubbed his palms on his jeans. Nothing like jump-starting his nerves too.

Before he shut the truck door, Lacey called out, "Tell Sarah we will be back to celebrate."

Celebrate. He wanted to do that with his cowgirl, but there were things to be said first. Apologies to give. Promises to be made.

He heard Lacey put her truck into Reverse, but his gaze remained fixed on his farmer. There was no chance he could have looked away. She was propped on his motorcycle. Her straw cowboy hat sat low on her forehead. The brim of her hat cast her face entirely in shadow. She wore his favorite red-and-white pin-striped overalls and cowboy boots. Her wildlife crew surrounded her, as if providing backup. He wanted to run over to her, sweep her into his arms, and tell her how much he adored her.

Instead, he forced himself to slow down. It was the possible start of the rest of his life with his cowgirl. There was no room for error.

He curbed his nerves and stopped within helmet-tossing distance of the motorcycle and everything he wanted. "Lacey claims you're making a stand."

She tapped the brim of her hat higher and eyed him. "It's more like I'm taking a leap."

"What kind of leap?" And please let it be toward him. Preferably straight into his arms.

Her hands were tucked in her overalls pockets. She lifted one shoulder. Her words were pleasant, almost cordial, as if she discussed nothing more pressing than her grocery list. She said, "It's the kind of leap that involves a farmer, a ranger, two hearts, and something like forever."

Talk about convenient. That was the very same kind he wanted to take. His nerves disappeared. His pulse slowed and everything suddenly made sense again. All because of a cowgirl.

"So, what do you think?" Sarah asked, hope threaded around the reserve in her words.

Don't worry. I will always catch you. He stepped closer to her and said, "I think forever sounds about right. And here seems like a good place to start."

She swung her leg over the motorcycle, yet stayed where she was. "I need to say something else."

Bodie stilled, worked to keep his arms at his sides when all he wanted to do was reach for her. To hold her and get to that apology and those promises.

"I love you, Bodie Taylor Hopson." Her smile was impossibly bright. Her words clear and tender. "My heart is yours."

Bodie would have laughed if anyone ever told him a wisp of a cowgirl would cause his knees to buckle. But then he'd never known a love quite like this. He heard the catch in his words and didn't bother to clear it. Instead, he said, "That's good. Because you, Sarah Rickelle, have had my heart—

my whole heart—since the moment I first saw you. It's yours and so am I."

Tears pooled in her eyes. Her smile stretched wider. Her boots fairly flew over the gravel as she raced toward him and finally leaped into his arms. Mav barked excitedly and the ducklings chirped as if cheering them on.

Bodie swung his cowgirl up against him and gathered her as close as possible. "I love you, Sarah." He pulled back and shouted, "I love you!"

Sarah framed his face in her hands, and they met for a kiss that swept his cowboy cynic right off his boots and made him believe in those so-called silly fairy tales and things like a love of a lifetime. Slowly, he lowered her back down until her boots touched the gravel.

"I know we have a lot to work out. Things to discuss." She smoothed her hands over his chest and framed his face again. "But I want you and I want this so very much."

He kissed her again. Because he could, and why not. He wanted to be hers and he wanted this. He finally pulled away, tucked her hand in his and tipped his chin toward the merry flock surrounding them. "I think we've made these guys wait for their swim long enough."

Sarah laughed and whistled for Mav, who barked happily and led the ducklings to the pond. Mav splashed in the water and the ducklings excitedly followed.

Bodie stood on the shore, wrapped his arms

around Sarah's waist and pulled her back against his chest. He waited a beat, before casually saying, "The first thing we need to discuss is water rights."

"What are you talking about?" She leaned her head on his shoulder and kept her attention on the pond.

"I checked the property lines," he explained, working hard to sound indifferent. "This pond is on my land, not Rickelle land."

She stilled, completely and silently. Only her fingers flexed around his arms. "Your land?"

"I signed the papers this morning to buy the property as is," Bodie explained. Thanks to his family and their connections in town, he was introduced to the appropriate legal team and the process was fairly seamless. There was still more paperwork to be processed, but the sale was official. He added, "It was why I was late getting here."

Sarah shook her head as if struggling to process his words.

"Pearl and Artie were thrilled to start their retirement, as you can imagine." Bodie kept talking, his words relaxed and easy. He pressed a kiss on his stunned cowgirl's cheek and added, "Did you know they already had a condo with an ocean view picked out in the gulf? We've been invited to visit whenever we'd like, of course."

Sarah wiggled around to face him, but he managed to keep her in his arms.

"Are you telling me that you bought the McGowan property?"

"It seemed like the right thing to do. I know I should have talked to you first." He reached up and tucked a piece of hair behind her ear. "It's just I got excited about the idea of building something together."

Her eyes filled again. One tear leaked down her cheek. Then another.

"You hate the idea." Bodie winced and tried to catch her tears with his fingers.

But they kept falling. Fast and free. She shook her head, sent more streaming down her face.

"It's just I figured we're going to need more land for your rescues," he rushed on, and set his palms gently on her cheeks to collect her tears. "And now you can expand your corn to a large-scale operation like you envisioned and focus on the crop you want." He paused, heard her sniffle, then he asked, "What do you think?"

"I think I couldn't love you more than I do." Sarah threw her arms around him and kissed him breathless.

Finally, and rather reluctantly, he pressed one more kiss to her lips, leaned back and said, "I was serious about starting our forever right here on this land."

"I can see that now." She was laughing and crying.

"Now back to this water-access issue." He dried her cheeks with the sleeve of his plaid shirt, then kissed her softly and quickly. "What kind of deal are you prepared to make?"

She sniffled and grinned. "Picnics in my sunflower fields for unlimited pond usage."

"Only if it's you and me and a blanket," he said, then smiled. "And all day to ourselves."

She took his hands in hers. Her gaze was affectionate. Her expression so very tender. "And maybe with our kids one day."

"We've got over a thousand acres collectively now." He gathered her into his arms again and said, "Our kids can get their own field. I'm calling dibs on our sunflower field."

She laughed and tipped her head to consider him. "Then we're doing this?"

"Yes. All of it." He'd never wanted anything more. He was itching to get started. "The wedding. The kids. Family dinners. Family game nights. Holidays and staycations and harvests. I want it all. With you."

"Now you're speaking straight to my heart." She curved her arms around his neck and tangled her fingers in his hair near his collar. Her eyebrows creased and she asked, "Wait. What about your job?"

"Well, it seems my chief has an opening here coming up, and another case already pending," he explained. "There are rumors of race-fixing at one of the local tracks not far from here. He wants me to look into it."

She grinned. "So, we both get to keep doing what we love."

"With the people we love supporting us," he

added, then frowned. "But you should know this means I will still be gone some of the time for work."

"As long as you are home for the harvest," she said.

"There's nowhere I'd rather be than with you, harvest or not." He reached up, smoothed his fingers across her cheek, and said, "You're my home."

"I love you, Bodie Hopson." Sarah pulled him closer and said, "Welcome home."

Home. That was where it all led. The engagement. The wedding vows. The building of a life together.

The *I* became *we*. The *my* became *our*.

Bodie finally found everything he had been missing. A farmer. A family. And a forever home.

EPILOGUE

Halloween

"GRANDMA, WHAT ARE YOU DOING?" Sarah adjusted the cowboy hat she had propped on the life-size skeleton sitting on a hay bale on the farmhouse's front porch. All part of the Halloween decorations Aspen and Bodie had selected to put the cowboy in the spooky.

Grandma Rose stopped fishing around in the extra-large candy bowl and shrugged from her seat in one of the rocking chairs. "I'm picking out the good ones."

Sarah chuckled and sat in the rocking chair beside her grandmother. "Am I going to regret asking why?"

"Shouldn't you be adding those final touches to your boo bash decor?" Her grandmother frowned at her and waved as if to shoo her away. "And not hovering over me and the candy bowl."

Sarah grinned and said, "As it happens, I've put out all our decorations. And I like the view from this very spot." Quite a lot. From her seat, she had her cowboy directly in her sights.

Bodie and Aspen were organizing their carved pumpkins on hay bales in the front yard while they waited for their family and guests to arrive to kick off what Aspen declared as their first annual Cowboy Boo Bash.

"This was always one of my favorite spots too. Got a good view of all the comings and goings on the farm." Her grandmother slipped a candy bar from the bowl into the pocket of her sweater.

"I saw that," Sarah said, and swallowed back her laughter.

"You've got more in the house," her grandmother replied. "Don't deny it. I saw where you hid those bags of candy."

Sarah's laughter spilled free.

Her cowboy took note and headed up the stairs toward them. His smile was warm and affectionate. "Everything okay up here?"

Her grandmother tipped her head toward Sarah and muttered, "It would be better if my granddaughter minded her own business."

"Grandma Rose is stealing the good candy," Sarah accused, amusement in her words.

Her grandmother harrumphed, yet her eyes twinkled in the evening light. "It's for a good cause."

"Your midnight sweet treat stash is not a good cause," Sarah countered.

"Of course it is." Grandma Rose patted her other

pocket, then slipped a candy bar into it. "Tell her, Bodie. Tell her all sweet treats are good."

"I think I'll let you two sort this out." Bodie shook his head and took the candy bowl from her grandmother. He rummaged around, then tossed a chocolate bar to Aspen when she stepped onto the porch with Mav beside her.

"Caleb says all secret candy stashes are good as long as you share." Aspen unwrapped her chocolate bar and took a bite.

"Sharing is all part of my plan," Grandma Rose stated and grinned at Aspen. Then she eyed Sarah and explained, "As it happens, I promised my water aerobics bunch I would return with chocolate incentives."

Sarah tapped her fingers on the armrests. "I'm not sure candy is on your friends' approved diets."

Grandma Rose swished that away with a flick of her wrist and said, "It's not for us. It's for our instructor, Miranda."

Bodie's shoulders shook silently, and he said, "Still haven't convinced Miranda to teach you any synchronized swimming routines."

"We're not giving up." Grandma Rose raised her eyebrows and grinned. "We've decided to bribe her with chocolate."

"I'm sure you'll wear her down eventually," Bodie said.

"We've already picked out our routine after watching videos on the computer," Grandma Rose explained, her smile still in place. "It's only a matter of time before Miranda agrees."

It was more than obvious her grandmother had not slowed down after she moved into the seniors' community. If anything, it seemed her grandmother was up to more now than she had been at the farm. And she was happy. That gave Sarah peace and joy. Sarah pushed out of the rocking chair and said, "Speaking of time, if we don't get changed into our costumes now, we will be out of time and our boo bash will begin without us."

Her grandmother picked up a helmet Sarah hadn't noticed until now and handed it to Aspen. Then Grandma Rose stood and wrapped her arm around Aspen's other arm and the pair headed inside.

"Grandma, we have a costume for you," Sarah said. "And the witch's hat will go better than the helmet."

"Oh, that's not for my costume," her grandmother said. "That's my safety gear."

"Safety gear for what?" Sarah stepped around the pair and opened the front door.

"Doc Sloan cleared me to race." Her grandmother paused in the open doorway and arched an eyebrow at Sarah, then added, "You didn't think hayrides was all that old tractor was doing tonight, did you?"

"You aren't tractor racing, Grandma," Sarah said, and shook her head.

"Of course, I am. Doc Sloan cleared me," her

grandmother retorted. "And besides, we've already got a pool going at the seniors' center."

Sarah rubbed her forehead and glanced at Bodie.

Her grandmother drew her attention again. "I would let you in on the pool, but you're clearly not on my team." Her grandma tugged on Aspen and the pair headed down the hallway. Her grandmother muttered, "I can't believe my own granddaughter bet against me. Aspen, we're going to need more chocolate now."

Aspen giggled.

Sarah let the door close and rounded on Bodie. "We can't let her race a tractor, can we?"

Bodie pulled Sarah into his arms and said, "I don't think we can stop her."

Sarah wrapped her arms around his waist and dropped her head onto his shoulder.

"If it makes you feel any better, we will have a doctor, a retired heart surgeon, and a trained EMT here for the boo bash," he stated.

Sarah was grateful for each and every one of the Sloan family. But even more she was grateful for the cowboy with her now. She smiled and said, "And you. I'll have you here."

"Always." Bodie set his fingers under her chin and lifted her face up to his. Then he kissed her slowly and tenderly, as if he had all night to stand on the porch with her. And nowhere else he would rather be.

Sarah pulled away and took his hand in hers.

"Maybe we could hide her helmet. Doc Sloan can't clear her to drive then."

Bodie kissed the top of her head and chuckled. "Before you do that, I should tell you that I already talked to Carter. We set the speeds on both tractors. They'll be lucky if they get up to five miles an hour."

Sarah's laughter burst out. "Are you serious?"

"Completely," he said, and squeezed her fingers. "It's what we do in this family. We look out for each other."

"And love each other," Sarah said.

"Always," he said. "I love you always."

"And forever," she said, and lifted up to kiss her cowboy again.

* * * * *

*For more great romances from
Three Springs, Texas, from acclaimed author
Cari Lynn Webb and Harlequin Heartwarming,
visit www.Harlequin.com today!*

Harlequin Reader Service

Enjoyed your book?

Try the perfect subscription for Romance readers and get more great books like this delivered right to your door.

See why over 10+ million readers have tried Harlequin Reader Service.

Start with a Free Welcome Collection with free books and a gift—valued over $20.

Choose any series in print or ebook.
See website for details and order today:

TryReaderService.com/subscriptions